Aunt Linda,
Thank you for all your love through
the years! We love you! I hope
you are encouraged as you read
what God put on my heart!
Blessings,
Zach

The
RESCUE
of the
BRIDE

Z. C. CYRUS

WESTBOW·
PRESS
A DIVISION OF THOMAS NELSON
& ZONDERVAN

Z.C. Cyrus
9-20-14

Scriptures taken from the Holy Bible, New International Version®, NIV®.
Copyright © 1973, 1978, 1984, 2011 by Biblica, Inc.™ Used by permission of
Zondervan. All rights reserved worldwide. www.zondervan.com The "NIV"
and "New International Version" are trademarks registered in the United
States Patent and Trademark Office by Biblica, Inc.™ All rights reserved.

WestBow Press books may be ordered through booksellers or by contacting:

WestBow Press
A Division of Thomas Nelson & Zondervan
1663 Liberty Drive
Bloomington, IN 47403
www.westbowpress.com
1 (866) 928-1240

Because of the dynamic nature of the Internet, any web addresses or
links contained in this book may have changed since publication and
may no longer be valid. The views expressed in this work are solely those
of the author and do not necessarily reflect the views of the publisher,
and the publisher hereby disclaims any responsibility for them.

Any people depicted in stock imagery provided by Thinkstock are
models, and such images are being used for illustrative purposes only.
Certain stock imagery © Thinkstock.

ISBN: 978-1-4908-4411-4 (sc)
ISBN: 978-1-4908-4412-1 (hc)
ISBN: 978-1-4908-4410-7 (e)

Library of Congress Control Number: 2014912238

Printed in the United States of America.

WestBow Press rev. date: 07/18/2014

Dedication

For Laura, my wife and best friend, your life inspires many.

Acknowledgements

First and foremost, this book is a reflection of my walk with You, Jesus: who as Savior you did something I can never repay and who as friend you never ask me to.

Laura, you made this entire endeavor possible through your love and support.

Adalyn and Elliott, you inspire me. Thank you for letting daddy use the computer and for going to bed when you were told!

Finally, special thanks goes to my friend and mentor, Alberta Kelly, for having the willingness to inspire multiple generations and for taking the time to help one of them with the burden of his heart.

Book 1

Out of the Darkness

"Isaac, slow down! What did the Council say?"

"I don't have much time. Justice is dead. The Council moved swiftly knowing we were splintered."

"How can he be dead? Isaac? Are you leaving?"

"I am afraid so."

"Please, slow down! I can barely keep up! What did they say?"

"Here. It's a copy of the Act. They are creating cities for us – reservations would be a better word. You know as well as I do this was their goal all along. Now they can wipe their hands of us and separate us completely from the populace."

"You mean everyone must go?"

"Only those deemed dangerous. You will have to stay."

"Eight years. This is all I know. I don't think I can go back to –"

"You won't. There are many here who are still loyal. I promise we will find someone you can stay with."

"Will I ever see you again?"

"I don't know."

"Where will you go?"

"North. They gave us a two mile square on the Pacific… only twelve thousand can go –"

"But there is double that in Sapphire! What about the rest?"

"I don't know. Maybe they will be granted land elsewhere. I wish I could do more, but if we don't leave now, we will lose our lot."

"Who are you taking?"

"Conner will shepherd us and Lloyd will lead. I believe Porter and Fair are coming. The Good Doctor will help run the government hospital."

"Is he administering the tracking dyes? Is it true everyone will be marked?"

"Yes, he injected me this morning. I wish I could tell you more but we must go."

"Isaac, promise me you will never tell him. I could never live with myself if somehow my existence lead to–"

"I promise."

Chapter 1

Still. That is how my mother described it to me. The feeling when I sit alone in the woods, my eyes focused blindly on a distant shadow as my senses devour the terrain in search of my quarry. As I sit, motionless, barely breathing, I can feel my heart rate, the steady flow of blood through my veins. Any slight sound or flash of movement and my eyes dart toward the disturbance without moving another muscle.

Still. It is the feeling I long for after an exhausting day. When all I desire is to sit in my favorite chair and melt into the cushions, daring not to move or even breathe deeply, afraid I might disrupt this feeling of bliss. You see, this is what I fight for and fight against. When my mind and body become worn out from the daily struggle of merely existing, I long for stillness. When this stillness comes, I can only stand its presence for so long before I become restless and long for some sort of movement, the next challenge.

"Be still, Sardis," Mom would say when we would have our quiet time in the mornings. "If you want to see God working in your life, you must be still. Faith is born of trust, and trust is found solely in God's presence. Only then will He reveal to you the assurance of all you hope for and the certainties of what you cannot yet see." We were both hunters, called to help provide food for the people of our community. She was the best. She was my mentor and my closest friend.

My eyes fix upon a brown mass hidden in the thick undergrowth. My breathing quickens as my focus slides from branch to branch. An outline of the mass begins to take shape. I shift my weight and tighten the grip on my rifle.

"*Pffh*," I exhale and release the tension from my chest as I realize it is the same stump that initiated a similar response ten minutes earlier. I chuckle quietly to myself. I wonder if Mom had ever been this anxious on her slow days.

I close my eyes and take in a deep breath of the fresh forest air. I catch the faint smell of salt from the Pacific and glance over the tops of the pine trees at the blue horizon. Between those pines and the ocean lies our town. At one time it was called Chinook Falls, in southwestern Oregon. After the Relocation Act of 2320, all the locals were forced to move south to Sapphire City. Our denomination settled here. It is a beautiful place, nestled between the ocean and the foothills of the Cascade Mountains. My great-grandfather, Isaac Alexander, was part of the original twelve thousand who recolonized the town and named it Shiloh. There were about 144,000 who settled throughout the Northwest Territory, but now the three or so thousand left in our town are all that remain. It is God's grace and our location that spared us from the spread of the virus.

"*Crack*." I jump slightly from the sheer decibel level of this new noise and shift my gaze from the motionless hillside to the small tract of woods to my right. Without noticing, I have released the safety on my rifle and am staring through the crosshairs at a pair of feet dangling helplessly over a fallen tree.

"Are you trying to get yourself killed?" I yell toward the now scrambling figure, who somehow has managed to right himself, possibly more quickly than he hit the ground. No doubt he was hoping I was sitting deeper into the woods and would not have noticed his graceful display.

"You saw that?" comes the weak reply from an all too familiar voice.

"I knew it was you before you hit the ground!" I yell back at my best friend Phil. "That is why God called you to cook the food!"

"Yeah, Sardis, the only reason you are out here is because God knew your people skills before you were even born."

That is why he is my best friend. It is true that I have a habit of not handling certain situations with the grace I have been taught, but Phil has never seemed to mind. He just gives me a look or fires right back.

"What are you doing here?" I ask, as I think back to the handful of times I have seen Phil outside of town during the nineteen years I've known him. The last time he snuck up on me during a hunt was six months ago to inform me that Lacy Fair had called off her courtship with Jeremiah Nelson. She was my childhood crush, and Phil knew how much it killed me when Jeremiah was given permission to ask for her hand. Another time was back in 2416, my first year solo hunting, to tell me about Mom.

"Put that gun down and get over here. It is coming today!"

"No way!" I feel the adrenaline begin to fade from Phil's loud entrance, only to be buoyed by the excited anticipation of what would be inside this month's shipment. It is true that I have been called to be one of the providers for our community, but I feel my real gift is my ability to feel things. I can sense animals in the woods before I can hear or see them. I can tell what people are thinking by just being with them. I also have this unique understanding of the operation of my body. Phil tells me I am nuts when I try to explain how I can feel the chemicals racing through my veins as I experience life. He reminds me that God gave us these feelings and they are to be controlled by our minds, not our chemicals. He may be right, but my mind sometimes thinks the chemicals have more to do with how I feel than God does.

When I reach Phil, he has his stupid grin. I call it the Phil face. Generally speaking, he is a normal looking kid with short brown hair, a stocky unathletic build, and brown eyes; but when he becomes excited he flashes this silly grin that makes me want to either laugh or slap it off.

"Hopefully it will be here today. I don't think I could wait another whole month. It almost killed me last month when it wasn't there!" Every month, two freight cars drop off supplies in our town, a sort of good-will offering from those in the Establishment. No one really knows why they started doing this. For ninety some years, no one ever was allowed to come in, other than the doctors and government officials of course. Then, six years ago they started coming. I think they felt sorry for the way we were treated after the epidemic, but my father thinks there is a more sinister motive – a way to corrupt the minds of this new generation of believers, to take away any possible threat of upheaval in the future by exposing us to "new and exciting technology," as he always says. It is true. Since the shipments started, two hundred people have decided to leave for the Establishment. My father is afraid that someday I will go. To be honest, I have thought about it – especially after Mom died. I have questioned a lot of things since then, but I know I will never leave. This is my home, where I grew up, and where I still feel her.

It is about a three-mile hike from the entrance of town to my favorite hunting spot across from Bright Meadow. It usually takes about an hour to hike out since most of the way is up the mountain. The trail is steep in parts, winding alongside Chinook River, and the views on a sunny day like today are breathtaking. Hiking in is much easier and usually takes half the time. Today we make it in twenty minutes flat.

"There they are!" Phil yells from a hundred yards behind me.

"You think? Come on, Philistine, get those oversized drumsticks in gear!"

"I might not be as fast as you are, Sardine, but at least I smell better."

As is customary, the train is no longer here. They have swapped out the two freight cars left from last month, and the new ones are now resting just inside the open city gate. I reach the gate and begin to wade through the normal crowd. Most people are either at work or school, so only the mothers and the eldest are gathered around the agape cars. Almost all married women with families do not work; each stays at home to take care of her child. One of the regulations of the Articles of Human Peace and Equality states that each family is permitted only one child. After the Relocation, this was enacted to control the human population, but now after the virus, it seems only in place to keep our faith system in check. In fact, there are rarely children born at all anymore in the Establishment.

"Oh man, we are late," I say to Phil as he finally joins me. "Hopefully no one has swiped it."

"Whose name did you put on it?"

"I obviously couldn't put my name on it, genius. If my dad found out, he would kill me."

"So whose name did you put?"

"Um..." I crane my neck to see the name on the box on top of the first pile. "Ephie's."

"Ephie!"

"He was the only one I could think of who wouldn't raise suspicion with an extra box," I whisper back.

"You do realize that he is always one of the first in line. It's as if he has a sixth-sense when the cars are going to show up."

"Yes, I realize that." I turn over another box to check the name only to toss it aside in disgust. "And we may be too late. I only have one more pile to check."

"Sardis, look at this."

"Did you find it?"

"No, this one has your dad's name on it. When was the last time –"

"Four years." I finish the thought for him. "Let me see it." He hands me the box and I turn it around to read the label:

> Jason Alexander, PHD
> 194 South Main Street
> Shiloh, Northwest Territory

"That's him," I mouth as I slowly spin the brown rectangular shape in my hands attempting to decipher what is inside. "This thing is ridiculously heavy. What could possibly be in here?" I say a little louder to no one in particular.

Dad gave up all contact with the outside world after Mom died, as if shunning those responsible would somehow avenge his wife's death. He has forgiven them, which is required by our faith, but his feelings have been made clear. He and his family were no longer to mention or think about worldly things ever again, and since I am the only one left, this mandate falls on me.

"Hurry up, Philistine, let's check this last pile. I have a feeling we will be making a trip to campus." We scour the last stack only to come up empty.

"Only the food supplies are left. Ephie must have been here already. Really, Phil, you need to lay off those cheese cakes. Ten minutes faster up that mountain and we could have beaten him to the stack."

That remark sours the Phil face, and I quickly duck to dodge the left cross targeted for the back of my skull. "Why is it that every time I bring up the name Ephie, there are punches thrown?" I chuckle as his grin returns. Ephie is known to everyone else as Dr. Porter. I have never really liked the guy. There is just something about the way he looks, tall and gangly with a mousy face – and the way his eyes shift behind his glasses – it just rubs me the wrong way. He and my father are professors at the University. Ephie is the Technology Dean and last semester Phil and I were both in his *Faith and Technology* class. Probably because most computer devices are frowned upon, we have always been fascinated by them – the newer and more advanced the better. In one particular computer lab, Phil and I happened to cause a small riot by "unintentionally" remotely activating a new device that was designed to catch cheating. It sat in the front of the classroom and scanned each student, detecting changes in their behavior or physiology. An alarm would sound if someone was deemed guilty and that person's name was announced loudly by the machine. Somehow Phil figured out a way to pick a certain seat in the classroom and have the alarm go off for that seat. We would be sitting in class and all of a sudden the alarm would start blaring, trumpeting the name of whichever student he deemed worthy. We would try so hard to sit straight-faced and contain our laughter, but more often than not we would fail miserably, especially the time I picked Jeremiah Nelson. He knew I didn't like him, so when his name echoed through our class, he jumped out of his seat and started throwing punches. He connected with one, but I quickly nailed him with two before the all-out brawl commenced. The whole class was in on it, causing Dr. Porter to scream, "If you kids do not halt these shenanigans this instant, so help me, if my name is not *Ephesus* James Porter, I will personally escort each and every one of you to your maker!" It was from that point forward that he was known to us as Ephie; and every time I hear or say the name I think back on that day and smile.

"We can drop Dad's package off at my place on the way. It looks like we will be breaking into the computer office once again!" I shout triumphantly. We both laugh as we jump off the platform and head up Main Street toward our houses and campus.

Phil grew up three houses from me, and we have been friends for as long as I can remember. His father, Levi Conner, is one of the Pastors at our church, and his mother, Mary, just returned to her calling as a nurse at the hospital once Phil finished classes last semester. Mary has been like a second mother to me, especially after Mom died. She would come over some mornings and bring breakfast for Dad and me; and the mornings I would have a big test or competition, she would make apple pancakes. My dad makes the best, but Mary's are a close second.

We hurriedly make our mile journey up Main Street. Technically I am on my lunch break so I really do not have much time to mess around. Children in our community go to grammar school until age fifteen and then four years at the University to hone their calling. Both Phil and I are in our final University semester which consists of all field experience. Phil was called to be a chef, while I am following in my mother's footsteps. During a normal day, I will hunt in the morning and the early evening when most of the game is moving. Depending on the time of year and where the herds are located, I may take overnight trips further away from town. It is the end of September though, so the deer and elk are just coming into their mating seasons. It is the best time of year to hunt.

"I'll be right back." I hurry up the front stairs to my house and fumble through my pockets for the keys. I open the door and quickly place my rifle in the gun case in the closet below the stairs and open the door to my father's study. As I place the package on the desk, I can feel a presence in the room. The chair facing the window slowly begins to swivel.

"We need to talk."

Chapter 2

I can feel the blood pounding in my neck as a wave of heat and nausea rises from my gut into my throat.

"About what?"

Dad slowly places his hands on his knees and rises from the chair. He takes two steps toward the window and puts his hands in his pockets. "Do you think I'm –" he rises on the balls of his feet, but quickly composes himself.

"Is there something you would like to tell me, Son?"

Thoughts are flying through my head. Does he know? Should I tell him? How did he find out –the shipment just got here?

"Um, I'm not sure what you are getting at. Seriously though, could this wait until later? Phil and I –"

He raises his shirt sleeve to his mouth. "Hi, Phil. This is Mr. Alexander. You should get back to work."

My jaw hits the floor. Not only does he know about the package, he is using it. I know I should say something but there is nothing to say.

"Dr. Porter and I have been fooling around with these. The things people invent these days." He looks down at his wrist and then lifts it toward me so I can see. "Last month they just showed up at the shipment addressed to him, but he claims he didn't order them. We thought that was quite odd. What do you think?"

I stand there for a moment staring at his wrist. Obviously I should have realized Ephie grabbed them last month, how stupid.

I cannot believe that thought never crossed my mind. How can I get out of this now? Dad knows. Ephie knows. I frantically search for a viable excuse but none surfaces. There is only one option left, the truth. I take a deep breath and go for it.

"I ordered them and addressed them to Dr. Porter so you would not find out."

My complete honesty catches him off guard. He looks at his desk as if rearranging the thoughts in his mind. "Why, Sardis? You know how I feel about this."

"I know, Dad – I'm just – I don't know."

"You're what? You're searching for something?"

"No, I'm not searching for something. I don't know. You wouldn't understand."

"Please, explain it to me."

I look past his stern gaze and see Main Street through his study window. Anxiety begins to bubble inside as I try and put into words what I feel. "It's because I'm – I'm sick of being punished for something that had nothing to do with me!"

"Sardis," he groans, shaking his head. "Outside these walls there is nothing but pain and suffering, lifeless beings who think that things like this," he throws the communication devices on the desk, "are what we are to live for. Is that what you want?"

"It's not as black and white as that."

"It is as black and white as that! This is how it happens. You let the desire spread and soon it's like – it's like a wild fire consuming your every waking thought. You allow their propaganda, how much easier and more fun life is when there are no consequences, to permeate your mind and soon that is all you long for."

"Every choice I make or any thought I have is not a referendum on my soul!"

"That is what they want you to think!" he screams.

13

He abruptly takes a step back and softens his gaze. "Look, you are a good kid and I love you but this infatuation has to stop. It will leave you empty, longing to be somewhere you cannot be and someone you are not, until you decide you do not want to be here anymore. I have seen it too many times." His shoulders slouch and he takes a seat on the edge of the desk. "I can't lose you, too."

I relax as well, as if that last comment soothes an open wound that has never been attended. We often fight about everyday things, things that don't matter. We fight for what seems like no reason at all. Only there is a reason. We are trying to cope with our loss in our own way. We both need and cannot stand to be around each other. I look at him and see how much better and easier things were when she was here, and he looks at me and sees the same.

"I miss her, too, Dad."

Those words hang in the air as I take a seat on the opposite corner of the desk.

"She would have liked these," he says smiling as he picks up a device. "I can hear her now, 'Jay, are you there? Can you pick up some milk on the way home from the office today?'" I had not heard him use the "Mom Voice" in a long time and it brings out an unexpected laugh. He smiles but then lowers his hands to his lap and lets out a heavy sigh. "I am sorry if I have been – distant these past few years. We haven't talked about Mom or things like that for a long time."

"It's alright, Dad."

"No. No, it's not." He stares blankly at the device in his hands, slowly turning it over as a faint smile returns to his face.

"I never told you what she said to me that morning. We had the census the day before, and she took the pregnancy test." He looks at me with the parent guise again. "That reminds me; we have the census tomorrow morning."

I roll my eyes, "I know, Dad, keep going with your story."

"Anyway, she came in to the study and plopped down on the corner of the desk, right where you are sitting. I could tell there was something was on her mind – you know how she was. So I set down the book I was reading and as serious as I could and still keep a straight face, I said, 'Did it come back positive this month?'" He snickers. "And she answered in that tone only she could do – 'So you are saying I look fat?'"

He starts laughing harder and I join in, remembering the times she would kid me using that same voice. He takes a deep breath and wipes his eyes.

"But then she got a serious look and asked, 'Do you think it's worth it?' 'Worth what?' I asked. And she said 'Worth dying for?' As you can imagine, I was confused as to what on earth she was referring to. So I said, 'I guess it depends on what 'it' is.'" He laughs again at his response as if she was the one sitting here reliving this memory.

"She stood up and said this – and it still sticks with me to this day – she said, 'I was reading from Luke during my devotion time yesterday before Sardy and I left for a hunt. It was the first time in a while we hunted together and I was just struck by how much he has grown. It got me thinking that someday he might be doing this with his child – and, Jay, I started wondering if that was a good thing. God tells us we are to die to ourselves daily and follow him. Is this life, this world, our future, worth dying for?'

"Before I could come up with a response, she got this wild grin on her face and said, 'Of course it is! It is the humanity we are fighting for. I want my grandchild, just like my son, to experience what it means to be alive, to feel the breeze in his face, and to feel the danger when you love someone so much that to lose them is to lose a part of yourself—'" his voice trails off as his memory overwhelms his usual composure. He raises his hand to his chin and lets out a deep sigh. "And then she winked at me and said, 'If this goes bad, make sure you tell Sardis to always let love guide his heart.'"

I smile. It would be just like her to wink before giving her final instructions.

"Then she met up with Dr. Pergo and went in for the procedure. I never thought it would be the last time I spoke with her. I expected to see her again soon. I didn't even cancel class that day."

"No one knew, Dad; it was just a freak thing."

"I know, but I feel like I should have known – or done something. I didn't even say goodbye."

We sit there for a moment reflecting on that day. I long for a measure of closure, a way to erase the memory of how I felt when I first learned she was gone. To have one last moment with her, even if only to say goodbye, would have been enough. Instead I am stuck; holding onto a fleeting hope that this is all some big mistake, as if someday she is going to walk through that door and make everything better. I know I need to let go but I am terrified of losing that hope – as if then all she will be is a memory.

Dad slaps his knee as if announcing he is back in dad-mode. "Well, there still is this business of deceit to address. There are consequences for our actions in Shiloh." He takes a moment to properly decide my fate. "No dessert cakes for two weeks and you need to stop by Dr. Porter's office and apologize."

I groan, but concede, realizing I have gotten off easy.

"He has been wracking his brain for a month trying to figure out who would forge his name. It just dawned on him one day when he saw me walking by. That was quite the semester you had last –"

"I'll be sure to stop by first thing tomorrow," I chime in, changing the subject before fist fights and detentions emerge in his memory and the punishment worsens. "Why are you home early anyway?"

"Oh, I was just on my lunch and I stopped to get a few things from my study on my way to get that," he motions toward the box sitting on the table. "Thanks for picking it up for me."

"What is it?

"Just something for one of the chemistry labs I'm setting up for next week."

"But I thought you gave up all contact with the Establishment..."

He walks around the desk and sits in his chair, opening the front desk compartment. "Yes. I did." He pulls out a pen and a small key. "This is an exception, Sardis; I need a block of palladium for an experiment and there is no more in town." He walks to the far wall and unlocks his safe. He pulls out a brown satchel and a few folders and places the package inside. I slide off the desk and head toward the door.

"Thanks for being honest with me," he says as I turn the handle. "I was prepared for a fight and your punishment could have been a lot worse."

"I may get my personality from Mom but I've picked a few things up from you as well. And not just the good looks!" It is true though, we do look a lot alike: tall, broad shoulders, reddish brown hair and bright blue eyes. "See you tonight for dinner? What do you think, Mark's or Martha's?"

"I think I'm in the mood for Martha. What's on the menu?"

"Not sure yet! I guess I should get back to it. I think I'll head to mom's favorite spot after lunch and take my bow in honor of her." He smiles and I walk out. After a few steps I turn around, walk back in, and put my arm around his shoulder. "Thanks, Dad, for all you do. I may not say that enough either."

"I love you, too, Sardy." He pulls me in close, then reaches down and picks up the devices off the desk.

"Tell Phil you wrestled these off me. I don't want him to think I'm going soft."

"Thanks, Dad."

"Just be careful – you never know who may be listening in."

I slide the devices into my pocket. I will have to meet up with Phil later and try these things out; but for now, I grab my shotgun and bow from the closet and head toward the hunting grounds. By the time I reach Bright Meadow, the sunshine that had ruled the early part of the day has disappeared. In its place is the overcast sky that dominates our climate.

There are twelve hunters in our community and I am by far the youngest. The food we harvest is vital for sustaining our population. The east side of our city is designated for agriculture, but there is just not enough area to grow crops and keep enough cattle to feed the whole city. The government allows us to hunt within twenty square miles of the city limits with no real restrictions on what game we can harvest.

Each person in Shiloh has a calling, that when melded together, allows our community to continue to survive. What I kill is taken to the butcher's shop to be processed, then to the chefs who prepare the meal at one of the fifteen restaurants. Each restaurant has its own flare. Mark's, for example, is known more for its fish and seafood, while Martha's is more wild game. We all eat together in the evenings and share communion and fellowship. No one is paid for his work but each person is an essential cog in the wheel. The pastor nourishes the nurse, who cares for the chef, who prepares the food for the professor, who teaches the next generation how to maximize the gifts with which God has blessed them.

I continue past this morning's hunting spot at the edge of the meadow and head deeper into the forest. I find a well-used game trail and follow it, my bow on my back and my shotgun in hand. A pair of grouse burst into the air as I pass a small thicket and I quickly fire off two accurate shots. With the quarry safely stowed in the pouch on my back, I continue through the familiar terrain. I reach the edge of another clearing and stop to observe. I notice the sun has peeked from behind the clouds and there is a slight breeze blowing in my face. This is a good spot to sit for a while. I place my shotgun against a tree and nock an arrow. Mom's favorite weapon was her bow. She never told me why specifically but I think it was the challenge. Anyone can take a deer from a hundred yards with a rifle and a scope but it takes skill to move close enough to your prey to use your bow; and she was as skilled as anyone. I used to practice with her all the time. I could never quite best her, but I came close.

Ten minutes goes by; twenty; life begins to reemerge around me. First the song birds flitter in, followed by the smaller woodland animals. Soon, the forest forgets I have taken residence below one of its pines. A hawk swoops into the meadow and grabs a field mouse, but only for a moment, as it loses its grip a few feet off the ground and the mouse tumbles back to earth.

I wonder if it were the abundance of life that made this her favorite spot. I remember the many times she brought me to this place. "Elk and deer follow the game trail and venture to the edges of the clearing to feed on the grass," she would teach, "but make sure you keep an eye on the dark forest behind the light. It is there you will find most of your success. Sure, the meadow is easy, but if we become comfortable in its light we will never reach the fullness of what God has in store for us. It is in the darkness, Sardis, where the greatest harvest lies." Every lesson was a life lesson.

I look down at my wrist and remember what Dad said about her liking the transmitter if she were still here. *If she were still here.* I don't understand. Why did you have to take her from me? There is so much I never got to learn and even more I never had a chance to tell her. I thought you were our protector? You say we are to die to ourselves daily and follow you, forsaking our families and all we have. For what? For you? For your satisfaction? Do you enjoy watching us suffer and die while those who curse your name, or worse, do not even acknowledge your existence, get to revel in the best of this world?

A rustle in the opposite pines grabs my attention. Instantly the adrenaline pours through my body as I peer through the light and into the darkness.

Chapter 3

I hear the noise again and rule out the possibility it was just the wind rustling a few limbs. The contrast between the bright clearing and the shadows in the opposite pines make it difficult to see deep into the woods. My whole body is tense, but completely still, as I stare intensely into the crisscrossed branches. I see no movement nor can I make out any shape; but from the sound I know whatever is lurking just beyond my sight is much larger than the small squirrels and birds that are playing around me. Whatever it is may have noticed my presence and is standing as still as I am, waiting for me to make the first move so it can determine the level of danger before leaving its hiding place; but that will not happen, because I know something it is only fearful of. It is being hunted. Its instincts tell it to freeze, to listen, to run back to the cover of darkness at any strange noise or smell, but this innate fear can only take it so far. A bear or wolf it knows but an arrow is a foe it has never faced. A step into the light means certain death.

I am frozen, my left hand on the body of the bow, my right hand clutching the nock and string. I wait. Ten minutes feels like ten hours, and then, movement. The cow elk having waited out the enemy steps confidently into the meadow and lowers its head to take its final mouthful. The arrow passes behind the right shoulder blade, piercing both lungs, and exits into the darkness. Dumbfounded, it jumps in the air and runs back into the pines.

I sit for a moment and collect myself. There is no other feeling like that of the hunt: the taking of one life for the life of another. I say a quick prayer of thanks for His provision and for the life of the creature. Existence is both brutal and beautiful whether one is the hunter or the hunted. Today, I am the one with the bow. Tomorrow, I may be the one who takes the final breath.

I walk across the meadow and see the evidence of the kill shot. The bright red blood and tissue on the ground is clear indication the lungs were the mark. I continue into the woods, knowing from many such encounters that a lung-shot will only allow the animal to live for a few moments once it has begun to run. I walk a hundred or so yards into the dense pines and I see the elk lying on its side. I radio Thomas, the butcher's son, to come and retrieve the animal. He enjoys the job because he gets to drive the all-terrain vehicle. Other than for certain tasks, like plowing the fields, or in this case, retrieving a six-hundred pound cow elk, vehicle travel is forbidden by the government. In fact, ground travel is non-existent outside our village; those in the Establishment will fly if they even travel at all.

While I wait for Thomas to arrive, I walk back to the kill zone in the meadow and determine the trajectory of the arrow's flight so I can retrieve it from the woods. I make the walk into the dense pines twice but see nothing. I check the elk to see if it is still lodged in the animal but it is not. Where is this thing? I take off deeper into the woods. Twenty paces or so in, I leave the dense group of pines and find it lodged at the base of a huge white oak. When I bend to grab it, I notice something shiny buried in the dirt. I brush the dirt away unveiling an old tin box. It is weathered and the image on the top is corroded. "S…" I uncover, wiping the grime away with my sleeve. "A…R…D…I…S… Sardis?" I gasp aloud. I hurriedly pry open the box. Inside are a letter wrapped in plastic and a military pin in the shape of a cross. I examine the pin and find an inscription, "Commander of Angel Armies." I slide it into my pocket and unwrap the letter. It is a single sheet of lined paper folded into thirds.

> *My dear Sardis,*
>
> *I pray this letter finds you and finds you well. It was the joy of my life to watch you grow from the peanut you were when I brought you home from the hospital that first night, to the young man you are becoming. I saw how much you loved life and I hope one day you will be able to follow the lead of your heart and take hold of all that God has placed before you. This pin is one that belonged to your great-grandfather, who fought in the battle of 2312. I have worn it ever since but I think that it should belong to you. I did not know how or when to give it to you but I trust God will bring it to you in His perfect timing. When you are ready, I know God will lead you to this letter and these instructions:*
>
> *Follow your heart. Don't ever sacrifice what makes you human.*
>
> *Follow the advice of Godly friends and never let them leave your side.*
>
> *Fall in love and never let that feeling go. It is the greatest gift from God.*
>
> *And finally, always trust in the Lord, He will never forsake you. You are a commander of Angel Armies. Never forget that.*
>
> > *With all my love,*
> > *Mom*

Tears are flowing down my face as I stare at the message. The way she writes – I can hear her voice speaking the words as if she were standing right here with me. I look up half expecting to see her, but realize my emotions are getting the best of me. Thoughts are swirling through my mind. When did she write this? How did she know I would find it? Did she know she was going to die that day?

I fold the paper and carefully slide it in my pocket. I grab my bow and gun and sprint toward home. My only thought is to show this to Dad. As I run, I am twelve again, running home for lunch after playing at Phil's house, wondering what Mom is cooking on the stove. I hope it is her venison stew. The way the vegetables soak up the flavor of the meat excites my senses just thinking about it. I will tell her about all the hunts I have been on since she went away: like the time I tracked the 8x8 bull elk for miles before finally taking it with my bow, or the time I jumped the brown bear that required four shotgun blasts to stop its charge within feet of making me his lunch. I will tell her how Dad and I have had our struggles, but have recently begun to patch up our relationship. When she asks which lucky girl I have my eye on, I'll explain that there has only ever been one, and she'll laugh because she knows my heart better than I do. We will sit at the kitchen table and talk for hours and hours, just like the talks we had walking to and from the hunting grounds.

The drone of Thomas' vehicle snaps me out of the illusion. I give him the grouse and explain the location of the carcass, then continue home. The rest of the way I try and determine when she would have hidden the box for me to find and how she would have known exactly where to put it so only I would find it. By the time I reach Dad's study, I have decided it must have been before

I started the solo hunts, and she put it close to her favorite spot knowing I would frequent it often.

I open the study door but Dad is nowhere to be found. "Does he know about the letter?" I blurt, still disoriented from the day. I shake my head to try and clear it. Obviously he is just not back from class, it's only – I look at the clock on the wall – 5:30, dinner at Martha's! I hurry back out the door and make for the restaurant.

On the way, I slip one of the new neural communication devices on my wrist. With all the excitement of the day, I had completely forgotten about them. I have to tell Phil my father didn't kill me.

"Phil, can you hear me?" I yell at it not knowing exactly how it works. I put the bracelet to my ear.

"Sardis? Is that you?" I hear Lacy Fair's voice respond as if she were *inside* my head. I spin quickly and see her walking on the opposite side of the street, wearing her nursing outfit, and huddled inside a heavy fur coat.

"Oh. Hi, Lacy." I feel my face flush. "I was just looking for Phil; have you seen him?"

"No," she says slowly. "I haven't." She looks at me strangely. "Am I losing my mind or was your voice just inside my head?"

"Oh," I say realizing how stupid I must look. "Yeah, I –"

"You what?"

I hesitate for a moment thinking how dumb I would sound if I explained that I had no clue how to work this thing. "I just got these new neural transmitters. They send messages through electrical impulses directly to another person's mind. I saw you walking by – and figured I would try it out on you."

"That's a little presumptuous, don't you think?"

I stare blankly at her, not sure if she is waiting for me to respond. "Well –"

"And why would I want you of all people inside of my head? And why did you call me Phil?"

"Well… I… Um –"

"Don't ever do something like that to me again!" She pulls her purse higher onto her shoulder and briskly walks away.

That was smooth, I think as I watch her pony-tail bob back and forth. Not wanting her to think I am following her, I pretend as if I am trying to tighten the strap on the transmitter until I notice her turn the corner toward the hospital. Why did it have to be Lacy standing there!

Martha's is located on the west side of town, behind the hospital, but before the dock and fishing district. Like most of the restaurants it is set up in a cafeteria format, with a buffet line in the front and tables lined in rows throughout. I walk in and locate my father sitting with a few other professors. From the amount of arm waving and the looks on a few of their faces, it appears as if they are in a deep debate over something. I decide this is not the best time to tell him my news and look for another place to sit. I spot Phil standing in the buffet line and sneak up behind him. I tap him on his left shoulder and quickly move to his right side, but a quick elbow to my gut suggests I have tried this trick one too many times.

"Nice to see you made it out alive," he jokes. "I almost had a heart attack when your dad's voice popped into my head."

"Yeah, he let me off pretty easy. I was expecting Armageddon."

"At least we know the communicators work!"

"Yeah, a little too well." I plop a spoonful of mashed potatoes next to an elk steak. "Here is yours. I guess you have to be wearing this in order for me to communicate with you."

"Why? Did you invade someone else's mind trying to reach me or something?" he remarks in a way that suggests only a real moron would do something like that. My silence suggests I might not be as technologically savvy as he thinks I am. "Are you serious? Who?"

"Take one guess."

"No way!"

"Yeah, shut up. Real funny. She already thinks I'm an idiot."

"And you just reinforced it!" he shoots triumphantly as we sit down across from each other. "What did she hear you say?"

"I was just trying to talk to you. I don't remember exactly what I said. She was on her way to work."

"Or on her way to dinner before work." He motions with his eyes toward a table in the middle of the open room. I glance over my shoulder and see her sitting with a few other nurses. She is laughing, and something about the way her eyes light up when she is happy, causes me to stare for a moment.

"So how do these things work then? If you are not wearing the other transmitter do my thoughts just randomly bounce into someone else's head?"

"No, not randomly," he answers between chews. "You have to be able to see the person. That's how your dad communicated with me. He must have seen me standing outside the window. But if you can't see who you want to reach, then it doesn't work."

"Good to know. At least we didn't have to sneak into Ephie's office −" I take a mouthful of mashed potatoes. "Although I do have to stop by tomorrow and apologize. That's part of the punishment."

He puts down his fork and grabs his glass. "I'll come with you; it was my idea, too. I won't let you face him alone. Besides, I don't want to miss the fireworks." He flashes his grin and takes a drink. It is times like these that I really admire him. Being a pastor's son he is expected to be a moral lighthouse. He has to choose his words carefully and make sure that his actions mirror them. For as long as I have known him though, that is who he is. He is not fake. He is truly the most humble and compassionate person I know. I would have been much more surprised if he would have not volunteered to come with me to see Ephie. I cannot say I would have made that decision.

"Thanks, Bud. I appreciate it."

"You would have done the same for me. By the way, did your dad happen to say what was in that package?"

"Yeah, he said it was some chemical he was using for an experiment in one of his classes. But I got this feeling there was something else going on with it. I can't put my finger on it though." I sit back in my chair and grab my glass to take a drink.

"I agree; that does not sound like your dad. He has nothing to do with the Establishment." He crinkles up his napkin, tosses it on his empty plate, and leans back in his chair. "What do you think he is up to?"

"I have no idea. The whole thing is strange."

"Yeah – What a crazy day."

"I didn't even tell you the craziest thing that happened!"

"Oh yeah? Something crazier than your dad's voice in my head?"

"Listen to this… I shot an elk with my bow this afternoon and went looking for the arrow –" a nervous tug in my gut causes me to hesitate. Should I wait to tell Dad first? Should I even tell Phil? "– I looked everywhere for this thing but couldn't find it. So I walked deeper into a section of woods I had not been to in a while and I found it stuck at the base of this big oak. When I bent down to pick it up, I saw something shiny buried in the dirt. It was an old tin box with my name on the top of it!" I emphatically lean forward on the table. If I can't tell my best friend, who loved my mom like she was his own, whom could I ever tell? "So I opened it up and found a letter and this pin." I pull it out of my pocket and hand it to him.

"Commander of Angel Armies?"

"Phil – the letter was from Mom!"

"What? That is awesome, Sardis! What did it say?"

"Well –" I sit up to take it out of my pocket when I have this overwhelming urge to keep the words to myself, as if sharing them would somehow diminish the connection that was rekindled. "It just said she loved me and was proud of me, and I should always follow where God is leading me."

"Wow. I am so happy for you, Buddy. That is amazing! I bet that really means a lot to you."

"It really, really does." His remark massages the uneasy feeling in my gut. I let down my guard and open up to him.

"Dad and I – we talked about her today – the first time in a long time. It was nice."

"Oh, yeah? What did you guys talk about? The letter?"

"No, I actually haven't told him about that yet."

"Oh?"

"I was hoping too, but he was already gone when I got home this afternoon."

"I see... So what did you guys talk about earlier?"

"We just talked about... her – You know?"

He nods his head. "She was a wonderful woman. I know how much I miss her."

I look down at my hands and let out a weak sigh, before looking over at the empty table where Dad and his colleagues had been sitting a few minutes earlier. "We both think about her all the time, but never talk about her. You know? Like – talking about her would make the other person hurt."

"Do you think he feels guilty for what happened?"

"Yeah, maybe. I know it's not his fault. I just wish —" I shake my head.

"What, Bud?"

"I don't know. I just wish — Oh, I don't know. Just promise me someday when we are old and gray, and we see each other for the last time, that we will remember to say goodbye. It really would make life easier."

He smiles. "I think I can remember to do that."

"And make me laugh, too."

"I promise. I will tell you one of my famous jokes."

"I said make me laugh, not cry."

"By that time I will have mastered my comedic calling."

"Yeah… forget I mentioned that. I forgot I can just take one look at your face and laugh for days."

He flashes his grin and sticks his chin up as if posing. "You must not realize how the years will mold this face into a priceless work of art."

I smile and nod. How else does one respond to that statement? We stand up to leave and I toss my napkin at him.

"Sardis," I hear a woman's voice say from behind. I turn and see Lacy. "I just wanted to apologize for how I acted earlier. What I said was rude."

"No problem. I should have learned how to work it before I used it," I confess in complete shock she is speaking to me.

"Yes, you should have." She cracks a smile. "And you still do."

My blank petrified stare must have alerted her to the fact that if she is referring to what I think she is referring to, then I might fall over dead from embarrassment; so she quickly adds, "I am not upset or anything, but could you figure out how to work your new gadget properly so your voice isn't in my head all the time?"

"Oh, yeah – sure – no problem, Lacy. I am so sorry about that. I really need to figure this thing out."

"It really is not a big deal," she reassures, but I am miles past the point where any reassurance will help. "And I also wanted to say I'm happy you found that message from your mom; I know how it is to lose someone."

"Oh, thanks. I appreciate that. Yeah, it was nice to hear from her again." Someone please shoot me! We stand there for a moment and I realize I am staring at her eyes. Embarrassed that she might think I am gawking, I quickly blurt out, "And she was the love of my life!" I am making a total fool of myself! If there were a cliff nearby, I would jump.

Phil awkwardly coughs and interjects, "It was nice to see you, Lacy," in an effort to stop the bleeding.

"Yeah, I'll make sure I stay as far away from your head as possible!" Phil puts his hand on my shoulder and ushers me out the door.

We walk briskly, staring straight ahead, and not saying a word. Phil is attempting to hold his laughter, while I am struggling to comprehend what just happened. We slow our pace when we have put enough distance between ourselves and the restaurant.

"Was that as horrible as I think it was?"

"Yes." He confirms with a straight face. He looks over at me to see if I am still conscious before he cracks his smile. "It could have been worse." He erupts in laughter. "And take that thing off before she hears you again!"

I hurry up and pull it off my wrist and shove it deep into my pocket. "What the heck is wrong with these things!" I run my hands through my hair and throw them forward angrily. "I can't believe this!"

"I'm not sure what is going on. My best guess would be you created some sort of telepathic link between you and her during your earlier mishap."

"But the thing wasn't even turned on!"

"You must have bumped it when we were talking; probably at the end there whenever you were telling the story about finding the letter. You got pretty excited and were leaning against the table. I'm sure she only heard the last little bit of our conversation. Besides, she didn't seem upset about it. She even came up to you and apologized. When was the last time she has even had a conversation with you?"

"I can't remember." A sheepish grin sweeps across my face. "I guess it is kind of a one-sided relationship." We both laugh. "Hopefully that is all she heard. Man, that was awful. What a day."

"Amen, brother." Phil concludes as we approach his porch.

"I'll see you tomorrow, Philistine. Thanks for having my back. If you had not herded me out the door, I may still be there digging my grave."

"No sweat, Bud. Tell your dad I said hi and make sure you fill me in on what he says about the letter." He gives me a playful shove then hops up the stairs to his front door.

"I will. See ya."

"Oh yeah, don't forget about the census tomorrow. I wouldn't want them to send the Dragons after you!" He waves and disappears through his front door.

I see the light on in my kitchen and walk in, full of nervous excitement to tell Dad about the day and show him the letter. He is sitting at the table reading the Bible with one hand and jotting notes with the other.

"I missed you at dinner tonight. Did you work late?" He asks, lifting his eyes from what he is working on.

"I was there. I saw you with guys from work, so I didn't want to interrupt." I sit quickly next to him at the table. "I'm sorry about that, Dad, but you have to see what I found today." My enthusiasm causes him to set his Bible down on the table and sit up attentively in his chair. I hand him the letter and the cross pin and begin to recite the entire story. He stares at the letter shaking his head as if he is trying to allow what I am telling him to enter into his conscience. There are points when he cracks a smile, as if he is actually witnessing her writing the letter or hiding it below the tree, but for the most part his reaction is tempered.

"So what do you think?"

"Who else knows about this?"

"Just Phil. I told him at dinner." I leave out the whole Lacy episode. I have no desire to endure another lecture on the dangers of technology. He looks at me and takes a deep breath. He closes his eyes and a small grin creeps across his face as if he was just let in on a great secret.

"Are you sure no one else knows?" He opens his eyes, revealing a wild look I have never seen before. "Sardis, are you sure no one else knows about this? Do not lie to me, son."

Taken aback by the tone of the question, I confess, "Well, Lacy Fair may have overheard. She mentioned something about it as we were leaving the restaurant."

"Does she know or does she not know!" he thunders, slamming his fist against the table.

"She knows, okay! What is wrong with you?"

"I apologize, Sardis; I just need a moment to digest this." He stands quickly and walks toward the closet. He grabs his coat and hurriedly throws it on. "I need to run to my office, and I probably won't be back until late." He jogs back to the table and grabs the letter. He turns around and gives me a hug, holding the embrace for a few seconds, and then grabs my shoulders and looks me in the eye, finally smiling. "You look just like her." He lets go and rushes toward the door. "Please stay here tonight, and if I happen to be gone when you wake up in the morning, don't worry." He forcefully grabs the door handle. "And whatever you do, do not forget about the census!"

I stand there in a daze, staring blindly at the empty room – the slamming of the door still ringing in my ears. A fear begins to rise as I attempt to comprehend what just happened.

Chapter 4

Tick... Tick... Tick... The sound of the second hand rhythmically starting and stopping in perfect intervals as it counts down the seconds until the end. I feel the cold steel of the table on my bare legs. The barren walls and sterile smell remind me of my location. I stare aimlessly at the round clock, wishing there was some way to halt its uninterrupted race against itself. Tick... Tick... Tick...

The door opens. A man enters wearing a white lab coat with blue sterile gloves and a white surgical mask on his face. I have seen him before, when I was young. His gait is rhythmic, robot-like, as he approaches my gurney and begins wheeling me down the hall.

"No need to worry, I have done this procedure thousands of times." The words put me at peace and my body relaxes. I stare straight ahead as the hallway continues on and on. Faster and faster we move. Fear begins to creep in as the sound of his footfalls become louder. "We should slow down," I advise as the speed continues to increase. Faster, faster. The lights on the ceiling are a blur. "Slow down!" I scream but no sound escapes my mouth. Faster, faster. I can hear him laughing as my fear shifts to panic. I try to look for a way to escape but we are moving too fast. I see the far wall approaching. "We have to stop or we are going to crash!" I bellow at the top of my lungs but still there is no sound. Faster, Faster...

I jump up, sweat pouring down my back. Gasping for air, I turn my head from side to side, scanning the dark room for my foe, but what I see is the familiar shape of my dresser. The tension retreats from my chest and I fall backwards onto my pillow. I lie there for a moment trying to collect my thoughts. What time is it? I roll over and search with my hand for the alarm clock. I locate it on the floor underneath my hunting coat. "Four-thirty," I mumble to myself and roll back over. It has been one of the longest nights of my life. Dad still has not returned, and I have been over the scene in the kitchen a hundred times since he left. He wasn't even excited, I think again, as I begin the mulling process for the one hundred and first time. It was almost as if he was expecting it. Maybe Mom had told him about it? But why would he run off like that? And why go to his office?

I throw my legs over the side of the bed and locate my slippers with my feet. I stumble downstairs and open the refrigerator for something to settle my stomach. I grab an apple and take a seat at the kitchen table, opening Dad's Bible. "Revelation chapter six, go figure," I mutter aloud, as I scan the familiar passage. He has verses ten and eleven underlined. "How long, Sovereign Lord, holy and true, until you judge the inhabitants of the earth and avenge our blood?" I recite from memory and take a bite from my apple. Both of my parents had a fascination with the book and this passage in particular, so much so that they named me after one of the churches in chapter three. I can remember them going to get-togethers with friends when I was younger, where they would study it for hours. I never really understood their interest. To me, it is just weird symbols and creatures with ten heads.

I stand and stretch in an attempt to either wake myself or have my body realize the depth of its fatigue. Realizing I am much more awake than tired, I wander into Dad's study to see if

I can find anything that might help me understand his actions last night. There are a handful of papers strewn across his desk along with the box, that at one time housed his shipment from yesterday, but is now open and empty. The door to the safe is ajar, so I look inside to see if there is something out of the ordinary. It is empty, other than a few papers. I see no sign of the folders or satchel he had there yesterday or the contents of the package. I decide to just ask him whenever he finally comes home. I let out a long yawn and give in to this sudden sweep of drowsiness and wander upstairs to bed.

When I awake, there is still no sign of him, so I throw on some clothes and grab some breakfast before heading to the government building. It is the tallest in the city, rising twelve stories above the town square. Per law, no building is permitted to be constructed higher. At the top sits the Emblem of Unity: two gold hands folded in the shape of a dove, surrounded by an olive wreath. It was created after the relocation as a symbol of global peace. The outside of the building is an intricate design of polished platinum sections and translucent glass panels. The large rectangular panels can display images or colors depending on what message the government is wishing to convey on that particular day. This morning there is a scrolling message with three dimensional fireworks reminding us the census is today. At the entrance are holographic people who are dressed in the finest clothing, dark purple and blue silk shirts and dresses with extravagant gold and gemstone jewelry. They wave and motion to any passer-by, happily inviting them to come inside and try some of the new devices and foods that have been developed within the past few weeks. As I approach, one figure calls out to me by name, asking if I am enjoying my new neural transmitter bracelets. I lower my gaze and increase my pace, ignoring the joyful faces.

As I step onto the bronze plated stones leading to the base of the building, four of the eight-foot tall panels slide into one another creating the entrance. Inside, there are sensors that analyze each person's tracking dye, alerting the humming propaganda machine to display images and objects that tempt each person's unique desires. I walk through the doorway and instantly am overtaken by the wonderful aromas emanating from within. The rich floral perfumes and sweet fruity smells tickle my senses and draw my attention to different brightly lit and colorful rooms full of decadent foods and beautiful artwork. There are displays of many new technologies, with more joyful figures eager for me to try. They are free, no strings attached, just choose and it will arrive with the next shipment.

I continue to the desk at the back of the first floor and grab my census card that has been created for me as I entered. I walk to one of the elevators and take it to the sixth floor, where all males go the first of every month to be counted for the census. Females go to the fifth floor, where they are also given a pregnancy test. I have made this trek dozens of times, and each time there is a different scene playing on the walls of the elevator. Today, it is an underwater reef. I reach to touch the elevator wall and it feels wet. Two bright blue and yellow fish dart to avoid my fingers. I slowly bring my hand back and place it on my face. It feels dry. I reach further to see if I can grab some of the coral when the door opens behind me. I quickly pull in my hand and walk out into the brightly lit hallway. Sitting at the desk is the same official who is always there, an I-Mort, just like everyone else in the Establishment.

An I-Mort is what we call the immortal bodies. The technology was developed during the twenty-third century. A human can transfer his conscious being from his human body to this man-made one, effectively allowing him to live forever. These bodies are inorganic, but they experience the same sensations as a human body and look and feel very similar. Their creation essentially changed the course of human history forever. Disease and hunger were eliminated. Eventually, the bodies were mass produced and sent around the world by peace organizations – a much more effective vessel to destroy poverty since they do not need food or water to exist. With a person's basic needs met, world peace became a reality. The Articles of Peace were written, dissolving all nationalities and merging them into one world. The only voice in resistance to the I-Mort revolution was the Church, which vehemently opposed the technology because it robbed a person of his humanity: stripping man of the Spirit that connected him to his Creator.

I hand the official my census card and she scans it into the computer. She motions me on and I follow the glowing green arrows moving along the floor tiles that direct me to the "bloodletting room," as Phil and I call it. "You cannot have atonement from your sins without the letting of blood," he often says reciting the tenet from scripture; and our sin, we joke, is still believing there is sin to be atoned for.

I walk into the room and sit in a remarkably comfortable chair. I stare tensely at an ornate sculpture in the corner of the room, deliberately avoiding eye contact with the I-Mort who is quickly and efficiently labeling and lining-up empty vials which are to be filled with my blood. He motions with his hand and I make the same nervous walk I do every month. I hold my breath as he inserts the needle and skillfully fills three vials.

He smiles cheerfully. "All done; now that wasn't so bad, was it?" I grin and thank him for being gentle, only because I have been taught to be Christ-like to everyone I meet. Truthfully I would rather punch the guy for making me do this every month.

"You don't have to thank me. It was my pleasure," he replies in that joyful tone that makes me want to hit him harder.

I fake another smile and head for the door. Phil is always lecturing me on how I need to be nicer to those in the Establishment. "It's the only way to fulfill the Great Commission in Matthew 28," he says with his pastoral tone; "We are to go and make disciples of all nations." I usually ignore him or say something sarcastic. Sure, once upon a time they were real people, but to me, they are soulless robots. If I ever met a human outside Shiloh, then maybe I would say something.

"Sardis Alexander." I turn back toward the bloodletting room and see an I-Mort I have never seen before. "You must proceed to the hospital immediately for further testing. Ask for Dr. Pergo at the reception desk on the first floor."

I feel the blood that is still left in me rush to my face, as an intense hatred mixed with rage begins to course through my body. I have not seen Dr. Pergo since he took my mother from me. I know I am called to forgive him but I can't. Not possible. I would rather kill him than forgive him, I realize as I pound the number one on the elevator and watch as the brightly lit sixth floor hallway disappears. I feel like spearing the stupid fish swimming around the elevator wall but decide against it. Instead, I stare defiantly ahead, ignoring their fabricated beauty and fixing my eyes on my reflection in the shiny door. What I see is something real, tangible, even if I am shamed by the anger in my eyes. I reach the bottom and storm through the first floor, blowing right past Lacy and several displays of gold jewelry and brilliant gem stones, similar to the necklace and earrings she was wearing last night.

As I walk, the events from the last twenty-four hours replay through my mind. I am still concerned for my father. I have no idea why he acted the way he did, nor do I know where he is now or what he is doing. The letter is still fresh in my mind, bringing up thoughts and feelings about my mother that I have not experienced in so long. The multiple episodes with Lacy are also weighing heavily on me. I have totally blown any shot I might have had to win her favor. Now, as I walk toward the hospital and this encounter with Dr. Pergo, I can't help but feel he is the one responsible. If Mom were still here, everything would be normal. She would know what to say and how to fix all of this. But she is not here and it is his fault. I walk up the steps with a clear and determined focus – I must repay him for what he has done to me. I step from the bright midmorning sun into the darkness of the dimly lit hospital lobby.

Out of the light and into the darkness – the thought echoes through my mind, through my soul, as I place one foot in front of the other. Images of hunts with my mother flash through my mind as my eyes begin to adjust to the dull shadowy surroundings. I see the desk. One foot in front on the other, I think as all willpower leaves me. I hear the words of my mother urging me to look beyond the comfort and ease of the meadow. She would want me to seek forgiveness. That is what is needed. But the temptation for retribution is too great. The opportunity to punish the one who did this to me is at hand, and I will not let it pass. "Dr. Pergo, please," I say to Mrs. Weaver, the receptionist, who motions toward an elevator to the left of the desk.

"Basement floor, third door on the right, room B-13."

I step into the elevator and barely notice the stark difference between the last ride and this one. I am consumed by one thought: kill Dr. Pergo.

The doors open to the basement floor and I walk out with purpose, confidently striding toward my goal. I throw open the door to room B-13, only to startle Phil, causing him to spill a glass of water.

"Phil? What are you doing here?"

"You scared the heck out of me barging in here like that." He bends to pick the glass off the floor. "You look like you want to kill someone."

"I must be in the wrong room," I say maniacally, turning around and walking back into the hallway. Who is this person who has taken over my body? I look at the placard next to the door—B-13. This is the room.

The hallway begins to spin as the reality of what I was about to do hits me. I fall heavily against the doorframe, my head in the crux of my arm. I can't contain it any longer. The emotional dam I created to guard my scared heart bursts open. I feel Phil's arm around my shoulder. "I'm sorry," I sob.

"It's alright, Bud. Come on. Let's sit down." We walk in and I sit next to the table and he hands me a towel. "What's going on?" he asks, using the same gentile tone I have heard his father use while ministering to someone in church on a Sunday morning. I wipe my face and then lean forward in my chair.

"I really think I was going to kill him," I say bluntly, staring straight ahead into the dull room.

"Kill who?"

"Dr. Pergo."

"Oh," he mouths softly and sits down in the chair next to me, finally comprehending the gravity of the situation. He loved my mother as well and knows first-hand the pain our family went through. We sit there for a few moments in silence. I am wringing the damp towel in my fingers, attempting to control my emotions.

"So he summoned you down here as well?" he asks lightly. He sits back in his chair as a quizzical expression begins to form on his face. "Huh… that's strange – I thought they picked me for genetic testing since I'm the best looking person in Shiloh."

I blurt out a sharp laugh. Only Phil could get me to laugh in a moment like this. "Oh, I get it. They wanted you as the model for the latest I-Mort prototype."

"That's what I figured. So I have no idea what you are doing here." We both laugh loudly. "But in all seriousness. Are you ok? I have never seen you like that before."

"I don't know." I shake my head. "I don't know what came over me. I heard his name and it was like a switch was flipped. All of the pent up feelings I had for so long just – boiled over. Not to mention all the stress from yesterday. I didn't even tell you what my dad did last night."

"I was going to ask you about that. What happened?"

"Well, I showed him the letter and told him the story. I was expecting him to be excited, or happy, or something like that; but instead he– he – kind of went nuts. Well, not nuts. It was as if he wasn't surprised by it or even upset by it. And then he grabbed the letter and took off to his office and I haven't seen him since."

"Weird. Do you think that has something to do with why we are down here?"

"I didn't think about that until now, but I guess it's possible." My mind begins to churn in search of a tangible connection between Dad and Dr. Pergo. "I remember seeing him at our house a few times when I was younger, but I never thought much of it since he was their doctor. I have not heard or seen him since the accident."

"Me neither. I know he was sent back to Sapphire City after the accident, and I was under the impression he was gone for good."

"Yeah," I mumble and stand out of the chair, finally feeling a bit more stable. "I have never heard of someone needing extra testing done for the census. I have no idea why we are here."

The door swings open.

"Lacy?" Phil and I blurt at the same instant, catching her off guard.

"What are you two doing here?" she asks, standing frozen in the doorway. "I can't seem to get away from you guys."

"Ha," I nervously laugh, but I begin to feel that something is not right. "We were told to come down here after they processed us at the census."

"Same with me," she says more relaxed and takes a seat next to Phil. "Do you have any idea what they want with us?"

"We were just discussing that," he answers. "We have no idea."

"I don't like this. Something doesn't feel right."

Lacy looks at me alarmed. "What do you mean something doesn't feel right?"

"This room, it is too small and confined. There is nobody else down here –" the door slams.

"What is going on?" Lacy screams. Fear has gripped me as well. I stand up and take her by the hand as she grabs my arm.

"What is that smell?" Phil yells and joins us in the middle of the room.

"Stay with Lacy," I instruct and head for the door. I try to open the handle but it is locked. I frantically pound my fist against the cold steel, shouting for help as I hear loud footfalls racing down the hallway, stopping directly outside. Then silence.

"Open the door! We're locked in here!" There is no response. I hear a thud behind me and then another. I race over and find Phil and Lacy lying unresponsive on the floor. I bend down to help and feel the room begin to spin. A wave of nausea overwhelms my stomach. I feel a tingling sensation in my fingers and numbness at the base of my skull as I fall backward.

Chapter 5

There is a flash of light, then darkness, as I strain to pry my thousand-pound eyelids open. I see the outline of my chest and feel a dull aching in my left wrist. I try to move it but nothing happens. Black sets in once more. A throbbing pain in the back of my head alerts my senses, and I watch the darkness slowly peel upwards as light begins to flood my eyes. I see my chest again and somehow force my head to lift, revealing the faint outline of my legs. I'm sitting, I think. The throbbing intensifies and I raise my hand to try and ease some of the pressure, but again, no movement, only a slight aching in my shoulder. I focus as much strength as I can into my arm but I am only successful in moving a few fingers, which brush gingerly against my back and the cool wall. I realize both of my hands are behind me. Lacy...

I look to my left and see both her and Phil sitting against the same wall as I am. Their hands are behind their backs and their heads are hanging forward, their chins resting on their chests. I shift my weight and try to stand, but the pain in my head is too much. The room starts to spin and I feel my head slouch against my shoulder.

"Sardis." I open my eyes once more, this time with much less effort. Phil is staring straight ahead while Lacy is looking toward me.

"I'm ok," I say groggily. I'm afraid to stand in fear of passing out again, so I merely lift my head and give her a feeble smile. "Are you guys alright?"

"I think so," she answers weakly, "but my head is killing me."

"Yeah." I try to move my hands but they are bound at the wrists. I look down at my legs expecting them to be constrained as well, but they are not. I gaze around the room and see a small yellow light bulb above a steel door. From the dull glow I notice the rest of the room is small, with concrete floor, walls, and ceiling. There is a small window in the door and I can see light coming through the square opening.

"I'm scared," she whispers, her lip trembling. "What is going on?"

"I don't know, but it will be alright." Normally I would be saying that half-heartedly, intent on convincing myself of its truth, but I unexpectedly feel a calm confidence. I am the protector here. My best friend and the woman I love need me, and I will be their rock.

"Phil, are you doing alright?"

"Yeah, other than the head thing. And I think we should pray."

"I agree," Lacy quickly responds.

"Go for it."

His head falls forward and he closes his eyes. "Mighty Deliverer, come and blanket us with your infinite protection. Give us wisdom on the decisions we are about to make, so we can walk out of here safely. We trust you with our lives. Amen."

"Amen."

"Amen," I breathe, feeling a hint of betrayal. Do they not recognize I am here to protect them as well? I quickly clear that thought from my mind. It is much better to have God on our side in this cell than not.

"What are we going to do?" Lacy whispers, breaking the silence. Her long dark hair is hanging haphazardly over her shoulder. Her eyes are dark, but with what little light there is, they are sparkling. Her lip is quivering, but somehow she is still managing to hold back the tears.

"We are going to get out of here," I say confidently. She takes a deep breath, clenching her lips and closing her eyes, before releasing the air from her chest a bit more assertively. A faint smile appears on Phil's face as well. I roll over to my side and sit up on my knees. The pounding in my head is so strong that it feels as if my ears are going to explode. I close my eyes and sit there for a few moments and the pain begins to subside. Carefully, I make it to my feet.

"Where do you think we are?" Phil asks, as I deliberately make my way around the room.

"I'm not sure. My guess would be somewhere in the hospital. Whoever did this would not risk dragging three lifeless bodies anywhere else. Though, everything is cement in here." I motion with my head around the room. "And as far as I know the hospital does not have cement ceilings anywhere."

"Maybe somewhere below the basement?"

"Maybe."

"I just want to know who is doing this and why they chose us."

"Chose us?" Lacy questions.

"Yeah – They said Dr. Pergo wanted to do some additional tests. We were singled out." I glance at her face to see her response, but the blank expression is still there. "As soon as you came, the lights when out. It had to be planned that way."

"Why me?"

"I'm not sure…" I answer hesitantly, but deep down I know the reason. I had stormed into the hospital basement so blinded by my own rage and hatred toward Dr. Pergo that when I saw Phil sitting alone in that room, I failed to realize something was not right. It was not until Lacy walked through the door that I figured it out. Whatever is going on has something to do with the letter and the way my father acted last night. Lacy is down here because of me. The thought turns my stomach.

"Whatever the reason," I whisper, "I think we need to keep our voices low and our words to a minimum. Who knows who could be listening." They both nod in agreement.

"That being said, I think we need to make a plan. Can either of you stand yet?"

"I haven't really tried," Lacy answers, as she moves her knees up towards her chin. "Ugh, am I stiff." Phil is already kneeling next to her, with his eyes closed.

I walk to the door and glance out the window. I can see a long corridor with three lights mounted on the ceiling every ten feet or so, connected to each other by thick black wires. The bulbs are dull yellow, creating small dimly lit sections of corridor between areas of shadows. I squint trying to make out the end of the hallway, but there is only black after the third patch of light.

"Whatever gas they drugged us with was some nasty stuff." Phil groans. He slowly rises to his feet. "So what are you thinking, Sardis?"

"I am thinking it is strange that are our legs are not bound and there are no guards or security cameras in the hallway. Here – Let me see if I can undo your hands." I examine the constraints on his wrists; they are merely a small length of rope with a simple double hitch knot. I grab the one end of the rope with my teeth and pull, easily freeing his hands. He brings them gingerly to his face.

"That's odd," he says, and unties mine. I free Lacy's wrists and we both help her to her feet. "Do you think the door is even locked?" I walk over and try the handle and it turns in my hands.

"What is going on?" Lacy squeaks, and loses her balance. Phil quickly catches her before she hits the ground and I help him lower her to the floor.

"I think we need to take a minute to think this through before we march down that hallway. Whoever brought us here evidently is not concerned with holding us in this room – I don't know if that is a good thing or a bad thing."

"How can it be bad?" Lacy asks.

"It can't be a good thing they went through all that trouble to bring us here," Phil answers.

"But it also can't be too bad if they are allowing us this much freedom," I reply. "Although I could see this being an Establishment mind game."

"Do you really think they had anything to do with this?" Phil rebuffs. He looks directly at me and then over toward the door. "You know just as well as I do this has something to do with the letter."

"Wait, you know who did this?" Lacy asks confused.

"Not exactly," I say quietly, "But…"

"But what?"

"But, I have a feeling Phil might be right. Last night I told my father about the letter. He responded strangely and then demanded to know who all knew about it. So I told him it was the three of us –"

"So you are saying if you would not have used that stupid mind-reader-talking thing, then I would not be passed out on the floor of this God-forsaken place!"

"That's what I'm saying – I'm sorry."

She closes her eyes and lets out a disgusted huff. I want to say something but nothing comes out. There is an awkward moment of silence before Phil sits down next to her. "Look, I understand what you are feeling. We are all in the same boat here. No one knew this was going to happen – but if we are going to figure out what is going on and how to get out of here, we all have to be in this together." She opens her eyes and takes another deep breath. She looks at him and then at me.

"What do you think we should do?" she asks and forces smile. I let out the air that had been trapped in my lungs for the past minute and return the small grin.

"I think we need to figure out who would be so bothered by this letter that they would capture the only three people who knew about it. My father must have suspected something. That is why he acted the way he did."

"Do you really think Dr. Pergo is behind this?" Phil asks. "Maybe the letter suggests the botched surgery wasn't an accident?"

Those words rattle around in my brain but do not instantly stick. I replay them in my mind until I comprehend the idea. Did he murder my mother? "I—" I start but can't get the words out of my mouth, as I feel the same intense anger rising up inside.

"Sardis, please, settle down." Phil cuts in. "I'm not going to let you do this again. We need you. You are the strongest of us; we can't have you losing it."

His words slice through my growing anger like a warm blade. I take a deep breath. They need me. "I really am glad you are here."

"I'm supposed to be here," he grins.

Supposed to be here. I was supposed to find that letter. Lacy was supposed to be there to hear it. I close my eyes and find that calm confidence I felt earlier. What would I do without Phil keeping me in check?

"I think Dr. Pergo has to be involved in it somehow. We have not heard about him in years, and he just shows up out of the blue the day after we find the letter? It is too much of a coincidence."

"I agree. And it sounds as if your father were concerned something bad might happen –" he continues at a whisper, "so I think we need to be cautious because whoever did this scared your dad as well."

"Or maybe your dad is responsible? In a good way, of course," Lacy adds quickly, alerted by the disapproval on my face. "Maybe he kidnapped us to keep us safe from the bad guys?"

"Yeah, I didn't think of that," Phil replies. "It explains why we are not shackled to the floor."

"It's possible, but I can't see why he would go to this extreme."

"You know him best so I think you should decide what we should do."

"I agree with Lacy, Bud."

I walk over to the door and peer out the window once more. The corridor is still and inviting. "I don't like the idea of lying around waiting for our captors to return – I guess we go for it." Their faces indicate they are in agreement. "I will go first, and when I see that the coast is clear, I will wave for you to follow." I check the hallway one last time and see no change. I grab the handle and slowly turn. Lacy takes a quick deep breath behind me. "Are you ok?"

"Yes, I'm sorry – I just got really nervous the door was going to blow as soon as you opened it! I've never been in a life or death situation like this before!" she squeals, and puts her hands to her mouth.

"Don't worry," I chuckle reassuringly. "This is nowhere near as terrifying as realizing I am spilling my deep, dark secrets into your head."

"Yeah, good point. I hope it does blow up."

I smile and take hold of the handle once more, turn, and begin to pull. The door is heavy and sticking towards the top. I pull harder and it scrapes open, reverberating loudly down the hallway. I look back and they are both wincing, realizing any chance we had for a stealthy operation was now gone. I wait a moment and see no one coming, so I quietly take a step into the hall. I peer past the lights and still can only see darkness at the other end. The paradigm between the light and the dark plays out again in my mind. What does that mean? I questioned God in the woods, and I lost myself upon entering the hospital. Am I giving into the darkness as Dad has always feared?

"You are supposed to be here," I hear inside of my head, not some trick of the Establishment but something deeper, something within me that was awakened in that dark cell. Again the calm sweeps through my body and this time I know for certain this is not a physical reaction. The presence is palpable. I look again down the hall and instead of seeing the areas of light, I see the expanse of shadow and I do not fear it. I understand what my mother was teaching: look past what is easy and you will find what God has put before you. Only I can do this. This is my calling. Whatever is at the end of that hallway is what God has put before me. At this moment, I am where I am supposed to be.

I move quickly but stealthily through the shadows until I am past the final splash of light. I stop. Peering further down the corridor I can barely make out the far wall another twenty feet or so ahead. I reach my hand to the floor and feel a draft – the exit must be close. I take three steps into the dark and stop, allowing my eyes to adjust. Above me I can see the dull reflection off the wires that connect the lights to some unseen power source. I follow the wires with my eyes and they disappear to my right. I walk silently, slowly, one foot in front of the other as if I am in the woods stalking my kill. I reach a corner and peer around the edge to my right. Ahead is another dark hall with only one light in the middle. There is a line of light on the floor at the far end. It must be a door. I observe the new hallway for any sign of danger, but notice nothing different from the first. It appears that Phil and Lacy may be right: our captors may not be hostile. I hear what sounds like voices coming from the far room, but they are too soft to make out who is talking or what is being said. I walk back to the last area of light and motion for the others to follow, before returning to the dark corner.

"Everything ok so far?" Phil whispers as they join me.

"Yeah, I can hear voices coming from the far door. Stay here. I will creep closer and see if I can tell who it is — then I'll come back and we can decide what we want to do."

"Sounds good."

I slowly make my way down the second hall. The voices grow louder and I can almost make out words by the time I reach the door. I stand motionless, barely breathing, trying desperately to make out who is talking and what is being said. I can distinguish a few different voices but no words; until I hear a loud smash as if someone slammed one's fist against a table.

"They are only kids!" One voice shouts, followed by a smattering of imperceptible responses.

"Go get them!" another yells, sending a cold shiver up my spine. I hear footsteps heading toward the door. My first instinct is to run, but I must protect my friends. I motion with my hands for them to head back to the cell, but I cannot tell if they see me through the shadows. The footsteps grow closer and the handle begins to rattle. I am trapped. I cannot make it to the dark corner before they see me. My only chance is to fight. I take what could be my last breath and prepare myself for imminent battle, when I hear a familiar voice from just behind the door.

"Wait," my father says. "Take this — Sardis may not come easily."

Chapter 6

The moment the handle turns until the shadowy figure emerges from the doorway is mere seconds, but to me it seems like hours. I have determined my first priority is to protect my friends regardless of who is behind this door. Even if I cannot fight them off, I will at least give Phil and Lacy a chance to escape. The light from inside the room illuminates my face as the door swings open. Before the man takes a full step, my fist lands squarely against his right cheek, and I tackle him to the ground. I can hear screaming from within the bright room but it sounds like white noise. I land another punch against the back of his head before I am hit from the side and pinned to the cold floor.

"Sardis!" I finally perceive my father yell from on top of me. "We are – " he cuts off as I feel his weight being lifted from my back and hear a guttural scream as Phil's body whizzes past mine, flattening my father to the floor. Instinctively I am back to my feet. There are half a dozen people in the room and another door which must lead to our escape. I prepare to jump over the bodies in the doorway and take on the next obstacle between us and our freedom, when I hear an unknown voice inside my head, "Sardis –" I spin around confused, unable to locate the source.

"Stop!" A different voice yells and I turn back to see Lacy racing toward me. "He has the letter!" The scrambling figure of Dr. Pergo rises in front of me with my mother's letter in his hand. Phil and my father are still on the ground behind him, both moaning and trying to catch their breath. I watch as a woman from inside the room leaps over the sprawling bodies and intercepts Lacy in the hall. My body tenses once again. I prepare to rush to her aid when I hear the woman cry, "Lacy!" as they embrace. I relax as Lacy's body goes limp and she begins sobbing.

"Mom..." she trembles, pressing her face into her mother's chest. "I was so scared."

I survey the scene in front of me. My father and Phil are now sitting upright but still in a daze. "What is going on?" I scream. Dr. Pergo takes a step toward me with the letter outstretched.

"Please, I mean you no harm. Come and sit with us. We have much to discuss with you."

I grab the letter and press it to my chest. Just knowing this man does not have it in his possession anymore puts me at ease. Lacy is walking toward me with her mother's arm around her shoulder, still resting her head against her mother's chest. I hold out my hand and help Phil to his feet. We both take one of my father's hands and lift him to his feet.

"Sorry about that, Mr. Alexander."

"No problem, Phil. It was a nice hit; I think you might have broken a rib," Dad wheezes, wincing with each word.

"So what is going on?" I reiterate, as I help him into the room. Still in pain, he places his hand on the back of one of the chairs to steady himself and motions toward the table.

"Why don't you three take a seat."

There are four people standing in the back of the room. Two of them are Phil's parents: Mary has tears in her eyes and is leaning against Levi, who is staring intently at us. Standing next to them is Ephie, who is peering over his thick glasses at a computer device of some sort. He is wearing a heavy jacket but still appears rather scrawny. Walking toward us is the governor, Jacob Lloyd.

He is the civic head of our town and the main ambassador to the Establishment. He reaches out his hand and I shake it. He pulls out a chair and gives me a dry smile. "Take a load off, young man." I sit down gingerly because my back is sore and Governor Lloyd has always intimidated me. Phil sits to my left and Lacy to my right. Strewn across the table are various objects, but my mind is too frazzled to comprehend what any of them are.

"Do we all know everyone?" Dad asks rhetorically as he sits at the end of the table. "Good. I am sure you are wondering what is going on." He sits up in his chair and winces. "You got me good, Phil." He flashes a wry smile attempting to both stall and lighten the mood.

"This is not easy for me, well, us to say," he begins slowly, looking at the others for approval. "There have been certain – events, which have shaped each of our lives and have brought us to this point. Some of these events were beyond our control, some others were not.

"You see, there is a battle being fought for our souls. Each and every day we are fighting off the advance of the enemy, and it is quite obvious we are losing this battle. Our community is all that is left of humanity as it was created in the Garden many millennia ago. We are on the front lines of the greatest battle in human history."

"What does that have to do with us in this dungeon?" I ask impatiently, annoyed at the deliberate pace of his explanation.

"I'm getting there," he answers calmly. "First you need to understand the gravity of our situation. Unbeknownst to you, each of your parents and I are members of a group known as the Fifth Seal. It has been in existence since the twenty-first century, actively trying to protect the fabric of human existence from the onslaught of the Evil One." Memories of our parents meeting for alleged Bible studies surface in my mind. "The Seal was created during the Information Revolution to try and stem the flood of moral decay. Man for the first time had the entire world as his audience, and the result was a systemic rise of individualism. No longer did man turn to God for his direction and comfort; he merely searched until he found something that could make him feel better in that moment. Soon his longing for comfort turned to a thirst for power and fame. Celebrities were treated as gods and each man thrived for that same feeling. Man's time was spent solely on bettering the way he was perceived in the world, instead of truly making a lasting difference.

"Our forefathers tried to expose the hollowness of man's desires, but for the most part their efforts were futile. When I-Morts were created, and all of man's basic needs were provided for, the battle was all but lost. Since each man's singular desire was his own wellbeing, and that desire could be met in this new body, then why would he suddenly turn away from all he had achieved to follow a God who demanded his complete individual surrender? The Seal's focus shifted from rescuing man to preserving a faction of the population to continue God's work.

"We were convinced the war of 2312 would bring about the Second Coming of Christ and the end of human suffering. But when it did not, and we were herded into these reservations like cattle, many grew tired and weary of the cause. It was at this time that the epidemic hit, leaving only our small community to continue the work God set before us. We have taken that responsibility to heart; it is our calling —" he looks at each of us, before settling his gaze on me, "and it is now your calling to protect humanity and bring about the future kingdom God has created for us."

I stare into his fiery eyes. There is a passion there I have yearned for these past four years. I am at a loss for words, so confused and frightened by this whole experience.

"What do you mean we are the only people left to do this work?" Phil asks, thankfully still mentally engaged enough to formulate a rational thought.

"As of six years ago the people in this community are the only humans left," Dr. Pergo answers. "I had the privilege to hold the hand of the last man alive outside of your community as he passed into the presence of our Lord."

"How is that possible?" Lacy asks, her voice still weak from the tears. "I knew that our territory was hit hard, but I thought others were spared?"

"You are correct. The first sweep of the virus was not universal but it frightened most people enough to receive the radiation vaccine."

"And one of the unknown side effects of the vaccine was that it caused both men and women to become sterile," my father adds, clarifying Dr. Pergo's explanation. "That was discovered a few months after it had been administered to all the territories around the world. Coupled with many choosing to abandon their bodies for I-Morts to negate any risk for further infection, the population dwindled to mere hundreds within decades of the Relocation Act. Those who remained, banded together in one territory outside of the Gold City before the second virus hit."

"Why were we never told about this?"

"That was my decision coupled with the recommendation of the Board of Elders," Governor Lloyd answers. "After the onset of the second virus, we decided it was in the best interest of our people not to know they would soon be all that was left of the human race."

"That is absurd!" I yell. "How could you hide that information from everyone?"

"That was the decision," he huffs, before shifting his weight and deciding to soften his approach. "We felt that people would not react well to the news and would choose to leave for the safety of the Establishment. We could not afford our city, the final beacon of hope for mankind, to deteriorate into panic and chaos."

I sit back in my chair and stare at the desk. I want to scream at these people for manipulating our lives like pawns in some cosmic game. Phil's face is locked in the same expression of disbelief. I wish we had the communication devices on our wrists so I could ask him what he thinks about all of this without the others hearing our conversation.

"So what is your plan? Do you want us to start some war against the Establishment? Three thousand against millions? And why us? We are not military leaders by any stretch of the imagination."

Dad stands up slowly, clutching his side. "A war? No, not exactly." I notice all the others, except for Dr. Pergo, have taken a seat at the table. "Truthfully, we are not sure yet of all of the details – and it wasn't until you found the letter that we knew when to begin and who was to be involved.

"You see – we have a plan; well, it is more of a theory, really. It is based on promises hidden in the Scriptures concerning the end of the ages. We know that God has an end game for this creation, a way to usher in His New Heaven and Earth promised in Revelation. According to Revelation 6, that time will come when the last of his saints on earth suffers a martyr's death." He picks up a Bible lying on the table and flips to the page. "We thought that would happen during the war, but obviously it did not. After the Relocation and the epidemics, the only humans left to satisfy this prophecy were us in Shiloh. But you see, that also does not make sense. As Christians, we are instructed – our main purpose – is to go and make disciples of all nations, as is instructed in Matthew 28." He closes the Bible and places it back on the table. "So we realized something was not right. The only souls who could benefit from the Good News of the gospel were with us in Shiloh, and each and every person here has already heard. Either God's Holy Word is not inherently true as we all believe it to be or we missed something along the way."

"Are you suggesting that we lead a final charge against Sapphire City, some sort of death march to bring about the end of the world?" Phil asks. "I don't understand." He shakes his head and looks at his parents. "Why us?"

"Why you three?" Dad answers directly, the intensity of his voice increasing with each word. "Because we believe you were chosen. Before the death and resurrection of Christ, or the Fall in the Garden, or even before He made man, He chose you to bring about the final chapter of history.

"And why do we think this? It is because of the letter!" he shouts breathlessly. Our faces must relay that we still are not following so he continues quickly with fervor, "Well, let me explain. It was a few years ago that we came to the realization it was time to act on our current situation. It was actually Tira." He nods toward me. I had not heard him use my mother's first name in years, and it brings a smile to my face. "She is the one who came up with the plan. We had heard a rumor that there was a new form of technology that could transfer bits of information through time. In other words, we could create a message, send it back in time, and warn previous generations of what was going to happen to our people. We went to Dr. Pergo to find out if this machine even existed and if it were even possible for us to reach it and use it."

"Yes, that is accurate. The machine was real. It was located in Gold City. I had seen it once before and knew the man responsible for creating it." He places his hand to his chest. "I was glad to assist with that first mission, and I will be glad once again to assist. I will always be faithful to the Cause – until our Savior arrives again, riding on his white cloud." I look at his eyes and see the light reflecting off his glass pupils. He is staring at the Bible on the table, and if his face could adequately show expression there would no doubt be one of pride. I have never seen that glimpse of humanity before in an I-Mort.

"I hope you don't mind my asking," Phil says candidly, "but I always thought a member of the Establishment was not allowed to be involved with religion, especially believe in Christ?"

"Yes, and I am an I-Mort, so I no longer have a spiritual connection to our Creator. I am one of only a handful of I-Morts who still hold to their beliefs, although we do so in secrecy. I did not –"

"We are getting off the matter at hand," Governor Lloyd interjects, fidgeting in his seat. "We need to move this along; we are wasting valuable time."

"I apologize. I can tell you my life story, Phil, when we meet later at Sapphire City." He turns mechanically toward my father. Maybe I am wrong about him, I think, as I continue to stare at his face.

"Right, moving on." Dad takes a deep breath. "Before we go any farther though, there is something that I need to tell you, especially you two." He motions with his head toward Lacy and me. Instantly I feel a rush of adrenaline. I somehow know that whatever he is about to say is going to shape the rest of my life.

I look over at Lacy and she is hunched in her chair. Her hair is matted and tears have displaced her eye make-up, leaving black streaks on her cheeks.

"What we did, we did with your best interest and the best interest of our people in mind." He looks up at the ceiling. "Lacy, your father, and Sardis – your mother," he gets out barely before choking up. He puts his hands to his eyes and sobs. Out of the corner of my eye I see Mrs. Fair place her arm around Lacy who is now staring intently at my father, tearful trepidation on her face. A mirror would show the same expression on mine.

"They did not die in the way you think," he explains through tears. "They were the ones chosen to complete the mission." He gives in completely to his emotions and walks over and takes me in his arms. I feel the corners of my eyes wet, as I try and grasp what he just said. "I'm sorry." I place my head against his neck and close my eyes tight. My mind is numb as I try to burrow into his body. I feel his chin rest against my head. I wish it would not have taken the end of the world to bring me to this feeling in his arms. I wish I could stay here forever.

"She was the best; that's why we chose her," Governor Lloyd says reflectively. "And he was the strongest man I ever knew, both physically and spiritually. They were perfect for the mission, and they performed admirably."

"Is Mom still alive?" I blurt out, as I try desperately to hold back the flood of tears, but when Dad grips me tighter, the dam bursts. I look up through the tears at my father, who is also crying. The pain on his face leaves no doubt of the answer.

"No," Dr. Pergo answers. "I was there when she died. They both died in Gold City. Tira passed as soon as she sent her message." He looks toward Governor Lloyd, seemingly for approval. "James died from palladium poisoning. His body did not take well to the chemical." I let out a heavy sigh, releasing the hope that had been building inside. My father lets loose of his embrace and gingerly walks back to his chair.

"Did they succeed in getting the message through?" Phil asks.

Governor Lloyd awkwardly shifts his weight and glances knowingly at my father. "The message was sent, but the effect we were hoping for was not achieved."

"So we are going to try again? It's not a three thousand man Death March, it's a three person suicide mission."

The last jab brings a disapproving furrow to Governor Lloyd's brow. "In the simplest explanation, yes, you are going to try again. You see, the original message was sent to warn the people of what the future would hold if they did not change course, but they either did not listen or the message was never received. If another – stronger – more persuasive message is sent, we are hoping the multiple attempts will increase the chance for success."

"But we are all going to die, aren't we?" He looks over at his mother whose tears have returned and asks loudly again, "Are we all going to die?" She lets out a loud wail and hides her face in her hands. Levi puts his arm around her shoulder and pulls her close to him.

My father wipes the tears from his face and clears his throat. "The Governor is right; we need you three to go to Gold City and deliver this new message – and judging from the emotion in this room, we are all aware of the consequences of this decision." He motions toward the door and the others stand. "This cannot be something we force upon you. You must individually decide this is something you are called to do. The mission will have no opportunity for success if you are being driven by our expectations. We need you to be led by something hidden deep within you. So take a moment and discuss this with each other. Pray about it and let the Spirit lead your decision. Once you decide whether you are willing or not, then we will discuss the details of our plan. We love each of you and will stand behind you no matter what." He stands and follows the others out the door.

The only sound in the room is the ringing in my ears. Phil is leaning forward against the table, staring blindly at the contents strewn across it. Lacy is still hunched, as if she is trying to make herself small and shield all that is going on around her. The silence lingers. My mind and body are numb but I know what I must do. I see the letter lying on the table.

"*My Dear Sardis* –" They both raise their eyes. I was reluctant to read these words earlier, holding onto some selfish desire to keep her to myself, but something has changed. I feel as if I reached the bottom while I was tied to the floor in that cement cell. I had been spiraling out of control for years and finally landed face down and naked to myself. The protective walls I had built up around my heart are shattered and I feel alive. It is not a physical or emotional awakening, but spiritual. I feel with all I am that I must step forward and become the man I know I am supposed to be. From the depths of my darkness, I can now finally look up and see the light.

> "*I pray this letter finds you and finds you well. It was the joy of my life to see you grow from the peanut you were when I brought you home from the hospital that first night, to the young man you are becoming. I saw how much you loved life and I hope one day you will be able to follow the lead of your heart and take hold of all that God has placed before you. This pin is one that belonged to your great-grandfather, who fought in the battle of 2312. I have worn it ever since*

but I think it should belong to you. I did not know how or when to give it to you, but I trust that God will bring it to you in His perfect timing. When you are ready, I know God will lead you to this letter and these instructions:

Follow your heart. Don't ever sacrifice what makes you human.

Follow the advice of Godly friends, and never let them leave your side.

Fall in love and never let that feeling go. It is the greatest gift from God.

And finally, always trust in the Lord; He will never forsake you. You are a commander of Angel Armies. Never forget that.

With all my love,
Mom"

I finish and lay the letter on the table. The words were not written for me alone. Lacy hears her father reading, as if he were sitting here in the room, staring lovingly into his little girl's eyes. Phil hears the voice of his heavenly Father, whom he talks with earnestly each and every day, and whose words now are lighting up his heart. The air is lighter and we all feel it: the odd peace in the room. There are no words spoken, but it is clear – we know what we must do. I look over at Lacy and she is smiling, and I realize I am as well. She catches my glimpse but this time I do not look away. It is not a stare of love but a moment of understanding. We both look at Phil's silly grin and laugh. Somewhere God is looking down and laughing along with us, three unlikely friends about to embark on the greatest journey in human history.

Chapter 7

The door opens and my father walks through. "I don't want to rush you, but we are short on time. Have you made your decision?" I look at Phil, then Lacy, and nod. "Good. I will summon the rest of the group." He turns and walks out.

I fold the letter and sit back in my chair. "I wonder what the plan is."

"I was just going to ask that," Lacy replies, "I want to know what message they want us to send?"

"I was wondering that myself. And who are we going to send it to?"

"Any guesses?"

"I would think it would have to be someone important on the side of the Cause, maybe a general or something," Phil answers. "It is going to be difficult to get someone to believe a message from the future. I would see it as a trick the Establishment is trying to pull."

"I think we should send it to someone on the Establishment's side," I say, as I pick up a steel box, about the size of a deck of playing cards, from the table.

Lacy grabs an apple and wipes it with the sleeve of her shirt. "Why do you say that?"

"Governor Lloyd said the first message was sent to warn those in the past of what would happen in the future if they did not reevaluate the course they were leading humanity. I think

67

the leaders of the Cause already were fighting for this change, so telling them would not solve anything."

"But do you think they will listen?" Phil asks skeptically.

"Probably not, but it might be our only shot." I finally manage to pry the box open. It is full of red and blue medicinal capsules. "Must be some super pills for the trek," I quip, and close the box. I toss it back onto the table where it lands with a loud clang next to the bowl of fruit. There are several other objects lying about: the Bible my father was reading, a map, a compass, four canteens, a few hunting knives, three non-lethal stun weapons, and some papers. In the corner of the room are camping gear and backpacks, along with my bow and quiver of arrows.

"The atmosphere in this room sure has changed," Governor Lloyd announces pleasantly as the party reenters the room. The others have more measured expressions, except for Ephie, who is looking very nervous. I still need to apologize to him.

"Oh well," I accidently say aloud.

"What was that, Sardis?" my father asks.

"Oh, nothing," I answer, embarrassed. "I was just talking to myself, that's all." He gives me a strange look as he takes his seat at the end of the table. He folds his hands in front of him and clears his throat.

"So, what did you three decide?" I look at the other two and they are staring at me.

"We are all in," I answer confidently, buoyed by the thought that they are already looking to me as the leader. I hear Mary let out a heavy sigh and see Mrs. Fair close her eyes, but not before a tear squeezes from the corner of one of them.

"Wonderful. So – what is the plan? Well, we need to get the three of you to the time machine in Gold City. We have a message, we hope, that will be convincing enough to sway the hearts and minds of the people. We have been brainstorming the best way to do this, taking successful ideas from the previous mission and adding new ones so hopefully the outcome will be successful." He grabs the map and opens it on the table in front of us.

"What is the message?" I ask.

"We feel it is best if you do not know that at this time," Governor Lloyd answers. "If you are caught, the less you know the better." His answer does not sit well with me as Dad continues.

"There will be three legs to the journey. First, you must travel by foot south from Shiloh to Sapphire City." He traces the three-hundred mile path down the Pacific coast with his finger. "You will need a week to travel the final two legs, so you will need to make that initial distance in three weeks. I did the math – you will need to travel about fifteen miles per day on average."

"Why is everyone looking at me?" Phil asks incredulously, flashing his grin. "I could make thirty miles a day no problem, Mr. Alexander."

Dad laughs and shakes his head. He looks at me and rolls his eyes. "Since Dr. Pergo can move freely from city to city without raising suspicion, he is going to go ahead and prepare a safe entrance for you into Sapphire and then transportation once you get there."

"Why can't we use a vehicle or catch a ride with Dr. Pergo?" I ask confused.

"There is too high a risk of being detected on the first leg of the journey. Even though the government is not actively patrolling our territory anymore, they are still monitoring our activity. Using vehicles or trying to stow away on an aircraft would be far too risky."

"How can we leave Shiloh with the tracking dye?" Lacy asks. "Once we get outside the city, the Dragons will be on our tail in no time."

"I will get to that in a minute. But, yes – you are right; you will need to be diligent in your efforts to remain invisible. If you are discovered, they will undoubtedly send the Dragons, and you know how excellent they are at tracking and capturing runaways. The mission would be over at that point." I shudder at the thought of being hunted by the Dragons. They are a Special Forces unit created by the government to hunt down and arrest anyone whom the government deems to be a threat. They were developed before the war to help restore order during the time of unrest. Those who fled the newly formed Territories after the Relocation Act were hunted and forcefully detained.

"Once you reach Sapphire City, Dr. Pergo will have arranged for you to travel to the outskirts of Gold City using one of the Establishment's aircraft."

"Professor Alexander is correct. We used the same technique during the first mission. Those in the Establishment do not expect sedition of any sort, so the security and surveillance inside any of the Great Cities is minimal. It is actually quite easy to move about once you have infiltrated the city."

My father nods in approval. "The final leg of the journey will be to enter Gold City, locate the device, and send the message. Sounds easy enough, right?" He grabs the steel box and stands up from the table, still moving a bit gingerly from Phil's take down.

"To answer your earlier question, Lacy, I developed a chemical masking agent several years ago that uses the metal palladium to bind to the iron in your blood. It is quite effective in blocking the transmittance of the dye. It acts as a type of chemical shield, that when bonded to your blood, in essence, deflects the frequencies from the Establishment's satellite tracking equipment. These pills," he opens the small box and pulls out one of the red and blue capsules, "when taken orally once per day, make you practically invisible."

"But before you take them you must be aware of the downside," Governor Lloyd interrupts.

"Yes, the side effects. Although I have made advancements in the chemical make-up of the drug, there is still the possibility your bodies may not respond favorably. You will undoubtedly feel ill along the way, but it may escalate to more severe symptoms. Some may be able to tolerate it better than others, but unfortunately, it is a very harsh treatment."

"When you said my father died from palladium poisoning, is this what happened to him?"

"Yes, his body did not respond well to the treatment," Dr. Pergo answers. "Tira fared much better, only a few slight side effects: fatigue and nausea."

"Being his daughter do you think I will have the same reaction?"

"It is very possible," my father answers. "I have added a special treatment for you that will hopefully lessen the symptoms. See, Lacy, your father was anemic. As a result, he had less iron in his blood for the palladium to adhere. The excess metal circulating around his body had extreme adverse effects. I added extra iron supplements, which I am hopeful, will help you tremendously.

"Even though the advancements in our methods may make for a smoother trip, the reality is the treatment, when continued for an extensive period of time, will be fatal. Once the body is saturated with the metal, continued usage will result in rapid health decline." He takes a deep breath. "There will be no return trip."

Those last few words hang in the air as each of us comprehends the meaning of them in our own time. I close my eyes and take a deep breath, before nodding in a confident manner, hopefully masking the horrible pit in my stomach with the assertive leadership I know my friends need.

"Alright. When do we start?"

"After we find something to eat!" Phil cries. "If you would have told me when I rolled out of bed this morning that I would be signing my death certificate before I ate lunch, I would have told you that you were nuts!" We all laugh heartily, even Mary cracks a proud smile.

"Yes, we will bring some food down here, pronto!" Governor Lloyd says through his laughter. "I am hungry, too! The Professor had me up all night mixing chemicals and packing bags!" His joke brings even more laugher to the room. "We should keep it down though; we don't want to alert the wrong people of our whereabouts."

"That reminds me. Where in the world are we, and why did you drug us and dump us in that prison cell?" I ask.

"You are one hundred feet below the basement of the hospital. Shortly after Shiloh was settled, the community leaders decided they needed an area that was hidden from the government's surveillance, where they could feel safe to discuss and execute matters of business related to the government without their knowledge of it," Governor Lloyd explains cautiously, as if he is not totally convinced the government is not listening at this very moment. "They figured people would attempt to develop places like this, so they created a law that strictly forbade doing so. The punishment was treason and an automatic life sentence to one of the Criminal of War prisons.

"It would have been easier to build a place like this under – say – the University, or some other place that was not directly staffed by government officials, but our leaders thought if the government searched for our chambers they would undoubtedly check those places first. It was actually Dr. Pergo who suggested we could develop a space under the hospital, and he, along with some of our great-grandfathers, built this place."

"I guess that makes me old," Dr. Pergo retorts, playing to the lingering joyful tension that is still heavy in the room.

"But wise," my father adds. "To answer your question as to why we went to such lengths to bring you here, we could not afford at this point to raise any suspicion amongst the Establishment on the eve of our revolution. We knew that summoning Dr. Pergo to make an unplanned visit would raise red flags, so we used the census as a cover and made up a series of fake tests that only he could administer."

"But that doesn't explain why I woke up on the floor next to these two," Lacy replies confused.

"We discussed different avenues to take in order to bring you three here," he answers slowly as if what he is about to say is something of which he is not proud. "We decided you needed to experience some adversity before you found yourself in that situation in the near future. We wanted to see how you would react, individually and as a group, to a life or death situation. Would you turn to fear and panic or would you turn inward and find the strength we know is in each of you."

Are you kidding me?

"I realize this all is overwhelming to you, but you have to understand it is just as overwhelming to us. What I wouldn't give to take your place. The thought of sending my only son out there; it's –" Tears begin to fill his eyes.

"And it's not just me – it's Mary, and Levi, and Deborah; we wish we were the ones God called to do this, but we were not – it was you. The decisions we had to make were ones we would never consider in a million years under any other circumstances, but when the God of the universe shows you this is what He wants done –"

"Then you do it," Phil finishes the thought. "I know I speak for the three of us when I say this: we trust you and we trust Him, so if this is what you are telling us we are to do, then we are going to listen and follow your lead." I look around the room and there are smiles and tears on each person's face. Even Ephie, who has been sitting at the far end of the table in silence this whole time, has a smile.

"Well, we have delayed this long enough," Governor Lloyd says and stands. "We need to get moving. I will find you a good meal. In the meantime, Professor, finish explaining the details of the trip and get these kids packed. Dr. Pergo, head to Sapphire and get the ball rolling on that end. We have one month before they are due to check in for the next census – every second counts." He turns briskly and exits the room.

"You heard the Governor, we have no time to waste. We have packed some essential clothes and toiletries in your packs. I will give you a minute to look through and decide if there is anything else you want to take, but be mindful that you must be able to move quickly and quietly.

"But before you do that, there are a few items I wanted to explain in more detail. First, is this map; it will be your guide for the first leg. Once you meet up with Dr. Pergo, he will be able to guide you from that point. Your best bet would be to follow the shipment railroad until your reach Sapphire City. Do so at a generous distance so as not to be spotted whenever the shipment comes. We are also going to send Dr. Porter with you on the first leg of the journey."

Ephie?!

"He will be able to help with the navigation, and he has the most extensive knowledge of the Establishment's technology, so he will help you stay undetected. Once you reach Sapphire City, his knowledge will be invaluable in infiltrating the city. Also, if you happen to be stopped along the way, you can use his position as a professor as a guise. You can say that you are on a university field study for his class. It may not be a necessary diversion, but it just may save the mission."

I look at Ephie. I never thought of him as the outdoors type, so I can imagine he is not looking forward to trudging through it with us. The way he is nervously wringing his hands leads me to believe my assumption is correct.

Dad sets down the map and picks up the steel box with the palladium masking pills. "Each of you will have a tin with thirty pills. I wish I could have made more but there just wasn't time. Please, take two of the pills right now. It takes a little while for the palladium level in your blood to reach a high enough concentration for the masking to work." He hands Phil and me a pill box, and we grab a glass of water from a pitcher that Mary had set on the table. He hands lacy a box with a blue stripe on the metal lid. "Lacy, this is your box. The pills have a special additive that will hopefully help with your physiology." I pop two of the pills in my mouth and take a drink. They go down surprisingly easy but leave an awful tangy metallic taste on the back of my tongue.

"Byuck. Pleasant."

"It could be worse," Phil says, as he sticks out his tongue and opens and closes his mouth repeatedly to try and dissipate the taste. "It could taste like those awful garlic and fish pills that Dad takes every day."

"What do you mean?" Mr. Conner appeals dramatically. "They keep me young and vibrant!"

"More like young and odd smelling," Phil counters.

I laugh and look over at Phil's parents. Levi has a proud glow on his face, while Mary is sitting with a simple smile, her hands folded neatly in her lap. As a pastor, he must be extremely proud of how his son has grown into the God-fearing young man he has become. He must feel privileged that his son was chosen for such a great purpose. Mary, though, has the look I feel Mary the mother of Jesus might have had the eve before He was taken away. It is sorrow, mixed with motherly duty, and masked with a convincing smile. She understands the magnitude of the moment, but that realization is clouded by the years of nurturing and guiding that have led to this point. She would never let him see that she is sad or fearful; her doing so would only increase his anguish. A simple smile – anything more and she may be unable to control the flow of emotions.

Dad picks up a canteen from the table. "One on the most vital aspects of the trip is making sure that you have plenty of clean drinking water, and not only to wash out the bad taste," he adds jokingly. I have never known him to be this funny. Maybe it is a coping mechanism we are all employing.

"In all seriousness, you can go several days without food but only several hours without water. There are multiple rivers along the way that flow into the ocean. Be diligent to have sufficient water in reserve so you can make it to the next fresh water source."

"Sardis," he states, as he picks up one of the small rectangular-shaped stun weapons, "you are the most experienced outdoorsmen, so you are responsible for protecting and providing for the group. However, we do not think it is wise to take any high powered weapons. The field study guise would be blown if you were stopped, and guns are illegal in all of the Great Cities. So having one will be more trouble than the protection it can provide. These non-lethal stun weapons are what the Establishment has developed to use instead of firearms. Point the end with the black arrow away from you and press the small round button on the top with your thumb. The end with the arrow will shoot forward and adhere to your target, sending a jolt of electricity that temporarily paralyzes them. Hopefully that can give you enough time to escape. Each of you will be given one. But since you need to be able to hunt for food along the way, Sardis, you can take your bow and arrows. Be careful not to be spotted with them. Though they are not illegal, they still are frowned upon. It might even be safer to discard them before you enter Sapphire City."

"Will these things work against an I-Mort?" I ask skeptically, as I turn the smallish weapon in my hands.

"Most certainly," Dr. Pergo answers. "They were designed for that purpose. The electric shock freezes the internal computer system of the I-Mort, causing the body to collapse to the floor before it can be rebooted."

"Is there any way to kill one?"

"Though an I-Mort can theoretically live forever under normal conditions, the bodies can be disabled. If you shoot one in the leg, it will not be able to run. If you shoot it in the head, it can deactivate the computer, causing the whole body to become disabled until the brain is rebooted. But to kill the brain function is a different question. An I-Mort brain is just an advanced computer with human memories downloaded into it. As long as there is a way to recover the code, then the I-Mort can be salvaged. Although, once the brain function has been transferred from the human body to the I-Mort body at the initial download, any subsequent attempt to transfer the brain function results in a loss of emotional connection to the downloaded information."

"I'm not sure I understand. These things truly are immortal, but they just get dumber over time?"

"Think of the human brain as the memory of a computer. That memory is information that is downloaded from the original hard drive, which is the human brain, to the new hard drive, which is the computer system of the I-Mort. The information is changed from memories to pieces of computer code. After the initial download, there is a certain disconnect that is created between the emotional meanings of the memories and the computer code of the memories. The I-Mort can still bring to mind a memory from the past, but the emotional attachment to that memory is lost. There is a quarantine time after the initial download where the I-Mort is flooded with pictures and videos of experiences throughout the I-Mort's human life, along with actual visits from family and friends, which help to form some emotional attachment to the downloaded information. This process is relatively effective, but the feelings are not the same as a human's. Each additional download of the information results in less emotional attachment. So if the I-Mort decided at some point to upgrade to a new body with more technological advancements, then it would lose some of its emotional attachment to its memories. After enough downloads, the I-Mort becomes nothing more than a machine with a unique hard drive."

"So, in essence, they are already dead?"

"Yes. The body that its memories inhabit is nothing more than a high functioning robot with extremely advanced motor and sensory abilities."

"Then why would people willingly choose to die in order to live like that?"

"The same reason you chose to willingly die in your daily life to live forever. The difference is: they put their faith in human hands, while you put your faith in God's," he answers ardently.

With that, he nods politely and walks rhythmically toward the door. Grabbing the handle, he turns smoothly back to us, "I will see you three in Sapphire City. Meet me at the eastern gate in three weeks. God speed young brothers and sister." He nods and closes the door behind him. I sit there for a moment thinking of what he has just said. I never realized the simplicity of what makes a person who he is at his core. When one's life hangs in the balance, to whose hands will he entrust it?

When the door opens again, Governor Lloyd backs in with two platters full of food. My mouth waters as I see the silver plates piled high with all types of meats, cheeses, bread, and vegetables.

"Eat up," Dad instructs. I pick up a piece of bread, slap a chicken breast on it, and dump a helping of gravy and potatoes on top. The next several minutes are a whirlwind as we stuff our bellies, only stopping to talk and laugh. When we are finished, Lacy and her mother disappear into an unseen room. Phil and his parents sit at one end of the table, while I sit with Dad at the other.

"Mom would be so proud of you," he says softly, as I sip fresh water. "She was so torn when she left. She knew it was her calling, but she also knew how it would tear up our family, especially you. She wanted to be there and help you to grow into the man you have become."

"I still haven't wrapped my brain around the fact that she didn't die on that operating table. What that means to me – I – I don't know what to feel." I slide my chair next to him. I am not sure if it is the reality that this is the last time I am going to see him, or if I am just scared and want his company, but at this moment all I want is be close. I rest my head against his shoulder and he puts his arm around me. "I guess I am proud of her, too." I firm my lips to keep from crying.

"Did I ever tell you why she kept working after you were born?" I shake my head, in fear that if I open my mouth to respond, I would not be able to control the tears. "She started out with every intention of staying at home and raising you, but when you were six years old there was a terrible storm that completely wiped out the fishing one summer. The elders decided in order to make up for the loss in food, they needed to supplement with additional wild game. Your mom offered to help for a few weeks, so you went to stay with your grandparents." As he talks, I close my eyes and see the story playing out in my mind. As always, mom is looking as strong and beautiful as ever, with her long dark hair, bright brown eyes, and engaging smile. "She hunted that first week and came home with twenty-one deer, twenty-three elk, and I don't know how many rabbits and birds. In total, it was something ridiculous like fifteen thousand pounds of meat. So much so that Governor Lloyd immediately called off all the additional hunting," he says through a chuckle. "After that, the elders had a meeting and decided she was too valuable to the community as a provider, and commanded she return to her calling – which she promptly refused. She told them being at home with you was where she was supposed to be. They pleaded and begged, and finally she conceded, but only after she convinced them to allow you to accompany her on the hunts." He embraces me as his tears begin once more.

"She loves you so much – more now than ever. Love is the greatest thing in the entire universe, Sardy. That is what God is, and that is why He created us: to share in that love with Him. The most amazing thing about love though, is you don't understand the full magnitude of it until you lose it. It is the pain and the passion that comes through loss that purifies the love each of us has been given. For God so loved the world that he gave his only begotten son..." I see the pain in his eyes, the enormity of that sacrifice now being realized in his own heart. How horribly helpless he must feel at this moment, knowing this is the last time he is going to speak with his only child.

"I love you, Dad."

"I love you, too, Sardy."

We sit in a quiet peaceful embrace for a long while. My mind slowly clears as the emotion of the moment begins to melt into the reality of the hour. I wish I did not have to leave, but at the same time, I know what must be done. I hug him firmly once more and sit up. "You said earlier that we could take a little something extra with us, all I want is the pin Mom left for me and your wedding ring."

"Why my ring?" he asks, as he slides it off his finger.

"I want something tangible that reminds me of you and Mom." I place it on the ring finger of my right hand. It fits perfectly. I stare down at the smooth gold surface and smile. "And I also want it as a reminder of what I am fighting for. We have been taught since we were little that God is love, but the idea has always been just a pie-in-the-sky notion." I spin the ring around my finger with my thumb. "It feels real to me now, though. I feel it through the love that you and Mom have. I feel it when I think about how much she must have loved God to have left you and me in order to do what she was called to do. When things get rough, I want to be able to look at it and remember what love is."

"I think you are ready," he says with a confident grin. I look over at Phil and his parents and they are embracing tightly. Lacy has not returned, but I imagine she and her mother are doing the same.

"Do we leave tonight?" I ask, as I begin to focus my thoughts and emotions to the task at hand. "What time is it anyway?"

"It is around six o'clock in the evening. The original plan was for you to leave shortly, but I think the three of you need to get some rest before you head out. There are cots set up, so let's get everyone packed and then you can get some sleep. You should leave in the cover of darkness though, so sometime before tomorrow morning."

I walk over to the packs and begin to take inventory of what is inside, as Lacy and Deborah walk back into the room. Lacy's hair and make-up have been fixed, and she looks generally more put together. She walks over and picks up her pack and examines its contents. Soon, Phil joins us and we rummage through our supplies and acquaint ourselves with our situation.

"Well, do you guys think we need anything else?" I ask as I zip up my pack. "I have everything I can think of: hunting gear, some protein bars, and clothes. It looks like you have the food Phil, and Lacy, you have the first-aid."

"Yeah, I'm ready," Phil answers. "My mom is going to get my Bible from home and my grandpa's harmonica."

"Are you going to play us lullabies at night?" Lacy kids. She closes her eyes and bobs her head back and forth slowly as if she is listening to one right now.

"I guess you will just have to wait and see!"

"How about you, Lacy? Do you have everything you need?"

"I think I'm ready. I just hope there are showers along the way," she adds jokingly, though it is obvious she is concerned.

"Well, Dad said we are to leave before sunrise tomorrow," I say, looking over at the table where the adults are gathered, talking amongst themselves. "There are some cots set up for us. Why don't we get one last good night of sleep. We can let them iron out the rest of the details."

"Sounds good to me!" Phil replies enthusiastically, as Lacy nods.

"Dad, where are these cots? We are going to try and get some rest."

"Through the door, down the hall, second door on the right. We will come and get you when it is time. Ephie is going to get the rest of the gear in order and attempt to figure out the best route to take through the wilderness. And Sardis, one more thing – here," he hands me the letter, "I think you should have this."

I fold it in half and slide it into the pocket of my jacket. He is right. As soon as the letter is securely tucked away, I feel much more complete.

"Good night, everyone," Mary says lovingly.

"Goodnight," we all echo in return.

It feels as if as soon as my head hits the pillow, I hear the door open. I sit up, realizing I have been asleep for some time when I try to lift my arm and it is numb and lifeless.

"Alright, It is time," I hear my father's voice say. I look over and both Phil and Lacy appear to have been asleep as well. That is good, I think, as I yawn and forcefully rub my arm, trying to return feeling to it.

He has an odd looking metal bar in his hand, which he waves back and forth in front of me. "Good," he says, and does the same to both Phil and Lacy. "Excellent, the palladium treatment has worked; you are as good as invisible." He places the bar in one of the side pockets of my pack.

"Grab your packs and follow Dr. Porter. He will guide you this morning and fill you in on the rest of the plan as soon as you are far enough away from town that you will not draw attention to yourselves." Ephie enters the room with a pack over his shoulder. For the first time he appears mentally engaged, with a determined look on his rodent face.

"Dr. Porter, I wanted to apologize for forging your name. I had all intentions of stopping by your office today."

"Apology accepted," he squeaks in his high pitched voice. "But as luck may have it, the neural transmitters may be invaluable on our expedition. I placed one in your bag as well as Phil's."

"Great," I reply with a forced enthusiasm. Of all the people to be stuck with on this trip, it had to be Ephie. There is just something about the guy that makes me uncomfortable. I don't know if it is the voice or just the fact that he always seems to bring the worst out in me. Maybe it is his face I determine, as I look again at those beady eyes, behind small round glasses, propped up on a pointy nose.

We start down the hall and head up a dimly lit flight of stairs. They turn and continue to ascend, and we climb for what seems like forever, until we reach an empty platform. Ephie moves his hand slowly against the wall, then stops and presses forward, releasing a latch. The wall slides open to a dark room. "We are just below the basement of the hospital," Dad says, and flips a switch on the wall to our left. Soft yellow light floods the room, illuminating what appears to be an armory. There are weapons of all types and ammunition lying in boxes.

"What is this place?" Phil asks, echoing my thoughts.

"This is where we decided to keep our military equipment after the war," Dad whispers quietly. "This is the only place we had to hide weapons from the government. People had them hidden in their homes after the Relocation Act, but after a few were caught and thrown in prison, we determined it was best to keep them all in a central location where they could have been retrieved if needed."

Too bad I cannot take some of these with me. There are hand guns, rifles, small palm-sized laser cannons, grenades, stun weapons, and more. I pick up a handful of ammunition and let it run through my fingers. It topples back into its box. "Impressive." I bend to one knee to pick up a bullet that skittered away. Instinctively, my hand reaches for one of the laser cannons, and as I rise to my feet, I stealthily slide it into my jacket pocket.

"This is where I say goodbye," Dad states soberly. "We will be praying diligently and anxiously awaiting word from Dr. Pergo."

He smiles and looks at Phil, myself, and Lacy and concludes, "The Spiritual leader, the Physical leader, and the Emotional leader: may God bless and guide your journey." He gives me a brief hug and a kiss on my forehead. "Sardis, when you see your mother, tell her that I love her and I will see her soon." Before I can respond, he turns and walks toward the hidden door. I want to yell to him, but no words come. I watch as his figure disappears down the dark stairs. I clench the shoulder straps of my pack tightly and turn back to our small company. I know I will never see my father alive again.

End of Book 1

Book 2

Through the Desert

Chapter 8

The early morning air is heavy and cool on my face as we make our way from shadow to shadow through the town square. Windows are dark, except for the government building, which has a beautiful waterfall cascading peacefully down its front glass panels, collecting in a small lake at the entrance. Normally passing this close would elicit a response from the overzealous holographic representatives, but our chemical camouflage seems to be working effectively. We head south toward the city gate, passing each of our empty homes along the way. Though I have walked this road countless times, it seems eerily different, almost foreign, as if I have disassociated the pleasant memories from the places I experienced them. We reach the gate without meeting a single person. I place my hand on the electronic lock, and the gate swings quietly open, surrendering meekly to my unique physiology. Though each opening of the gate is monitored by the government, I am one of the few people with security clearance to leave freely whenever I desire, one advantage of being a provider.

We move quickly and silently away from town following the rail shipment tracks. Ephie has the map and the initial instructions, so he is the lead. I am last, keeping Phil and Lacy moving steadily along. The tracks reflect what little moonlight is visible through the patchy clouds. We are surrounded by the forest which seems to hover ominously, engulfing us in still blackness. It feels as if the further we travel, the closer the dark walls are pressing in. I am used to walking through the woods at this hour, so I can only imagine what the other three must be feeling. For the first time I feel as if I am the hunted, and as the skies begin to brighten above the mountains to the east, I sense we need to get deeper into the safety of the woods.

"We should move into the forest and take a rest," I whisper to Ephie. He nods in return. We walk through the wet grass and undergrowth and continue into the trees, until we can no longer make out the railroad tracks through the dim morning light. I slide the pack off my shoulder and place it and my bow next to me, and plop down on a fallen log, leaning against the base of a large pine. I grab the canteen from the side pocket and take a long drink.

"How far do you think we have gone?" Lacy asks, as she unscrews the lid from her canteen.

"About six or seven miles, I would think," I answer. "How are you holding up?"

"I'm doing ok. I'm not used to this hiking stuff," she groans and takes a drink.

"Me, neither." Phil adds, also a bit winded.

"We will take plenty of breaks. We need to make sure we have enough energy to sustain us for the whole journey," Ephie replies. "Barring any setbacks, we should have no trouble making it to Sapphire City in three weeks' time."

Three weeks… Ephie… The reality of his fate hits me. I just assumed that since he was not making the trip to Gold City, he would find his way safely back to Shiloh; but one week travel by foot will not bring him home in time for the next census. He will also die on this quest. As I watch him fumble with the lid on his canteen, I gain a newfound level of respect for him; and, for the first time, I feel as if he belongs.

"Our goal for today should be to make it past the twenty-mile hunting perimeter. From that point, there will be much less government monitoring until we come up on Sapphire," he instructs as if we were sitting in one of his lectures.

"How will we know when we make it past the perimeter?" Lacy asks.

"There is a red laser line marker," Phil grunts, as he struggles to coax his sore muscles to lift him from his reclining position. "It stretches the entire length of the perimeter."

"I thought that was a myth?"

"Nope, it's real," I answer. "Mom took me to see it during one of our overnight hunts. The laser is not harmful, just an imaginary fence of sorts, but when you pass through you are scanned by tracking sensors."

"So, theoretically, no person should be able to approach Sapphire City without the government's knowing hundreds of miles in advance," Lacy concludes.

"That is their assumption," Ephie replies.

"That's why it is imperative to get outside this area. It's where they most expect to see people," I add. "So grab a quick bite from your pack, and let's get back at it. We have – about ten hours to make it fifteen or so miles," I say as I reference the sun rising above the mountains. "We need to stay out of the open during the day, so the travel will be slower. We also will need to leave ourselves a little bit of time to make camp for the night and find food and water."

"Aye, aye, Captain Sardine," Phil remarks and puts his hand to his brow in a salute. I am not sure if he is making an angry sarcastic remark or trying to lighten the mood a bit. Either way, I give him a dirty look and chuck a rock at him. He ducks just before it skips off his head and flashes his stupid face.

"I feel like I'm on a camping trip with middle-schoolers," Lacy groans.

"You know he has had a crush on you since we were in middle-school," Phil zings with a sinister smile. I feel my face flush, and I take a step forward to pummel him.

"Oh, knock it off," Ephie yells. "Good grief, talk about a sick cosmic joke to be stuck out here with you two."

I decide against the fist to Phil's skull. Instead I pick up my pack, grab a nutrition bar from inside, and toss it to him. "Here, make yourself useful and shove this in your mouth."

"You're going soft!" He grins and pries off a large bite with his teeth.

Lacy is staring awkwardly at the ground, chewing a bar as well. I had not really thought about my feelings for her during this whole ordeal; but now, as Phil's words are still thick in the air, I can't help but sense the nervous energy I experience each time I see her. I don't know if it is the stress of the situation or the new inner confidence I have gained, but all the inhibitions I have felt towards her over the years are now gone. I don't care that she knows how I feel; in fact, I am surprisingly ok with it. Maybe now I won't act like a total idiot around her.

"He's right; I have always had a crush on you." Out of the corner of my eye I see Phil crack a smile. "There – that's over and done with. Now we can get on with what we are out here to do."

"I kinda had a suspicion that may be the case," Lacy answers sheepishly. Phil gives me a knowing wink, and it dawns on me that he did it on purpose. He must have realized there would be uneasiness or animosity between us, until the elephant in the room was exposed.

"Alright, alright, let's get moving," Ephie interjects loudly, jolting me back into reality. He heads off into the woods and we follow. I give Phil a playful shove.

"Thanks, Bud," I whisper, and he gives me another wink.

As we go, I look up occasionally and watch as Lacy's pony tail bobs back and forth. I think back to what Mom wrote about falling in love and never letting that feeling go. I wonder if this is what she was referring to. Regardless, the atmosphere has changed from that of a death march this morning to a pleasant hike in the afternoon sun.

We keep the railroad tracks between us and the ocean, following game trails if we can find them. The flat terrain has been replaced by a gradual incline as we begin to move up Lookout Mountain, the southernmost landmark in our territory. I have been this far on hunts a few times in the past, so the area is vaguely familiar. As midday approaches, we reach the spot Mom and I called Lookout Point: an open field at the edge of Infinity Gorge, where one can see for miles in all directions. We skirt the outside of the field, staying a few paces in the woods. The railroad tracks cross the three-mile wide gorge over a high bridge, which is far too conspicuous for us to attempt.

"Look, there is the perimeter," Ephie calls from ahead. He is standing at the point where the tracks leave the forest and head out across the gorge and gazing across the expanse at the laser fence at the base of the mountain on the other side.

"Wow, that's incredible," Lacy whispers with an awestruck smile. "The view up here is amazing!"

"I didn't realize the perimeter marker was more than a single laser line. That thing is like a monstrous red fishing net or something," Phil says as he sees the red crisscrossing lines for the first time.

"Yeah, that is intimidating!" Lacy replies giddily, still overtaken by the view.

"The good thing is, it is only a few more miles and most of it is downhill. We should be able to make it there without much trouble," I add and grab my canteen from my pack.

"Who could ever say something this awe-inspiring could be made by nothing more than chance," Phil says with a wry smile, as he takes in the majesty of the view. "It is as if God took his thumb and '*pfft*' pressed down leaving his thumbprint in the heights and depths of these ridges and valleys."

I have become relatively numb to the beauty of the wild over the years, but now, as I stand here for the final time, I am once again awed by the magnitude of the splendor. Rugged mountain peaks with pockets of white snow rise high against the blue sky. Far beneath, a glistening blue ribbon follows the contours of the mountain, winding in and out of view as it flows toward the Pacific. In between are countless acres of untamed beauty, represented by several shades of green tree tops that are hiding from view the untold struggles of life and death being waged beneath their watch. What a picture of our God. From the needs of the smallest of the unseen creatures to the enormity of the task we are called to complete, all playing out in simultaneous harmony within the beauty of this scene. As we start down the mountain, I cannot help but smile. What a feeling to know the deft mountain-making fingers are on our side.

The trek down the slope is a welcome change, as the steady decline in elevation eases the sharp aching that had been building in my upper legs. I cannot imagine what Phil must be feeling. A quick stumble and a groan confirm my suspicions, as he attempts unsuccessfully to step over a small branch strewn across the trail.

"You should have steered clear of that last helping of mashed potatoes last night," I jab. He only shakes his head in response. Maybe he is even more exhausted than I realize.

Ephie's shadow, lengthened by the late afternoon sun, approaches the crisscrossing red lines first, as we begin the ascent up the far side of the ravine. We all soon join him, and I slip the pack off my shoulder and grab the canteen once again.

"Nice work everyone, we made it," Phil musters with conviction and takes a long drink from his. I echo his enthusiasm but know we are far from being able to celebrate. Today is most likely the easiest day we will endure. We are all healthy and in relatively good spirits, buoyed by the adrenaline and excitement of the moment. Each subsequent evening will lead us one day further from our comfort and draw from each of us unknown amounts of strength and hope from our ever-dwindling reserves.

"It was a good day, but we still need to set up camp," I say to energize the group for one last push this evening. Lacy's shoulders slump as she sits resting on the ground, staring up at the fence. It is human nature to begin to relax as the completion of a tiresome task is clearly at hand, but with this much at stake, human frailty cannot be an option.

"Come on; let's keep moving. The sooner we put the perimeter behind us, the sooner we can make camp, and the sooner you can show us some of those fish-catching tricks you learned from your dad." I hold out my hand and help her to her feet. "I saw a nice salmon stream when we were at the top of the gorge; and I don't know about you, but a nice salmon filet sounds pretty good right about now!"

The mention of her father softens her tired face. She brushes a loose hair away from her sparkling eyes and pulls her pack further up onto her shoulders.

"So do we just walk through this thing?" she asks, rubbing her shoulder and looking up at the glowing lines. I nod as I gaze upwards as well. This close the fence appears massive, climbing high above the green canopy. If the Establishment were hoping for a sense of intimidation from the perimeter, they have definitely achieved their goal.

"I will go first and you can follow in single file behind me," Ephie instructs. He has been quiet for most of the day, maybe trying to establish his niche within the group. It must be difficult for him to digest that he is no longer the authority figure here, but rather a peer with three students who have caused him grief the past few years.

He walks quickly and confidently through the laser lines. Lacy begins to follow, but stops, looking blankly into the air, as if she is waiting for someone or something to swoop from the tree-tops and tackle her to the ground.

"It's alright," I encourage. "We are invisible, remember?"

"I know, I know. This is my first time walking through laser beams, okay? Geesh – cut me some slack." She cautiously reaches her hand through the lines but quickly pulls it back, shaking it to and fro, before examining to make sure the lasers have not zapped off her skin. Apparently satisfied with the result, she takes one step back and then jumps swiftly forward through the red lines, landing hunched and wincing on the other side. She slowly stands, tapping her body with her hands, as if she is taking mental inventory of the condition of her anatomy, before letting out an excited laugh.

"This is so much fun!" she squeals. "Come on, Sardis. You are right; I *am* in the mood for some fresh salmon!" I smile and shake my head. Phil and I walk through the perimeter with much less drama.

"Alright, I think the stream is a few hundred yards further into the woods. Why don't you and Ephie head down there and see if you can find us some dinner, while Phil and I walk upstream and find a place to camp for the night."

"Don't you think we should stick together?" Ephie interjects hastily. "The last thing we need is to get split up out here. We would never find each other."

"Why don't we use the neural communicators?" Phil adds.

"No way," I say emphatically. "Too risky this close to the perimeter."

"If you want to split up, Sardis, then I think the communicators are a great idea," Ephie responds aggressively. "You may think you have all the answers out here – in – in –" he waves his hands around pointing aimlessly at the forest, "this God forsaken, bug infested, wasteland – but when it comes to important things, like things made with some actual intelligence, you have no idea what you are talking about."

I can feel the anger bubbling in my gut. "What has gotten into you, Ephie?" Both Phil and Lacy have the same disbelieving look on their faces as I do, but decide not to butt in, possibly still trying to balance Ephie's position as both Dean of Technology and substandard traveling companion.

"It is Dr. Porter to you," he says crossly. "I may not be the prototypical outdoorsy type, but that is no excuse for you to refer to your elder with that patronizing name!"

I clench my jaw, and it takes everything in me to hold back my response. I see Phil quickly shake his head to the side, urging me not to go there.

"You are right," I concede unconvincingly through clenched teeth. "I apologize. But I don't appreciate your tone either." I dart Phil a defiant scowl. "And when it comes to decisions on where to camp and how to navigate this terrain, I will have the final say."

Ephie peers angrily over the tops of his glasses, perhaps debating whether to continue this verbal power struggle. "Fine; but all decisions in regards to trip strategy and the Establishment belong to me."

"Fine."

"Great, now that we have that established," Lacy interrupts sarcastically, with still a trace of the exuberance she displayed after jumping through the perimeter, "I'm hungry; and I don't care who comes with me, but I'm going fishing."

"I'll come with you," Ephie responds briskly. "But you two stay within sight of the stream. If we do get split up, we can find each other."

Realizing Ephie has conceded a little, I soften my glare. "If you really think the communicators will work without being detected, then we can use them. You and Phil can wear them, because I can't seem to operate one properly."

"You've got that right!" Lacy quips. I shoot her a playful dirty look. She raises her eyebrows and flashes a grin, then turns and heads toward the stream. We follow until the stream is within sight, then Phil and I head eastward toward slightly higher elevation.

"Hopefully we can find a nice cave to sleep in tonight," I say as I lift my hands above my head to wade through a patch of thick vegetation, before finally locating a decent game trail. I grab an arrow out of my quiver and nock it, just in case we jump something along the way.

"Ephie kind of lost it there for a second," Phil says quietly, after we are out of earshot of the others.

"Yeah, I don't know what got into him. Maybe he is struggling with the whole 'not having full authority' thing."

"It is kind of weird seeing him in this forum."

"Forum?" I mock. "You are starting to talk like him now."

"Ok, this *setting,* you dummy; but you know what I am saying. And I kind of feel bad for him. He is far from his comfort zone."

"Yeah, he is not much for the outdoors, but I would say that neither you or Lacy are much for it either."

"It is nor. Neither you nor Lacy." He flashes the Phil face.

"Fantastic, I am walking next to the human dictionary."

"Actually, you would not find simple grammar corrections in a dictionary. So I am more like your human middle-school English textbook."

"You are about to be an ex-human middle-school English textbook if you keep this up." He laughs heartily and punches me playfully in the shoulder.

"You are right, though; I am kind of intimidated by the great outdoors. It is a good thing you are here to protect me!"

We make our way slowly upstream, until we find a rocky outcropping that, upon close inspection, seems suitable for our first night in the wild. There is ample room to sleep four people under the overhang as well as an area to make a fire.

"I will go and find some fire wood. Let Ephie know where we are and I'll be back in a few minutes. Make this place cozy," I instruct and then head into the woods. After locating some good kindling and several prime pieces of dead birch, I walk back to the campsite and see all three of them sitting there.

"Back so soon?" I ask Lacy curiously. She holds up two nice-sized silver salmon and flops them next to where Phil had set up four rocks for dinner chairs.

"I thought that would be sufficient for one meal," she responds glowingly. "Plus, I figured you would have supplemented our fish dinner with some nice grouse or something."

"I didn't have any luck hunting, but I did find some fiddleheads along the path; so we can have a little greenery with our meal."

"Do you really expect me to eat those things?" Ephie huffs. "You just grabbed them off the ground over there."

"You should try one before you stick your nose up. They taste like asparagus. I'll cook you up a couple in case you change your mind."

Within a few minutes, the air is thick with the aroma of seared salmon. I spoon a few of the now boiled young fern plants onto a plate and hand it to Ephie. He hesitates for a moment, but pops one into his mouth. He chews a few times before raising his hand to his mouth, letting out a loud gagging sound, and hastily swallowing.

"I thought you said these things were good!" He growls.

"I said they tasted like asparagus; I never said they were good!" My retort brings a rare smirk to his face.

"The best thing I can say about them is they are edible." He picks up another and begins chewing.

"So how did you catch these fish so fast?" I ask Lacy as I take my first bite of the salmon. The flesh melts in my mouth, and the taste is out of this world good. There is nothing like fresh fish over a campfire, I think, as I wait for her to clear her mouth to respond.

"Wow, this is good," she says smiling as she swallows. "My dad showed me a few tricks on how to catch salmon in the river. Really, it is pretty easy, especially when the stream is as loaded with them as this one is." She takes another healthy bite. "You just kind of herd them into the shallows and grab them with the net," she explains between chews. "Excuse my rudeness; this is just so good and I'm starving!"

"That sounds easy enough. Do you think you could teach me?" Phil asks.

"Well, you have to be quick…"

"I'm quick!" He responds with a half-offended shout.

"As quick as a hungry cat. You should see him at the buffet line in Martha's!"

"You're right, Sardis; I have seen him swipe a few cakes from the desert table – So fast I couldn't even see his hands moving!" Lacy zings, causing me to burst out laughing.

"What is this, team up on Phil day?" he attempts to say with a mouthful of salmon, only to have a half-chewed piece sail out of his mouth and land on one of Ephie's fiddleheads. We all laugh hysterically. Even Ephie lets out a few genuine snickers.

The mood is jovial the rest of the evening as we sit and talk about trivial things that have nothing to do with the enormous task before us. Soon the evening is replaced by twilight, and after listening to Phil play a few hymns on his harmonica, we each slip into our sleeping sacks. I had instructed everyone to change clothes and hang them outside of camp until morning, as well as clean up anything that may smell like salmon, so as not to attract any unwanted visitors during the night. The new comfortable shirt and pants feel almost heavenly as I nestle into the warmth of the bag. I lie there looking up at the stars beginning to emerge from the last rays of light in the early night sky, my ears still ringing from Phil's serenade, and I cannot help but feel at peace. The group has come together in a way the leaders at home could not have foreseen when they selected us, although, I guess they were not the ones who did the selecting. I turn my head and see Lacy lying on her side, the orange flicker of the campfire reflecting in her eyes. She quickly shifts her gaze past mine as our eyes meet. I smile as her eyes focus back on mine. She smiles as well.

"Good night," I say and turn back over.

"Good night," she replies and does the same.

I wonder what she was thinking as she was lying there watching me. I have never known her to be this outgoing and full of energy, at least since her father died. When we were young, we used to spend a lot of time together. Her father and my mother were on the Board of Elders, and we would have play dates during those meeting times. We would also see each other while our parents had their Bible studies. I can remember playing hide and seek in our basement one particular evening. I would always try and find the best spots, and since the Bible study was at my house, I knew a perfect place: under an old pile of Mom's hunting clothes on the floor next to the washer and dryer. No one would ever think to rummage through a pile of dirty, smelly clothes to find someone hiding there. Phil was usually "it," partially because he was terrible at hiding, but mostly because he was equally bad at finding people. I had situated myself underneath the pile of clothes and was lying perfectly still. I could hear other kids rustling about, searching through the unfamiliar space for a good hiding spot. As I was lying there, I heard the dryer door open, someone tumble in, and then close the door behind them. Not wanting to give away my prime location, I did not say a word or move a muscle. Soon I could hear Phil bumbling around and muttering to himself. He walked past me several times before opening the door to the dryer and squealing with glee when he actually found someone. I heard Lacy groan as she attempted to get out of the dryer, only to stumble and fall directly on top of me, squeezing the air out of my lungs in a muffled moan. Phil yanked off the dirty clothes and jumped up and down, overjoyed with actually finding me, since I had bragged to him earlier how there was no chance he would. I can remember looking at Lacy and being so irate that she had given away my location, wanting to yell or say something mean to her, but instead it was the first time

I noticed her beauty. As boys, we do not think about that type of stuff; she had always been just another friend – Phil with longer hair. But in that moment, I saw her eyes sparkle for the first time in the dim basement light, and I was awestruck. No words came from my mouth. I remember her apologizing, and I think I may have grunted something back to her or I possibly could have said nothing, I don't really remember – I just remember the feeling.

After her father died, we did not see each other much. She was much more concerned with her friends and seemingly trying to impress everyone, whether it was with the latest fashion trends from the Establishment, or the jewelry and make-up that came for her at almost every shipment. The less we talked, the more she seemed like a glittering jewel on a pedestal, always out of reach and never really something that could be obtained. Tonight though, as she lies next to me, the only image I can see is the sparkling eyes of the young girl in the basement. Here – with no make-up to hide the pain caused by losing her father and no fancy clothes and shiny jewelry to define her worth – here she is real. Here she is finally free to be who God created her to be, and she is beautiful.

I turn over once more and her eyes are closed and her face looks serene. I close my eyes as well and quickly begin to dream. I see a young girl, about my age, with bright green eyes and short red hair. Her face looks pale and there are markings on her arms and legs. Her shirt is black and oddly short in the middle with a bold white pattern on the front. She is walking in a field full of white wild flowers, wilted brown by the scorching midday sun. She appears lost or confused as she walks aimlessly through the desolate landscape. There are tears on her cheeks and a look of fear in her eyes, and it becomes evident that she is either running from or chasing something as her gait begins to quicken. It's Lacy,

I think, as my consciousness somehow enters this dream world. The girl then stops running, looks directly at me, and shakes her head as if to rebuff this idea. "Help me," she whispers. She continues running until she leaves the field and heads for the edge of a cliff, with nothing but darkness below. I run to her as fast as I can and try to keep her from falling. "Stop, you are going to fall!" I yell but she doesn't stop. She turns back toward me and I can see bruises and scrapes on her arms and neck, and her eye is swollen. "I'm tired of the tears, the pain, and the fear," she sobs and turns back toward the abyss. "No!" I cry but it is too late. She leans forward and tumbles over the side.

"No!" I scream again, this time waking me from the nightmare. I sit up quickly, drenched with sweat and breathing heavily. The fire is almost out but I can see Lacy is sitting in her sleeping bag as well. The others are still asleep.

"Are you ok?" She asks quietly. "Seems like you were having a bad dream?"

"Yeah, I was," I reply, still groggy from the experience. "I actually am used to waking up in a cold sweat from nightmares, but this one was different."

"You, too? I have them almost every night. How was this one different?" She pulls her bag up further on her.

"Until two nights ago, I would always have these dreams about Dr. Pergo and my mom," I whisper before stopping. She is peering at me intently, but I am not convinced she is interested in hearing my problems.

"What happened in the dreams?" she asks gently, and I realize losing her dad might have brought about some of the same feelings I struggle with.

"Well, they are kind of personal…"

"You don't have to tell me if you don't want to."

"But I do though, that's the thing – If you really are interested."

"I am, Sardis," she says with a kind softness that puts my anxieties at rest.

"I have these dreams that my mom is going in for her procedure, because that is how she died." I shake my head. "That is how I thought she died anyway."

"Yeah, I am still struggling with that revelation as well. I can't believe after all these years –" she places the back of her hand to her mouth and squeezes her eyes shut to try and hold back the tears, but she cannot and begins to sob. I bring my bag closer and put my arm around her shoulder.

"I know. It is both life-shattering and unbelievably inspiring. To think they were picked for that mission – it's crazy."

"I miss him so much," she mouths through tears. "There is so much I wish I could ask him. I know he wouldn't be proud of how I've –" she fails to finish her thought, as she breaks into a heavy sob. I pull her into my chest and she burrows her head underneath my chin.

"I often times have these flashbacks where something will trigger a memory I have of her, and I will instantly be back in time," I say reflectively, staring into the smoldering pile of ash. "She will be there and everything will be back to the way it was. I'll be twelve again, eating dinner and listening to her stories about her hunt that day. I can smell her and even taste her venison stew."

"I have those, too." She sits up and wipes her eyes. "I will see one of his fishing buddies, or go to a place where he took me fishing once, and I'll be there with him. One time," she lets out a quick, short laugh through a heavier sniffle, "I was on my way to the hospital and I was passing by the holograms trying not to have them talk to me, and I literally walked right into his friend Francis. As soon as I went to apologize, it was like he was my dad. It was the weirdest thing. I said something to him fully expecting my dad's voice to answer, but when it wasn't, I was so confused. It was – oh, I don't know. It is so hard to explain what it is like."

"I know. It is impossible to put into words. It is just a feeling – a horrible empty feeling." I pull my arm back and rest my chin in my hands, as I continue to stare into the glowing embers. "There are some nights, after waking from my latest dream, that I lie there and think, and everything seems to make sense. It's like a moment of clarity or something, and the empty feeling has a purpose – something real or tangible. Something that makes me feel like everything is going to be okay. Like the hole that is there will be – not closed or healed – but used for something. But when I wake up in the morning it is gone, and all that is left is the pain."

"What do you think it is? The purpose?"

"I don't know. You know – I guess maybe something to do with all this? I don't know. I don't really think that's it either. I just think too much sometimes, I guess."

"I'm sorry; I didn't mean to pry so much. I just never talk about this with anyone and I feel like we have a connection or something because we both went through the same thing."

I smile and nod, "Yeah, it is nice." We both stare at the fire a few moments more before I sit up and move my bag back over to my spot. "We better get some more sleep; we are going to need it for tomorrow."

"If it's alright, could you stay over here? This is my first night alone – and – well, I haven't been able to sleep –"

"I'd love to."

"Plus, you never told me about the dream you had tonight."

"Oh yeah, of course," I say, going along with it. I tell her about the strange girl with the bright green eyes. She seems as confused about it as I am, and we both agree to ask Phil in the morning. We exchange goodnights and I lie there, *still*. Soon her breathing becomes more rhythmic and I steal one last glance before surrendering to the most peaceful night's rest I have had in four years.

Chapter 9

"Do you see the big one over there... under that branch?" Lacy asks, pointing to a large shimmering shape underneath the surface of the swiftly moving water. Phil cranes his neck before settling his gaze upon the prize.

"Yep, I see it."

"Okay, now you need to move slowly toward it and see if you can scoot it over to that shallow pool next to the far bank." He takes a few steps toward the fish and it moves away from him and into the targeted pool. He turns around and gives me a wink and a silly "I'm the man" grin.

"Now what," he whispers, knee deep in the cold flowing water with a net in one hand and a stick in the other.

"Now put the net in the water and slowly move it in front of the fish. Leave it there for a few seconds so it gets accustomed to its being in the water, and then take your stick and tap the back of the fish so it will swim into your net."

"Gotcha," Phil says confidently, and slowly moves closer to the fish. Cautiously, he places the net in the water and inches it nearer to the front of the fish, but it quickly darts away from his reach, out of the shallow pool, and into the faster moving water.

"Yeah, quick like a cat," I tease, as he takes the net and swings it through the air in frustration.

"Here, let me show you," she says. She places the net in front of another small school of decent-sized salmon. She stands still, staring stoically into the stream for a few moments before a quick move of her wrist, and like magic, lifts the net and a wriggling six-pound trophy into the air.

"That was unbelievable!" Phil yells and sloshes over to her, grabbing the net out of her hand. "This thing is huge! I can't believe it!" he gushes, as happy for her success as he would have been for his own.

"It will go well with the duck that Sardis got earlier." She looks at me, sending a light airy rush emanating from my gut to sweep over my body. We lock eyes for a brief moment before exchanging guilty smiles. Phil is too busy gawking at the fish to notice, but I'm sure throughout the past few days he has picked up on other cues. I am not sure if it is the heightened emotions brought on by the weight of our situation, or the connection we discovered that first night around the fire, or more than likely a combination of both, but something has definitely changed between Lacy and me. Our interactions have been overtly awkward, but at the same time, welcomed. It is undoubtedly the beginnings of something stronger; but without saying, we both realize we have at most twenty-seven days left on this earth with a monumental task in front of us. The whole situation has left me somewhat drained, yet, I have never felt so alive. My thoughts and movements seem lightning sharp, and I feel as if I could jump over a mountain and take on an army of I-Morts with just my bare hands.

Unfortunately, not everyone in our company has been doing as well. Ephie seems to be struggling with the palladium side effects, as he is quite sluggish and has complained of awful stomach cramping and debilitating nausea. We decided to stop early for today, to allow him to rest and get a good meal, hopefully helping his worsening condition. We did make a little over ten miles before making camp and attempting to fulfill Phil's desire to catch a fish.

"I've got to try this one more time," he states and grabs the net off the bank, as Lacy begins to clean her catch. I watch in awe as she skillfully produces two perfect fillets from the fish carcass.

"I guess I never realized how at home you are out here," I say as she tosses the remains up onto the bank.

"I used to go camping a lot with Dad. All we would take with us for a whole weekend was our tent and sleeping bags. Plus, I helped out at the cannery one summer before I started my calling. Truthfully, I really wasn't as excited about the nursing stuff as I should have been." She kneels near the stream rinsing the fillets in the water. "My mom loved it. Caring for people like that. It was her calling and so it became mine as well. Don't get me wrong, I enjoyed helping people and being able to comfort them in their time of need, but I *loved* being outside with Dad. I never got to go with him on the boats because women weren't allowed, but I used to wait for him on the dock, sometimes all day, until I could see his boat coming into the mouth of the river."

"Splash!" We both turn quickly to see Phil flailing on his stomach holding the net above water, while attempting desperately to get back to his feet without losing the fish he somehow has snared. He slowly stands up, water cascading from the pockets of his pants and dripping rapidly from his hair and the tip of his nose. I swear the flopping fish pauses its thrashing for just a moment to stare in shocked amazement at its unlikely captor, as Phil raises the net into the air in triumph.

"Way to go, Phil!" Lacy cheers.

"Alright, Philistine!"

He scrambles to the shore with the net bobbing in his hand. "How about that!" he yells victoriously. "See, Sardine, I told you I could do it!"

"I don't know what to say, Phil; I am amazed."

"You don't have to say anything. You could just stand there and revel in my awesomeness. I think that would suffice."

"At least you didn't have your stun weapon in your pocket; that could have been interesting," I say not wanting him to get the last word.

"Good, I was expecting something condescending. Now I know you are genuinely happy for me!"

"Yeah, yeah. Now you can clean it."

"Clean it? How can it be dirty; it lives in water?"

"*Pfft*," Lacy blurts out trying to muffle her laugh, not knowing if Phil were serious or just trying to be funny. I know Phil. He is not that funny.

"What?" He says confused, not realizing he is either a comedian or an imbecile.

"I can help you fillet," she offers innocently, as Phil lifts his chin in sudden realization of the alternate definition of the word "clean," before lowering it in embarrassment.

"Oh,yeah, that would be great, Lacy. Thanks," he says nonchalantly. "I would probably mess it up anyway." He sets the net down on the bank and flaps his arms, attempting to dry off. I resist the urge to say something; instead, I hand him the two other fillets.

"Why don't you take these back to camp and get dry clothes while we finish this fish?"

"That sounds wonderful," he replies through chattering teeth.

"We'll be right behind you," Lacy adds as he waddles away.

She quickly handles the fish while I clean up the rest of the gear. I sling the pack over my shoulder and take a step toward the creek, where she is rinsing the fillets, when a faint sound catches my attention. "Shh, do you hear that?" She stops and sits up straight, listening intently.

"I don't hear – wait – that low rumbling sound?"

"Yeah, it sounds like a – The shipment!" I yell and quickly grab her arm. "Come on! We need to get back to camp *now*!"

We sprint into the woods as the sound gets louder. My mind is racing, trying to decide what action to take when we reach camp. Can they see us? Why is the shipment so early this month? Should we get deeper into the woods? Smoke. I see it billowing white above the pines in the direction of our camp. Why would they make a fire during the day! We have become too relaxed since we left our territory, as if we were in a lull between the perimeter and Sapphire City. How stupid.

Our footfalls are now drowned out by the sound of the approaching menace as we reach the camp. Phil and Ephie have already packed most of our gear away, and we quickly help them with the rest and throw dirt on the fire.

"We need to get deeper into the woods," I command and we take off into the wilderness. "If they see the smoke they will send the Dragons!" The thought is terrifying, something out of one of my nightmares. We crash through the woods as the train passes by, easily within a quarter mile of our location. Please keep moving. Please keep moving. I say to myself over and over again, listening for any sign the barreling freight cars may be slowing down. Please keep moving. Please keep moving. I look back and notice the smoke has cleared from above the trees. Please keep moving...

I am in the lead and realize I have put a little distance between myself and the others, so I slow my pace. It would be disastrous to get split up now. Come on; come on! I yell to myself as I stand there, waiting for them to emerge from the thick undergrowth.

"*Screech!*" The sound of steel brakes grinding on steel track sends a chill down my spine. I feel adrenaline pumping through my body. My breathing quickens. This can't be happening.

"Come on!" I scream, this time loud enough for them to hear. "We have no time to lose; we have to hide. They are coming!"

The Dragons will be deployed within moments. A campfire smoke signature outside of a territory is an automatic red flag. They will be sent from Sapphire City, and at this distance, they will be here in half an hour.

"What are we going to do?" Lacy yells frantically. "There is no way to run from them!"

"They can track our body heat, so we need to get out of the open," I reply.

Visions from school lectures of I-Morts with green-clad Special Forces uniforms appear in my mind. The Establishment only chose the best soldiers to become Dragons, ex-military in a previous life. They are ruthless, relentless in their search. Once you have been targeted, you will be hunted – until you are caught – or killed. Their leader is a master tracker, nicknamed "Serpent" for how he can slither through any terrain, always locating his prey. He wears a red uniform, fitting for all the blood that has been spilt by his hands.

"Wait, stop!" Ephie yells, hunched over trying to catch his breath. "Listen to me; it is useless to keep running. We need to find shelter. *Now.*"

"We need to get as far away from our camp as possible!" I object.

"Listen to me, Mr. Alexander. I know the Establishment – there are certain protocols. This isn't a hundred years ago."

"What do you mean, a hundred years ago?"

"I'll clarify when we are safe in a cave somewhere; now please, we must go."

"Fine," I say and spin around, searching the surrounding terrain for the best direction to take. If we can find a river with this elevation change, we may be able to locate a cave in the rocky face of the mountain. That is my hope anyway. Our last hope. If we cannot find something soon… I shake my head to clear the negative thoughts. All they will do is cloud judgment. To second guess at this point would be a mistake. Go with your first instinct. "We need to head that way, south east, up that mountain," I instruct. Ephie nods in approval and we depart once more.

We crash through the underbrush, abandoning stealth movement and the ease of the game trails for the most direct route toward the highlands. Running water, yes!

"Keep up with me; we are going to follow this up the mountain. If you see a crack or crevice in the rock, point it out; that is what we are looking for!"

As we follow the river, I am constantly scanning the horizon for approaching aircraft and listening to see if anything may be coming up behind us. Nothing yet.

"Ah, hold on a moment – my leg…" Ephie yells. I turn to see him struggling to free his leg from a deep muddy hole along the bank of the river. Come on… Come on… I mumble audibly to myself, disgusted by the delay caused by such a novice mistake.

"Here, give me your hand," I yell, kneeling next to the mud pit and reaching my hand out toward him.

"Almost got you… There…" I grunt, as I pull him, minus a boot, up out of the muck. He looks down at his mud caked sock and places his hand to his head.

"I can't do this," he moans defeatedly.

"Yes, you can. Come on," I reply defiantly. I reach down and pull his boot out of the mud and hand it to him. "We need you, Dr. Porter."

"Over there! Look! I see a crack in the rock," Phil yells. "Do you see it? Over there on the other side of the river next to that mossy patch."

"Yes! I see it, too!" Lacy confirms excitedly.

I scan the river and locate a narrow section that appears easy to cross.

"*Wooooo!*" the freight train's whistle howls, indicating it is about to start moving again.

"They are leaving!" Phil announces excitedly. "We are going to be ok!"

"There are protocols!" Ephie shouts and gets back to his feet, outwardly revitalized. "Don't slow down now!"

We cross the river and tear up the opposite bank. The crack in the rock is just wide enough for us to slide in sideways. Once inside, it opens into a larger cavern. My eyes have yet to adjust to the dimly lit area, so I cannot tell how deep into the mountain the cave travels, but at this moment, we are safely tucked away from the government's gaze.

"I can't believe this. I can't believe this," Lacy is crying over and over again, bent at the waist with her hands on her knees, her mind trying to catch up to the last adrenaline-soaked ten minutes.

"Now what?" I ask Ephie, who is also bent at the waist trying to catch his breath. He starts dry heaving and falls to one knee before puking. I hear Lacy gagging and I turn away, focusing on the light coming through the rock-face, trying to keep from suffering the same fate. We stand there for a moment, all trying to gather ourselves.

"As I was saying earlier, there are protocols," he begins, laboring heavily with each word. He slowly stands, wiping his mouth and beginning to regain his composure. "The government set up a checklist after the war to follow when a possible threat is triggered. A campfire outside of a territory is low on the threat scale, especially since there has been little dissension from the territories in years."

"So what will they do?" I ask.

"They will do one of two things. Either they will have an I-Mort from the train physically investigate the scene, or they will, more than likely, scan the area remotely."

"With like a satellite or something?"

"Yes, they have a very elaborate surveillance system in place, using infrared and motion tracking as well as scanning our tracking dyes. Once the I-Morts on the train relay the coordinates, one of the government agencies will immediately scan they area. Hopefully we made it safely here before we showed up on their radar."

"The train has moved on, is that a good sign?" Phil asks.

"Not necessarily. It means they did not send someone to check the campsite, which then means they probably relayed our coordinates before we crossed the river."

"So they know we are in this cave?"

"It is a good possibility," he replies flatly. "But they can't see us now, so this gives us time to formulate a plan."

"How long do we have," I ask hesitantly.

"That is a loaded question, and what I am struggling with at the moment." I look at him funny, realizing he knows more than he is letting on.

"Spill it. What are we up against here?"

"Your father should have known better than to send you three out here into this inferno. You're just kids, up against forces you never had a chance to defeat."

"He didn't send us; we were chosen," Phil replies angrily.

"That was the first mistake..." Ephie mutters under his breath. "This is what will happen. They will send the Dragons, not the whole unit, just a reconnaissance team. Normally that is more than sufficient to subdue the average runaway. They will be here within a few hours." He searches through his pack and pulls out a canvas bag. "In here I have four cloaking devices. You place them around your neck and they act as a heat diffuser, virtually hiding your body heat from their scanners. Now – if we place these on, we could sneak out of this cave and find a new spot miles away before they get here."

"Excellent!" Lacy says excitedly.

"The problem is, if we are not here when they arrive, our security threat then escalates and we enter a whole new realm of troubles. They will immediately call for an emergency census back home in an attempt to determine who is missing. When they discover it is us, they will capture and detain our families until we are returned. At that point, we will all be at the mercy of the Justice System, and we know how that will end."

"So then we stay here and wait for them. We can use the field trip excuse; and when they escort us back home, we can try again in the future," I reply.

"Oh, that ruse was never going to work. It was just something your dad made up for Deborah and Mary's sake. To put them a little more at ease letting their kids leave. As soon as they found us, they would realize we had a dye-blocking agent, and we would all be as good as dead."

I put my hands on my head and nervously pace back and forth in the small space, while the others stand there quietly. "What kind of chance do we have eluding the Dragons until we reach Sapphire?"

"You know the answer to that, Sardis."

I take a few more blank steps before responding. "It seems to me though, it is the only chance we have. If we stay here, they find us, period. If we try and run – at least we have some shot."

"Yeah, but if we run, then our families..." Lacy stammers.

"I know, but if we get caught they will have to answer for us as well. I say we go for it. Take off deep into the pine forest and move under the canopy as far as we can make it."

"I don't think I can..." Ephie says, taking a seat on the cavern floor. "Not in my condition. Besides, who am I kidding – out there in the wild you do not need me. I will only slow you down."

"What are you going to do when the Dragons get here then?" I ask, irritated with the thought of his quitting just like that. "They will interrogate you unmercifully."

"And I will tell them the truth, more or less. We were on a school camping expedition. I got sick and separated from the group. I can even tell them your names, hopefully lessening the impacts back home."

"But what about the palladium in your system?"

"I don't know – I have not figured out how to massage that one. Hopefully I can come up with something in the next few hours. Regardless, leaving me here is a much better option. If I go with you, we are all caught."

I mull the idea over in my mind for a few seconds. "What does everyone think?"

"I don't know," Phil replies slowly. "The whole thing is just overwhelming; I can't think straight at the moment."

"I say it is our only chance..." Lacy begins reflectively, "Sardis, if your mom or my dad were out here, they would press on and see this thing to the end. We can't give up this easily."

I nod in affirmation.

"Then get out of here; you have little time until they arrive," Ephie orders.

"Dr. Porter," I say as I walk toward him and extend my hand, "it was an honor serving with you." He grabs my hand firmly.

"Thank you," Lacy says through tears and gives him a quick hug.

"We will be praying for you," Phil adds.

We each slip a body heat diffuser over our heads and slide quickly out of the cave into the bright sunlight. We head away from the open mountainside and into the pine forest. We are practically sprinting, hoping to put as much distance between ourselves and our last known location. Over the past few days Lacy and Phil have become much more adept at moving through the woods, and we are able to keep up this pace for several hours.

"Do you still have the salmon fillets?" I ask Phil after we stop for a moment to catch our breath.

"I think so," he replies opening his pack. "Yep, here they are." He pulls out the fillets, wrapped in a paper bag.

"We can't afford to make a fire so we are going to have to eat these raw." I look at the other two for objections. They nod in agreement.

"If the bears can do it, then so can I!" Phil says, lightening the heavy mood.

We each tear off chunks of flesh and eagerly eat. I did not realize how hungry I was as I devour handfuls at a time. I look up and all I see are pinholes of light through the dark, green pine branches. I am taken back to the many times I have waited for elk to emerge from dark thickets such as this. So far, we have not heard an aircraft fly over or any other sign the Dragons are hunting us. It is entirely possible we were never spotted, although we cannot afford to assume we are safe.

"Give me a minute," Phil says grabbing his pack and racing over towards a brushy area of smaller pines.

"That raw fish must have gone right through him!" Lacy jokes. I chuckle and set my pack and bow down to rest my shoulders for a few moments until Phil returns. I take a few drinks of water and scan the surroundings, searching for the best route to take as I hear him rustling toward us.

"Feel better?" I ask cheekily, looking up and seeing instead a brown bear cub, snout in the air, following the wafting smell of our dinner. A wave of fear sweeps over me as years of training have taught me the perils of this moment. I hear the roar of the protective mother before I see the charging brown mass, approaching from the direction Phil had taken. At that moment, he emerges from the pines with a sly smirk on his face, only to be knocked to the ground by the thundering animal, neither realizing the other was there. I reach down and grab my bow, hurdling an arrow into the side of the beast as it rises to its feet and Phil scrambles to get to his. The bear lets out a deafening roar as I let go another arrow, this time into its shoulder. I watch as it turns toward me, before turning once more and charging Phil. I stand helplessly as Phil falls to the ground, raising his hands to the air, as the brown bear crashes upon him.

Chapter 10

"No!" I scream, seemingly frozen outside of my body, watching as my legs move this alien form in the direction of my best friend. I see Lacy standing, mouth open in an apparent scream, her face disfigured with a look of absolute terror. I hear no sound escaping her as I sprint by. I hear no sound at all. A second stretches into a lifetime as I urge each fiber of every straining muscle to move faster, only to feel as if my boots each weigh a hundred pounds. As if in a dream, I watch as I leap onto the back of the beast, grab the knife from its sheath around my waist, and plunge it repeatedly into its side. Instinct tells me to brace for the monster's counter attack, but the only movement I see is Phil's scrambling figure as he attempts desperately to free himself from the weight of his adversary. I regain conscious thought as I jump down and barrel into the side of the bear with all my might, lifting it off the ground and rolling it onto its side. I realize it is not trying to get to its feet, so I turn to grab Phil, but he is already up and stumbling towards me. I grab a fist full of his shirt to keep him from falling as he flails about, blinded by the innate urge to flee.

"I shot it in the tongue! I shot it in the tongue!" he is yelling still in shock, as I usher him hastily away from the scene. I hear Lacy sobbing as she runs to join us. She hoists Phil's other arm over her shoulder, and we move further into the forest, out of sight of the lifeless bear.

"I think I'm alright," he groans as we carefully lay him at the base of a tree. "I don't think I am badly hurt."

"What happened? You shot it in the tongue?"

He lifts his right hand in the air; his fist still clenched around the base of a stun weapon.

"I shot it in the tongue," he replies matter-of-factly.

"You shot it in the tongue," Lacy repeats as if trying to comprehend the words, and then shakes her head. "Only you, Phil."

"I thought you were dead," I mutter loudly. I feel tears welling in the corners of my eyes, as the adrenaline is replaced by sheer emotion. My body feels weak. I bend and place my hands on my knees, collecting myself for a moment. "Are you sure you are okay?"

"I think so," he replies, getting to his feet. "I bet I'll be sore tomorrow, though."

"When did you grab the stun gun from your bag?"

"I actually did that when we left the cave. I wanted to be ready in case we ran into trouble. When that thing knocked me down, I blacked out for a moment. Before I realized what was going on, it was charging for me, and I just kind of put my hands up to protect myself. I saw the gun in my hand so I pulled the trigger...."

"God is definitely looking out for you."

"He has been guiding this whole trip," Phil replies, staring at what is left of the stun weapon in his hand. "I don't know what we are doing out here, truthfully. It sure doesn't seem like we are saving the world, trudging through briar bushes all day long." He pauses for a moment before looking up at both Lacy and me. I can see vigor in his eyes, something new, alive. "But you know what? This is what it is all about! Faith: to be sure of what you hope for and certain of what you cannot see. You know, I prayed everyday – *everyday* – for God to help me to live each day by faith. That is what we are taught to do – but I never really knew what that looked like, you know?" I nod as he rolls to his side and stands up slowly.

"You know, I should be dead. That bear should have ripped my head off. But look at me! And — and everything just seems like it is going wrong, like we have no hope....

"But do you know what I see? I see Satan trying his best to stop whatever it is we have going on here. You know, I'm not sure what we are going to find when finally make it to Gold City, but I know for a fact we are going to make it." He forcefully grabs his pack from the ground next to Lacy and storms into the woods.

I have never heard that emotion from him before and it moves me. Phil, the rock, the one who has always been the voice of reason, talking me off the ledge more times than I can count has done it again. In the depths of my soul I never thought we had a chance, but as I follow him deeper into the dark forest, I see a flicker of hope. I take Lacy's hand as we walk. I look up and instead of seeing a coffin of crisscrossed limbs, entombing us under the weight of their protection, I see a divine purpose for every branch, every needle. In order for us to make it, we must believe that. We must believe we are not alone out here; and in our darkest moments we must remember that the One who is with us is the One who is actually fighting the battle. He is the great Victor. Undefeated. Unstoppable. The battle has already been waged, and we win.

The drone of an aircraft breaks my thought, splintering the fortress that was being erected around my heart and replacing it once more with the human frailty that forever encompasses it. We have to keep moving; we have to make it to Dr. Pergo.

"They are really coming," Lacy whispers, grasping my hand more tightly as the sound of the engine dissipates in the direction of Ephie's cave. I squeeze it back.

"Let's keep moving until dusk; then we can find someplace for the night." My body is numb, my mind blank. I am so tired, so physically and emotionally drained. The war being waged inside of me is leaving me hollow, torn between carrying the weight of the responsibility for our immediate survival and a need to release these tensions altogether and completely trust. I am the leader here. I cannot lose my grasp on reality or my purpose. Or am I supposed to? I don't know. Right now, I can only put one foot in front of the other.

"Come on guys, keep up," Phil commands from ahead. I give Lacy's hand one final squeeze and we jog to catch him. He is moving quickly, his eyes still focused in a determined scowl. The encounter with the bear appears to have set something inside him ablaze, a righteous anger of sorts, as if it were not a coincidence that it was he who was attacked, and he is out to settle the score with the antagonist.

"I think we should look for a place now," he states, slowing his gate a bit and allowing us to finally catch up. "It doesn't matter how far we make it from the cave, if they are going to find us, they'll find us."

"Are you doing okay, Bud?" I ask. He does not break stride, head bobbing as he probes the darkening forest for a suitable location for the night.

"I'm fine. Never been better," he answers without acknowledging the question enough to crack his concentration. "I'm tired and hungry and ready to get off my feet."

"Look, I'm hungry and exhausted as well, but we can't give in to it."

"Give in to it? Sardis, you really don't get it, do you?"

"I guess not. Would you like to explain it to me?"

He growls and shakes his head in frustration, before turning and continuing his search.

"What is it? What don't I understand? I know what you are going to say; you're going to quote some scripture or something and tell me that everything is going to be okay. Well, right now that isn't good enough for me. I want it to be, but it's not. Not when –"

"Not when what?" he shouts.

"Not when we are running for our lives from things that are trying to kill us!" I yell back. "I need something concrete to hold on to. Not just some good feelings that everything is going to be ok. I'm not just going to stand here and let them find us and jeopardize our mission, when we can do something about it."

He lets out a disbelieving chuckle and shakes his head again. He looks at Lacy, raising his eyebrows and shrugging his shoulders, and walks toward a very thick area of scrubby pines.

"You're just going to walk away?"

"Sardis, I agree with Phil – I think we need to hunker down for the night," Lacy says gently.

"What?" I quickly turn toward her. Her eyes look tired and her features worn. She has mud splashed on one side of her face and a wad of burrs nestled underneath the collar of her coat. I let out a deep sigh and relax my shoulders. "Alright," I concede softly. I still think it is foolish not to continue while we have daylight, but we are all exhausted and it might be for the best to take some time and recharge.

"Sardis," Phil starts, emerging from the brush. "Do you remember the story of Peter walking on the water?"

I give him a strange look, but soon realize he is waiting for my response. "Um, yeah, well I remember Jesus walking on the water."

"Right, it is the same story. Jesus and his disciples had just finished feeding the five thousand when he told them to cross the lake and he would meet them on the other side. During that night, however, the wind kicked up and the disciples were struggling and afraid, wishing that Jesus were out there with them. Well, lo and behold, after a while Peter looked out and saw what at first he thought was a ghost, but soon realized it was Jesus walking toward them through the waves," he explains, his voice rich and full of life – telling the story as if he were there with them in the boat. "Peter was so excited that he jumped out of the boat and ran toward Jesus. He got part of the way there before he realized he was out in the middle of the water. As soon as he looked down, he sunk into the waves. Jesus grabbed him by the hand and said, 'Why didn't you believe you could do it? You were already half way here. You of little faith.'" He gives a confident smile. "You see, Peter had all the faith he needed. Shoot, he is one of only two men in history to walk successfully on water! Don't you get it?" He slaps me on the chest. "Sardis, don't look now but you are standing in the middle of the ocean and the waves are crashing all around. You have led us here, Bud. You did that. You found something inside of you back in that cement cell that has carried us this far. It is inside of you. God is inside of you. Don't you feel it? Don't you realize what that means?"

"I'm trying to," I reply heavily; "with all that is in me, I want to be able to trust like that."

"Then do it." Lacy says abruptly. "I felt it too back there, the confidence and hope rising up in me. It was exhilarating – but when I heard the Dragons fly over I looked down into the waves, just like you did, and I was shocked back into the reality that I am out here in the middle of nowhere doing this by myself –"

"But that's what you missed," Phil interrupts. "We are not here by ourselves. We don't have to do it alone. It wasn't Peter's trust that kept him from drowning in the end. It was solely the arm of Christ. That's the key! No matter what we do or how little faith we have, we are always held securely. *Always*."

"So do we just lay out here in the open and trust that God is going to protect us, and then somehow – oh, I don't know – beam us safely to where he wants us to be?"

"No, that is much too simplistic a definition of our God. Don't you think if He wanted to, He could have just snapped his fingers and whatever injustice we are out here dying for would have been made right without all this? Why would He go through all of human history: the fall of man and the reclamation of man through Christ's ransom, if He could have just skipped that whole thing and made us perfect? How much more awe-inspiring is it to create man who has the choice whether to follow him or not, instead of making him automatically do it? He crafts us each individually with a purpose and a design that if we choose to follow it, then we will be used and He will be with us. That is what you don't get, Sardis; He chose us for this task. He created us uniquely for it; and if we believe that, then we will succeed. Period."

I stand there for a moment, taking in Phil's sermon. I do not know what to say, but the silence seems to speak for me. We walk for a few moments, each thinking about what was said and digesting it as best we can. I wish I had the faith Phil does. I understand what he is saying and what I need to do. I just cannot do it. I don't feel it. It is there; it is in me; yet I am still numb, swimming desperately to keep my head above water.

"Alright, let's find a place," I say, breaking the lingering silence. "But I am not convinced these heat diffuser things Ephie gave us work that well, so I think we need to find someplace less conspicuous."

"That sounds like a great idea," Phil replies with his pastoral tone back. Dad was right; Phil is without question a spiritual leader. Even if I struggle with making the complete connection between what I see and what I believe, I am glad Phil has not given up on me.

We walk for a few minutes and find a series of small caves created by several large boulders at the base of a rocky hill, in a less dense section of forest. With my flashlight, I quickly peer into each and determine the one furthest from us is the best option. It has ample space for three people to sleep and also a necessary second escape route through a smaller crevice in the back. Once inside, we each grab a small bite from the food rations Phil has in his pack. There is enough packaged food to supplement the entire trip; but, if we are using it as our sole food source, we may only have enough for a few more days.

"We will need to be on the lookout for food as we go," I say, thinking out loud. "And we will need to be diligent to keep well hydrated – I forgot to fill my canteen today." I shake the container and a small amount sloshes in the bottom.

"If you need some for your pills tomorrow, you can have some of mine," Lacy replies. She is already inside her sleeping bag, her pack underneath her head for a pillow. "I'm going to try and get some sleep. We at least have a few hours, I would hope, until they would be in our area."

"I can keep watch. You get some sleep too, Phil."

"No way, Sardis. We all need our sleep. We need to let God handle some of this stuff, remember?"

I close my eyes and let out a long sharp breath, trying to relax the frustration that has been making a habit of quickly springing up in my over-stressed and completely exhausted body. I take another, easier breath and concede.

"Yeah, ok."

"Don't worry, Bud. Sweet dreams." He slides into his bag.

"Speaking of dreams," I reply, his response jogging my memory, "I have been meaning to tell you about this weird dream I had the other night."

"Oh, yeah? What was it about?"

"There was this girl about our age, bright red hair and green eyes. She was kind of pale and had on this dark shirt with strange markings on it." His face perks up as I get further into the dream. "And she was wandering through this barren field, almost as if she were lost. When I see her again she is beat up and running toward this cliff. I try to stop her, but she falls off –"

"Are you messing with me? Seriously? Of all places to be busting my chops. You are ridiculous sometimes."

"What are you flipping out about?"

"Yeah, real funny. Did you talk to my mom or something?"

"Okay, I really don't know what you are talking about. I just thought you might be interested. Forget it."

He looks at me skeptically for a few seconds. "That's my nightmare – I've had it ever since I was a kid. The girl with the red hair and green eyes, the girl I can't save – It's *my* nightmare."

"What?" I reply, the revelation causing my mind to spin.

"And you really saw the girl?"

"Yeah, she was about our age, bright green eyes and short red hair. Honestly, I had no idea!"

"Did she say anything?"

"Yes, she asked me to help her; then she said something about not wanting to be afraid and in pain anymore."

He puts his hands to his head and looks at the ground. "I can't believe this." He looks at me with a pained expression on his face. "It has to mean something, that you had the dream when we were out here. It has to."

"I was thinking the same thing. What else happened in your dreams?"

"Usually it was the same thing. She was running through a field and asking me to help her. I would watch as she kept running until she fell." He stares past me at the dimming light on the cave wall and shakes his head. "Although, one time I was in the dream with her. I was trying to figure out what it was she needed me to do. I was running after her, until I finally caught up and put my hand on her shoulder. She stopped, turned around, and then she...."

"She what?" I ask loudly, absorbed in his story.

"Well, she kissed me – and – afterwards we stared at each other for a moment, and I was – well – mesmerized by her eyes. They were like nothing I had ever seen. I didn't know what to say, I was in shock. And then she told me she loved me and for me to save her."

"And..."

"And, that was it. I woke up."

I give him a disappointed glare. I can tell there is more he wants to say. Sensing my frustration, he sighs and scratches his head, his face wincing as he braces for what he is about to say.

"But..." he starts slowly, looking down at his lap. "But I feel like she is my soul mate. I know. How stupid – but the dream was so real. I feel like I know her – like she is as real as you are."

"I don't think it is stupid, Bud. Not at all," I reply sincerely. "Well, maybe if we were home and everything were back to normal, and we were not chosen to save mankind, and you told me this over dinner one night at Martha's – maybe then I would think it was kind of odd. But, right now, I think it is fairly normal."

"Thanks, Sardine," he says smiling. "So what do you think it means? Your having the same dream," he asks as he slides back into his bag.

"I really don't know, but there has to be something to it." I think for a moment. "I don't know. Maybe Dr. Pergo will have some idea."

"Yeah, that's a good thought. We'll have to remember to ask him," he concludes and rolls onto his side.

"Yeah. Good night, Philistine."

I look out of the cave opening some ten feet away. I have intentionally chosen the spot closest to it. If they do come while we are sleeping, I want to be the first one they find. Now the sun has set and the forest is eerily gray. I see shadows moving in the distance, but they are just branches dancing in the wind. I wish we were home. I wish we were anywhere but where we are. I feel like the girl from the dream, running for my life – beaten, broken, and afraid. I wonder whose dream I am in. Maybe they will come and rescue me before I reach the cliff.

Chapter 11

When I open my eyes the cave is completely dark. I can tell I have slept soundly so it must be close to dawn. I lie there for a moment, listening intently. I hear the usual sounds of the forest at night, which is a good sign. Phil and Lacy are both quiet, and the regular cadence of their breathing leads me to believe they are also sleeping. My neck is sore, and I feel the hard frame of the heat diffuser when I reach my hand there to rub it. I wonder how Ephie is. Hopefully everything will turn out alright for him. Being the Dean of Technology, he has an extensive relationship with the Establishment. Maybe that will help him now. Even if he is to be punished, if we can get the message sent back in time and change the past before the punishment goes through, then he can be spared the pain. We will not exist. Then how am I here now? Does that mean we fail?

I reach into my pack and pull out the small metal box with the palladium pills inside. I pop one into my mouth and drink the final mouthful of water from my canteen. I shiver, preparing for the awful metallic taste and it does not disappoint. My stomach for the first time feels queasy, but I am not sure if it is from the pills or from the lack of food. Fortunately, none of us seem to have had any real issues with the palladium treatment. It is especially encouraging that Lacy seems healthy. Apparently the iron supplement has worked. I attempt to place the metal container back into the pocket of my bag, when it falls out of my hands and clanks loudly on the cave floor, causing Phil to sit up quickly out his sleep.

"What was that?" he whispers groggily.

"Sorry. I dropped my pill box. But at least it didn't spill."

"Yeah," he yawns. "What time is it?"

"I'm guessing around six-ish; another half hour or so until we should see some light."

"Okay," he whispers quietly. He rubs his hands together and then rubs them up and down his arms before letting out another big yawn. "I'm exhausted."

"Everything alright?" Lacy asks. I can't see her, but I think she is still lying down.

"Yeah, all good. I just dropped my pill box."

"Did they spill?"

"Nope."

"Hey, Sardis," Phil whispers again.

"What?"

"Did your pills spill?" he asks sarcastically. I cannot see him either, which is good, because he no doubt is flashing the Phil face.

"Let me guess – you already answered that before I woke up?"

"Yep," I reply matter-of-factly.

"That's what I figured."

"And it is six o'clock and we should see some daylight in about half an hour," Phil adds. "Now you know everything I know." I can hear her chuckle and then sit up and rummage through her bag.

"So what do we have for breakfast today, Master Chef," I tease Phil.

"Oh, I think I can cook you up something real nice." He opens up his bag. "How about some granola and dried apples?"

"That sounds pretty good to me."

133

"Guys, I can't find my pills," Lacy says panicked.

"What?"

"I always keep them zipped inside this side pocket, and they are not there. And I can't find them anywhere else in my bag."

"Maybe check your clothes pockets?" I offer, now alarmed.

"No. No." She replies exasperated. "I always put them in my bag so I wouldn't lose them. They must have fallen out at some point yesterday when we were running." She groans and drops the bag abruptly. "I can't believe this!"

"Don't panic. It will be ok. We will find them or figure something out," Phil soothingly replies.

"I am panicking. This is not good. Not good at all. Okay, Okay – breathe Lacy." We each search our own bag and the cave floor, but find nothing. Lacy checks each of her pockets to no avail.

"What are we going to do," she says almost in tears.

"Well, I have twenty-four pills left. Add in Phil's and we should have forty-eight. Divide that by three –" I look upward, doing the math in my head, "– we have sixteen pills each."

"But the iron…"

"And that is eight less days we will have," Lacy adds, demoralized. "I can't believe this."

"I don't see any other options. We are going to make it as far as we can and have to believe that will be enough."

"Not to change the subject, but you're blinking," Phil declares. I look down to see a small red light blinking on the heat diffuser. I take it off to examine it when the other two start blinking.

"Sardis?" Lacy quivers.

"Turn them off," I instruct. "We are in a cave; they can't scan us in here."

"But why are they blinking?"

"I don't know; just do it. I don't trust these things."

"Shh..." I say, as they slide them over their heads. They both freeze, and we listen intently. Silence...

"They are here," I mouth almost inaudibly.

"How do you know?" Phil whispers back.

"The forest is too quiet." I have hunted long enough to learn the sounds of the wild. Silence means the forest has been disturbed. Silence means danger.

Lacy is breathing heavily, almost hyperventilating, frozen, staring straight ahead. I echo her fear, but I cannot show it. Not now. This is it. The moment why I am here, why God chose me for this mission.

"Let me think," I utter aloud. If they know we are here, we cannot flee; we will be overtaken. Maybe if we stay still, they will pass by... My mind goes to the many times this scenario played out during my hunts – the prey, waiting patiently in the shadows. Waiting... waiting... Instinct telling them any movement means certain death. Waiting... waiting so long they determine their initial fear was misguided. That is when they make the fatal mistake. They did not know I *knew* they were there. The same mistake I will not let us make. They are here, and they know we are as well. But how? I made sure to cover our tracks the best I could. Did they hear us?

"We have to do something. They will see the blinking lights," Lacy anxiously moans.

The lights... A series of events begins to unfold in my mind. "It can't be," I whisper aloud.

"What can't be?" One of them asks. I am not sure who. My mind is too occupied connecting the dots of the past six days.

"Ephie..." I stammer, the sound of his name leaving my lips confirms it. "He's one of them."

"What are you talking about?" Phil whispers angrily. "Spit it out."

"I am trying to figure out how they found us. We covered our tracks. We are deep in the forest, miles from where they should be looking – when it hit me – Ephie always knew when the shipment was coming. *Always*. Remember?" I look Phil directly in the eye. "'He has a 'sixth-sense' we would always say. So was it a coincidence he stayed back yesterday and started a smoky fire on the day the shipment came?"

"Why would he do that?" Lacy asks, shocked and confused. "I don't think he would turn on us."

"He was sick, probably dying, and he thought if he turned on us and alerted the Establishment, with whom he had a good relationship, he could save himself. Think about it. Why would he just stay in that cave and wait for them? He figured out a way to save his hide. Then he gave us these things and tells us they are heat diffusers, when I'll bet anything they are homing devices."

"No, I can't buy that," Phil rebuffs, shaking his head. "We have known him forever; he wouldn't just ditch us like that. Nope. No way. These are master trackers, Sardis. Come on. This is what they do."

"My pills... I bet he took them, too. He was probably suffering from the same thing my dad did and thought my pills would help."

"Ahh," I groan. "How stupid. Even the night we left home he was so jittery. He must have known how this was going to turn out."

"I don't believe it, but that's not the point right now. We have to focus on how we are going to get out of here."

"Okay," I say firmly. "You're right; we can worry about Ephie later. Even if he did turn on us, he won't be here now."

"What is your plan, Sardis?" he replies earnestly.

"We only have one thing going for us: we know they are here and they don't realize that. So we have to use that however we can to our advantage.

"These are the facts as I see them. They no doubt found Ephie in the cave. Even if he did not turn on us, I'm sure he would have told them we have limited weaponry; so they would not be concerned that we would be able to defeat them in a battle. If I were them, I would just wait until we crawled out of our hole and then capture us.

"They are probably someplace where they can see us, but we cannot see them. And I would guess there are at least six of them: two of them for each one of us."

"So we just make a run for it?" Lacy asks hesitantly.

"At this point, there is no chance we make it if we run. There is nowhere else around here to hide. We have to fight."

"We can't beat them," Phil objects vehemently. "We don't have weapons; and even if we did, we wouldn't be able defeat that many."

"They will not be expecting an attack. Plus, they don't know I have this." I pull the laser cannon I grabbed from the armory out of my pocket.

"What is that thing?" he asks, the tone of voice suddenly more open.

"It is a laser cannon. The Cause developed them during the war specifically to use against I-Morts." I hold the smallish weapon for him to see. The barrel is a fat cylinder, roughly ten inches long, with a hand grip and trigger.

"It looks like a flashlight with a handle," he scoffs. "Where did you get that thing?"

"I grabbed it out of the armory the night we left home," I reply with a sly grin.

"So this is what I am thinking: we need to get cleaned up and act like nothing is amiss. Here," I hand Phil my stun gun, "both of you hide one of these in your hand in case you need it. According to Dr. Pergo, they should drop any I-Mort you hit; but you only have one shot, so make certain you can hit one before you let it go." Lacy searches through her bag and pulls out hers.

"You two will head out the front of the cave first with your heat diffusers on. I am going to slip out the back with mine off, because I feel strongly they are tracking us with these. If that is true, then they will not be watching for our heat signatures, only monitoring our movement through sight and these homing devices. Any objections to this rationale?" I look directly at Phil as the first glimpse of dawn begins to soften the night sky.

"I trust you."

"Good. Now, when you walk out, stay in the open as best you can. If you get too far into the forest, I won't be able to cover you."

"Wait, so we are going to be the bait?" Lacy interrupts.

"More or less – I need to be able to mark how many there are. It's the only way I can think to draw them out."

"Ok…"

"Once I start firing, make for my location. Don't try to fight unless you absolutely have to. Alright?"

"Ok," Lacy offers weakly again.

"Let's do it," Phil asserts.

We quickly pack our things and Lacy takes one of my pills. The thought of what she is going to go through is almost too much for me to bear. I collect myself and Phil prays over us. When he is finished, we all embrace for a long moment. I take a deep breath and nod toward them both before slipping quietly through the small crevice at the back of the cavern. The morning air is thick and smells of rain. The sun has not yet made it over the horizon, but I can see sufficiently in the dull gray mist. The blinking of Lacy's heat diffuser catches my attention, as I watch my two friends emerge from the safety of the shadows and enter the open woods. My eyes are fixed straight ahead, waiting for the slightest movement. Nothing.

I know they are here, somewhere, maybe waiting for me to emerge as well before pouncing. The blinking lights move slowly from my right to left – still no sign of movement as I devour the terrain with my eyes.

Another ten seconds goes by. Nothing. A fear begins to emerge. What if they do not fall for the bait? Lacy and Phil have passed in front of me and are now moving away. The further they move, the harder it will be to protect them. The longer it takes, the more nervous the two of them will get and the better chance they will act unnatural. Our cover will be blown.

Ten more seconds. I am frozen, my hands clutching the laser cannon, my body resting against the outside stone wall of the cave. Come on, make a move. Move! My breathing begins to quicken as my heart races. They are winning this game of cat and mouse. I am the cow elk, frozen in the shadows. I smell something strange in the breeze, something new. I know I must not move, but I see nothing. I have waited long enough, as long as I have waited in the past when something did not feel right. I'll wait another moment more, and then I will emerge into the meadow to fill my belly... but not me, not today. I know better. A shadow emerging from behind a tree catches my attention; my eyes dart there to make out a silhouette moving toward Phil and Lacy. Another develops out of the gray shadows moving toward the cave entrance. That's two...

A small noise on the hillside directly above me and another shadow following the first – Three… Four… My mind is telling me to make my move, but my instinct is keeping me frozen. Another glides toward the cave. I wait a moment more. They must know I am the biggest threat, so they will send the most troops to the cave, I think, as a feeling in my gut tells me it is time to act.

Sparks and metal fly to the right of Phil as I squeeze the trigger and release the bolt of energy. More sparks up the hill to their right, as another glowing dismembered figure tumbles down the hill in front of them. I have never fired a laser cannon before, but at this moment, no one would know it. I jump down to a lower rock ledge, spin, and search for the Dragon behind me but do not locate it. As I turn, I feel the rush of something past my face, and pieces of rock splinter behind me. I fall to my knees and release another blast toward the scrambling figure at the cave mouth, and watch as it crashes to the ground in a burning disabled heap. The enemy is now fully aware of the battle, but they are down three men. I see a flash from behind a tree and more rock pieces fly behind me, as a dark round object falls at my feet. Yes! I think as I recognize the nature of the object: a stun bag. Those pompous Establishment creeps are using non-lethal weapons. They must have figured we were going to come easy. They figured wrong.

I rise from my crouch and peer around the rock as another green-clad figure slowly jogs from the tree line and leaps toward Lacy. I stand and easily dispatch of that threat as I feel a pressure around my neck and am thrown backwards against the rocky hill. How stupid, falling for their diversion!

I struggle to breath and pull off whatever is crushing my windpipe, but my arms are unable to move. I try to stand but my body feels paralyzed. I watch helplessly as Phil and Lacy sprint to my aid. "No!" I try to scream as I watch a Dragon dive from a tree heading directly for Lacy, but the only sound that escapes my mouth is a wheeze caused by an I-Mort landing directly on my chest, having leapt from the hillside behind me. It lowers its face to mine and cocks its head to the side, blocking my view of what is happening below. Its eyes are fixed, staring blankly at me, its countenance completely deprived of emotion. I hear Lacy scream, sending a chill down my spine and bringing a sinister smile to the creature's face. It raises its fist above its head, and I close my eyes as a searing pain emanates from my cheek and travels to the back of my skull. I brace the best I can for the next blow, but it does not come. I open my eyes to see Phil standing over me. He bends down and yanks off the device from around my throat. I get to my feet, evidently now freed from the paralyzing effect of the Dragon's weapon. I grab my laser cannon from underneath the still pulsating corpse of my oppressor and motion toward the forest. The three of us take off in that direction, both Phil and Lacy having used their stun weapons successfully, now bringing the I-Mort body count to six.

"Take off your heat diffusers," I direct as we race toward the cover of the thick forest. I have my cannon raised, following closely behind my friends. My legs are unstable, but I manage to keep my balance as I watch for any movement in the brightening woods. A rumbling noise catches my attention, and I turn back toward the cave as an aircraft lowers itself onto the hill and more green-clad forces jump out.

"Move!" I fire two shots into the unloading army, before turning and sprinting. I did not anticipate reinforcements this quickly and now we are down to one weapon.

"Keep going! I'll cover you!"

They race ahead and I duck behind the trunk of a large tree. I am deep enough into the woods where the Dragons cannot see me, but I can see them. I quickly pick off two, but there are easily a dozen on the ground and twice that inside the aircraft. The aircraft – that's it! I point the gun at the engine and hold down the trigger. To my surprise, the weapon does not fire; instead, it makes a high pitched squeal and begins shaking. I let go of the trigger and an intense beam blasts into the craft, blowing a gaping hole in its side and sending several I-Morts flailing into the air.

"Wow, I love this thing!" I rapid-fire several more rounds into the fray before being buzzed by return fire.

"Drop your weapon or they both die!"

I spin quickly toward the deep forest and see a towering I-Mort, dressed in red, holding Phil and Lacy off the ground by their necks. I release the cannon and it falls harmlessly to the ground. I want to scream to him for mercy, but nothing comes. I am paralyzed once again, only this time by sheer terror.

"Put your hands on your head! If you as much as flinch, I will gladly remove their traitorous skulls!"

I slowly raise my hands. My mind is frantically searching for a way out, but there is none. I have failed. It is over. I close my eyes and begin to pray. I hear the brush crashing behind me as the army closes in. I feel the cold steel of a weapon against my neck as they yank my arms down to my side. I open my eyes and the scene is in slow motion. The Serpent lowers my friends to the ground and motions toward his comrades. Two run over and grab Phil by the shoulders and another two escort Lacy. Tears are streaming down her bloodied face. I want to hold her – to protect her – to tell her everything is going to be okay.

I feel them tug my arms behind my back. The Serpent motions angrily toward me, yelling something to a minion that I cannot make out. Another Dragon appears with a restraining device and hurries toward me. It raises it to my neck and I feel the cold steel press against my flesh. I wince, preparing for the paralyzing effect, but instead watch as the Serpent explodes into pieces in front of me.

I frantically free my hands from the Dragon behind me and knock the restraining device from my neck before it activates. In one motion I fall to the ground, grab the laser cannon, and fire two shots exploding my two captors. I turn my weapon toward Lacy's escorts, but they are already on the ground. An I-Mort I have never seen appears behind her and rips the restraints from her wrists. I blast the two Dragons near Phil, as the new I-Mort motions toward us.

"This way!" it yells and runs back into the forest. We have no option but to follow. I send two more rounds into the advancing forces, and we sprint into the woods. Tree bark and pine needles explode around us as round after round are fired into our fleeing party. It is only by the grace of God we are not hit.

"There! Follow me!" The I-Mort races toward a small aircraft parked in a clearing in the woods.

"Get in!"

I spin back toward the woods as Phil and Lacy charge up the loading ramp. I blast cover fire into the dense pines as the engines of the aircraft ignite. I dive into the small cabin, and the craft rises straight into the air. We clear the canopy and the I-Mort throws the throttle forward, tossing me backwards toward the closing bay door.

"Sardis!" Phil screams, reaching out his hand. I grab ahold as the door closes behind me.

In moments we are racing toward the rising sun, well out range of their weapons. I grab both of my friends, overcome with emotion. The tighter we hold, the further away the outside world is. It is not until we let go that I actually compute what has happened.

"Who are you?" I ask our I-Mort savior, wiping the tears from my eyes and noticing for the first time the blood oozing from my cheek.

"My name is Myrna." Bright morning sunlight has broken through the dissipating rain clouds, and I squint in an attempt to make out the I-Mort's face through the light pouring in the cockpit window. "I was sent by Dr. Pergo."

"Dr. Pergo sent you?" I shout. "How did you know where to find us? And that we were in trouble?"

"He overheard two government officials discussing a breach in security outside the Northwest Territory." The tone of her voice strikes a chord in my memory.

"You seem very familiar. Have we met before?"

"That is a complicated question, Sardis," it replies slowly. "I have been known as Myrna since the battle of 2312, the year I fought alongside your great-grandfather against the forces of –"

"You knew my grandfather!"

"Yes."

"How? Who are you?"

"God led me to him so I could remember who I was in another life. He brought context to my memories and helped me recall my real name – Thyatira Alexander."

"Mom?"

Chapter 12

The cabin of the aircraft begins to spin around me. I grab Lacy's arm to try and steady myself. My brain attempts to string together a series of words to ask how this is possible, but it is all I can do to keep breathing and not pass out.

"Yes, Sardis. I am your mother."

"What? How?" Lacy and Phil spurt at the same moment.

"Oh dear, I suppose I need to start from the beginning." She presses a button on the control board of the craft, then walks back into the cabin and sits next to us.

"As you are aware, Mr. Fair and I were chosen to complete the first mission." She grabs Lacy by her hand. "Miss Fair, your father was an inspiration. He was the backbone of our mission and the only reason we succeeded. Do not ever think he was insufficient in any way." I watch a smile crawl across Lacy's tear-soaked face as Mom speaks, the words healing dark corners in her heart that have been locked away for years. "He loved you dearly child, and he would be so proud of the woman you have become."

She lets go of her hand and grabs mine. "Just as I am with the man you have become."

I do not know what to say or what to feel. I want to yell "Hallelujah" at the top of my lungs, and, at the same time, I want to curl up in a ball on her lap. I stand up and hold her in my arms, squeezing as tight as I can. At first she is resistant, but soon relents and holds me in return. Her body is unfamiliar and her hair does not smell the same, but I do not care.

"Dad says he loves you," I whisper into her ear. "I love you, too, Mom."

"Oh, Sardis," she replies softly. "I have waited over a hundred years to tell you the same."

I hold her a short time more and then sit next to Lacy. I have dreamed about this day, what I would tell her and how I would feel if I ever saw her again; yet now that it is a reality, it is oddly different from how I had envisioned it to be. She seems – distant, cold even. Her voice is rhythmic and mechanical, a far cry from the sweet melody I remember as a child. Yet, just being in her presence I feel safe for the first time in years.

"As I was saying, you are now aware that we were chosen for the first mission. What you do not know is the nature of the message and how effective it was in helping the Cause. You see, the damage the war caused the relationship between Christians and non-Christians was irreparable. The plan was to send a message back to Colonel Luke Justice and convince him to change his future course of action. He was the head of the Cause's war efforts. If we could only get him to reconsider – to try and reconcile differences through Christ's love rather than an ill-guided war – then maybe humanity's outcome would be different. At least that was our thought. We coupled that with the truth from Revelation 6:11, that Christ would not return until after the last of his followers was martyred, and we formulated a plan. Instead of a simple message, we would use the time-bending machine to send a human by downloading his brain information using the same process that creates an I-Mort. We enlisted the help of Dr. Pergo and others inside the Establishment who were loyal to the Cause and traveled with them to Gold City where the time machine was located. Once there, they performed the operation to transform me into an I-Mort; and yes, I did die on that operating table, just as you thought for these past four years. It is true that my mind was downloaded and sent through time, but my soul has been worshipping at the throne of our God ever since. In our eyes, I was to be the final martyr; but naturally that was not the case, as should be evident when man tries to determine and manipulate the will of God."

Her words are fluid and cool, flowing over me and soothing my parched soul. I am comforted by the notion that I have not been fooled these past several years, and warmed by the idea that the creature sitting before me is not my mother, only a mere shadow of her – a glimpse of her charm and wit, but without the love that was always present.

"When I awoke, I was in this body. I did not know my name. I did not know where I was or what I was doing there. All I had were memories: pictures running through my mind with no context to them. I quickly learned I was in a lab created to transfer information through time. The scientists had just finished creating their machine and were attempting to send information backwards in time, when I arrived. They were absolutely flabbergasted when my computer code appeared in their system. I was proof their machine worked and was in operation sometime in the future. The only problem was, I could not tell them when or where I traveled from, or any information that was worthwhile. They were generous enough to allow me to keep the I-Mort body into which they had downloaded me, probably because they were hoping I could give them some valuable piece of information for their purposes. Unfortunately for them, I could not make the connections between the images and their meanings.

"Eventually I discovered I was in the year 2311, December twelfth, to be exact. Though I did not realize the significance of the date, it was exactly one year before the start of the War. I left Gold City and traveled around the country and was terrified by what I saw. There were riots constantly, mostly between the human group consisting of those deemed the 'very-religious,' and the I-Mort populace. The government named this religious group the 'Anti-Establishment,' because they were resisting the evolutionary change that was taking place to humanity. The government was solely concerned with the physical wellbeing of its people, and to have a citizen whose body would not suffer from ailment or disease was highly preferable to one that would. I watched many people being beaten, some to death. And you have to remember that I was a stranger to this world. I was slowly regaining some of the mental connections, but for the most part, I was wandering blind.

"You would think since I was an I-Mort that I would have been drawn toward them instead of the humans, but I was not. The I-Mort population was soulless and universally self-absorbed. Since they could not reproduce, there were few family units, and the human family they had before they chose to become I-Morts deteriorated rapidly as well. They did not have to eat or sleep to satisfy their bodies. Humanitarian groups diverted their resources to shelter needs, and the government followed suit with the Equal Housing Initiative. Soon every I-Mort was allotted a house, flush with technology of their choosing. Homes were equipped with a 'reality-room' where most I-Morts spent, and still do spend, the majority of their time. You can program essentially any scene or scenario into them and experience it instantly. With their basic needs met and any pleasure they wanted at their fingertips, people lost interest in doing everyday things. Each being was a world of one.

"Needless to say, I was not drawn to this lifestyle. The longing within instead led me to a church outside of Sapphire City. It was there, Sardis, that I met your great-grandfather, Isaac. He was a great man, a leader in the church – a humanitarian in every sense of the word. His love for people was second only for his love for his God. He took me under his wing, and the more we talked, the more the pictures in my head made sense. He had your smile and your father's love. We would talk for hours about all sorts of issues, but I soon discovered my favorite topic was you. As you could imagine, he was eagerly interested in the stories as well. To think, he was learning about things his grandson and great-grandson did a hundred years before it happened."

"Wow." I shake my head in disbelief. I glance over at Phil, and he is as absorbed in the story as I am. Lacy has composed herself and is leaning forward in her seat, engrossed as well.

"It was about this time that rumors of a militia being formed to oppose the government were spreading. We investigated and learned the group called themselves 'the Cause.' They were invested in bringing justice for humanity. The more we learned about the group, the more we realized this was our calling. So we sought out Colonel Justice, and to our delight we discovered he operated out of Sapphire City. We met with him and enlisted in the rebellion. He was an engaging and thoughtful man who always had time for anyone, no matter who he was. Many thought he was a prophet. People would come from all around to see him, especially those who had diseases or ailments. They felt if he just laid his hands on them, then they would be healed by the power of God working through this great man.

"Shortly after we joined, conflicts began to arise between small groups associated with the Cause, and soldiers from a new agency, we dubbed 'the Dragons,' who were created by the government to quell the uprisings. I began as well to recall bits and pieces of information from our mission. I remembered being a member of the Fifth Seal, and I convinced Isaac to seek out others in the group. We were caught up in the atmosphere of the times, and I never remembered the purpose of my mission until it was too late.

"After the eight year war ended, Isaac went north and helped settle Shiloh, while I was forced to stay in Sapphire City. Before he left, I made him swear he would never speak of the stories we had shared. Now alone, I decided to seek out Dr. Pergo because he was a good friend and loyal to the Cause. I became his personal assistant, and until recently, I never told him who I was. My greatest fear was that I would somehow change the future, so I decided never to return to Shiloh. When Dr. Pergo would travel there, I would stay in Sapphire and look after his office. I was diligent with this until you were born Sardis, and then I could not contain my desires any longer. I would accompany Dr. Pergo on his many trips, and I watched you grow up from a distance. So many times I wanted to catch you before you fell, or protect you from something I knew was going to happen; but thank God I never did. I never interrupted the future save for one instance."

"The letter."

"Yes, the letter. It was the only time God spoke to me in this body. You see, it is impossible to grow in your relationship with Christ as an I-Mort because there is not that connection between created and creator. I longed for that: the ability to communicate and hear from God. I cannot explain to you why or how it occurred, but for a short while I could feel again. It was as if He breathed my soul back into me for a moment and guided my hand while I wrote you those words. I placed the letter and Isaac's pin in the box the day Tira left, and hid it under that oak tree."

A beeping noise from the cockpit catches her attention, and she stands up and walks smoothly toward the controls. "Ah, we are getting close to our destination. Please take a seat, we are about to land."

"Are you okay?" Lacy whispers into my ear.

"Yeah, I think so." I pat her hand with mine. "How about you?"

"Yes. I feel much better actually – well my spirit anyway – my head is pounding."

"What is wrong?"

"Oh, it's nothing. I think I just need a drink."

"What do you mean? Are you sure you are alright?"

"Yes, I'm fine. Phil, what do you make of what Myrna said?" she asks, changing the subject.

"I am blown away. Absolutely blown away."

"What stuck out –" Both Phil and Lacy start at once.

"Sorry, you go ahead," Phil yields with a chuckle.

"I was just going to say that it is so inspiring to hear the story of your grandfather and to understand a little better just what it is we are fighting for. I had this image in my head of the Establishment as some terrifying place, but at the same time I always thought they had everything I could ever want there. To hear how they actually live – it was eye opening. It is as if we are fighting to help them in a sense by freeing them from their self-inflicted prisons."

"Yeah, they have no purpose for living," I add.

"Sorry, Phil, what were you going to say?"

"I agree with what you said. It gives me a different perspective as well. But what I was struck by was how Myrna lived for over a hundred years as a different person in order to protect us. I can't imagine how difficult that must have been not to tell anyone." He shakes his head. "To think, she was in the same room as you countless times and never so much as touched you. Wow, that is something."

The aircraft slows rapidly forcing me to grab the armrest of my seat to keep from sliding to the floor. I look out the window and see another aircraft in an open meadow, though we are still in the wilderness.

"Alright, we made it to our destination. Dr. Pergo will take you the rest of the way to Gold City."

"What?" I cry perplexed. "You're not coming with us?"

"I am sorry, but this is where my part in this story comes to an end."

"What?" I dart again angrily as the craft lands softly in the grassy clearing. "I don't understand. I just got you back and now you are leaving again?"

"My dear, Sardis, I am a shell of who you remember. I am nothing more than that. The love you feel is not for this mechanical device, it is for the original masterpiece. Never lose that love or that memory, but do not waste a second more worrying about Myrna, okay?"

As she finishes, the cabin door opens and an unfamiliar I-Mort steps inside. Before I realize what I am doing, I have the laser cannon in my hand and pointed at the creature. "Who are you!"

"Whoa, Sardis. Don't shoot!" Myrna yells as the I-Mort raises its hands in the air.

"Sardis, it is me: Dr. Pergo."

"What?" Phil huffs. I echo his uncertainty and continue to keep the weapon locked on its torso, prepared to fire.

"Yes, I transferred my brain to this new body. Please, be at ease."

I lower the weapon but keep my finger on the trigger. "Why would you choose now of all times to switch bodies?"

"I have friends in opportune places, and one such friend has access to newly created bodies that have yet to be registered into the government's database. Since I am now also a fugitive, we can all move outside of the Establishment's surveillance web."

"And the main reason why I cannot come with you," Myrna adds. "When we learned of the dire situation, we knew we had to act fast. One of us needed to come to your aide while the other one prepared for the trek to Gold City."

The explanation makes sense but I still am unhappy with the situation. I relax my trigger finger and get to my feet.

"Ok. What is the plan then?" I briskly ask Dr. Pergo.

"The plan is to switch aircraft. We will head directly to Gold City. Unfortunately, the route we need to take to avoid detection from their satellites is indirect. We will need to travel through the most remote wilderness we can find between here and there, and fly as close as possible to the ground. I calculate it will take two full days to make the distance. Myrna will take this craft back to Sapphire City and attempt to interrupt the Establishment's search efforts as best as she can. We know that Dr. Porter was in contact with them, and he undoubtedly informed them of our plans, so access into Gold City and ultimately into the facility will be much more difficult."

"So, Dr. Porter did turn on us?"

"I am afraid so."

"Unbelievable," Phil mutters disgustedly under his breath.

"As far as I can tell, he was not compromised until sometime during the mission. Hopefully that limits the scope of the knowledge they gained of our plans."

"Why would he do that?" Phil asks dumbfounded.

"People act differently when they are faced with their mortality. He found a potential avenue that would lead to his survival, and he took it. I believe it was nothing more than that. I surmise his prior standing with the Establishment allowed him to assume they would be lenient if he divulged what information he knew. Judas sold out the God of the universe for a few silver coins. It is not difficult to believe that Dr. Porter would do something similar for his life."

I shake my head in frustrated disbelief. I wish he was here now; there is so much I would say to him. His beady little eyes and cowardly face, begging for mercy at the feet of the Serpent – the thought turns my stomach.

"It is over and done with then," Phil says succinctly as we follow Dr. Pergo off the initial aircraft. "However horrendous Judas' crime was, it was not outside the scope of God's will, so we must trust that this is not either. We have to realize the magnitude of what we are trying to accomplish. We are on the frontlines of the ultimate battle of human history, and it is first and foremost a spiritual battle. The Evil One will be sending all the forces he can muster to defeat us. We must be prepared for anything and everything."

"And we have no time to lose," Dr. Pergo adds, echoing Phil's impassioned sentiments. "The enemy has no doubt already regrouped and is preparing counter measures."

"At least Myrna took care of the Serpent," Lacy says as we jog up the stairs to our new vessel.

"Unfortunately, that is not the case. His computer will be saved and his information downloaded into a new body. The process has, more than likely, already begun."

Her shoulders slouch a bit as she understands the reality of the enemy we face. No matter what damage we inflict upon them, they will never stop coming. We will never be comfortable again, perpetually on the run, one false turn costing us our mission and our lives. At least we can take some comfort in knowing it was not a mistake that lead us to this position: it was the unforeseen selfish act of one of our own.

The cabin of this craft is a bit larger than that of the first. We each strap a harness around our waist and shoulders and settle in for the long trip. Dr. Pergo is seated a few feet in front of us, behind a short glass wall. He is hurriedly examining gauges and tapping a computer screen.

"Farewell," Myrna calls from the aircraft's entrance. She turns and begins walking down the steps. The same feeling that overcame me when I watched my father walk away for the final time returns. I failed to cry out then...

"Wait," I yell earnestly. She stops and spins mechanically toward me. I do not have anything readily available to say; I just do not want her to go. At this moment I do not care that she is not wholly my mom. All I want is to be in her presence a little while longer.

"What is it, Sardis?" she asks softly, when I do not initially respond.

"Why did you take the name Myrna?" I ask when nothing else comes to my mind.

She smiles and takes a step back toward us. "She was a girl I met early on while I was wandering lost, from city to city. She was about your age. She was bright, vibrant, and attractive, although she was always hard on herself for not measuring up to what her family expected of her. Her father had recently become an I-Mort and had grown increasingly distant and violent. He was a doctor working with the Establishment, and he had no patience for her lifestyle. I only knew her for a short while before she tragically took her own life. I had been going by Eve, the name the scientists initially gave me, but I changed it to Myrna to honor her memory."

That is just like her, I think, as I nod my head in contented approval. She stands there a moment more, apparently waiting to see if I have any further questions in my attempt to postpone the inevitable. When she realizes my tormented mind cannot muster any additional requests, she eases my pain. "Have a safe trip, and do not fear for me. I never expected to have this time, and I will treasure it always. I have nothing further to offer you. All that God gleaned from me is in the letter. Read it and trust it was written to you by your mother, echoing the very sentiments of God the Spirit dwelling in her heart."

With that, she turns and walks out of sight as the door slowly closes. I stare longingly at the closed door, my heart aching more and more with each beat. The dull roar of Dr. Pergo's firing the engines breaks my gaze. I readjust my body in the seat, lie back, and close my eyes. I know my friends are waiting for me to say something, but I don't care. I just want the world to go away for a while. I just want to be alone.

Chapter 13

"Let the morning bring word of Your unfailing love,
For I have put my trust in Your hand,
Oh, Lord fulfill Your holy purpose for me,
Never abandon the work of Your hand."

Phil's song saves me from the bondage of my restless sleep. He is seated next to Dr. Pergo in the front of the craft. Lacy is reclining in the seat next to me; her head is resting on a sweatshirt that she has balled into a pillow, and her eyes are closed. I yawn and stretch my arms for a few seconds until I become light-headed and they fall slowly to my side.

"How did you sleep?" Lacy asks, sitting upright and clutching the pillow tightly to her chest.

I yawn again and shake my head to try and restore some alertness. "Alright, I guess."

"Not the most comfortable sleeping arrangements."

"Ha. You got that right. How are you feeling by the way?"

"Honestly, I've been better – I don't know if it is psychological or what, but ever since I took that pill this morning I have felt terrible."

"I wonder if being shot at and captured by Dragons has anything to do with it?" I attempt to smile, only to moan when a searing pain burns my cheek.

Lacy winces. "That doesn't look so good. Maybe I have something that might help." She opens her bag and searches for a moment before pulling out a tube of some type of ointment and a bandage. Phil begins playing a new hymn on his harmonica, as Lacy slides over in her seat and looks more closely at my wound. She frowns and slips back toward her bag and grabs a towel. She turns a bottle of liquid upside down a few times into the fabric and once again slides close. She leans in, her face close to mine, peering intently at the injury.

"Now hold still; this may sting a little bit." She lifts the towel to my cheek and wipes gently, but it still sends waves of intense pain through my face. "Sorry," she mouths, with her focus still on her task.

"It's alright."

She sets down the towel and picks up the salve, squirting a small amount onto her finger. "Thankfully, Phil pulled that Dragon off you when he did." She brushes off my cheek below the wound with the back of her hand and brings her face close once more. She gently dabs my cheek with the salve. I can feel her warm breath on my face. I watch her eyes as she concentrates on her job. They are confident, yet hiding something. I feel a flutter in my gut when I realize she is staring intently at her work so she is not tempted to make eye contact. The thought makes me smile, and this time I do not feel the pain. The subtle movement of my cheek causes her to lose her concentration and our eyes meet. She begins to smile and turn away when I reach forward and kiss her cheek. She turns and I press my lips against hers. She does not pull away; instead I feel her pressing back. My heart is beating out of my chest. I open my eyes and watch as her eyes slowly peel open. We pull apart slowly until I feel the last connection of her lips against mine. I stare into her eyes, mesmerized, wanting desperately to move in and kiss her once more, but the moment has passed. She smiles and slides back to her bag. She fumbles with the paper backing on a bandage and giggles shyly. She composes herself and successfully separates paper from fabric, before sliding over once more and quickly placing it on my cheek.

"There. Good as new."

"Thank you," I reply as if nothing had happened. We sit there awkwardly for a few moments, but neither one of us care. It is the first normalcy we have felt since the fishing expedition yesterday morning, and it feels wonderful.

"I wonder what it is going to feel like, becoming an I-Mort," she asks after we have sat there for a while longer.

"I don't know what to think about it. I was not prepared for that – I guess I don't know really what I was preparing myself for – but that thought never crossed my mind."

"I guess I'm most scared of waking up and not knowing anything: who I am – where I am." She lifts the armrest on the seat between us and moves closer. I place my arm around her and she nestles into my body.

"I'm hoping Dr. Pergo thought of that and we have a plan for it, or we are going to end up just like Mom."

"They have to have planned for that. That was the whole reason the first mission failed."

"I know. I can't believe they didn't think of it the first time." I shake my head. The more I think about it, the more confused and irritated I become at their lack of foresight. All the planning and all the hard work that went into that moment, and they forget that I-Morts need to have context given to their memories?

"Hey, do you still have the letter with you?"

I slide my hand inside my jacket and pull out the folded paper. "Dad gave it to me before we left home."

159

"Do you mind if I read it? Just seeing Myrna and realizing the backstory of the letter, I am interested to read it again."

"Sure, go ahead." She takes the letter from my hand and opens it, the creases so sharp that she has to flatten it on her lap. Though I have the words memorized, the message does seem more alive. I have envisioned Mom writing these words the night before she went in for her operation. Reading them now, they have new meaning. Instead of an encouraging life lesson, I begin to see instructions: a roadmap for the final leg of our journey.

"I can't believe we didn't see this before," Lacy says aloud, echoing my sentiments. "She wrote, '*This pin belonged to your great-grandfather who fought in the war of 2312, and I have worn it ever since....*' Um, obviously that makes different sense now."

"Yes," I say as Lacy sits up. "And look at this – how the instructions are laid out." I grab the letter from her hand. "They look more like a check list – or a guide to correct the mistakes she made along the way. Of course! That is why Dad was so excited. Don't you remember? We kept asking him about the mission and what we were going to do, and he kept referencing the letter – the letter – And this is why – Look!

"Instruction one: '*Follow your heart. Don't ever sacrifice what makes you human.*'"

"It has to be some reference to how she lost her humanity when she became an I-Mort!" Lacy cries, realizing where I am leading.

"Yes, I was thinking the same thing! Let's keep going with this. Instruction two: '*Follow the advice of Godly friends and never let them leave your side.*'

"Instruction three," I cry, my voice almost at a roar. "'*Fall in love and never let that feeling go. It is the greatest gift from God.*'" I move forward and give Lacy a quick kiss. She smiles. I hear Phil mumble something about it as he walks back into the cabin.

"Instruction four," I shout, ignoring him completely. "'*And finally, always trust in the Lord, He will never forsake you. You are a commander of Angel Armies. Never forget that.*'" I lay the letter down on my lap and look at my friends.

"What do you think that last one means?" Lacy asks.

"I'm not sure, but I would bet anything we will find out at some point."

"What's going on with the letter? And did you just kiss her?"

"Yes, I'm in love and I think she is, too," I blurt, my mouth moving faster than my mind. "And the letter, we read it again and we realized that instead of just some feel-good sentiments, it is actually a hidden message: a guide of sorts for the mission."

"Oh yeah?" he says a bit overwhelmed. "She told you to kiss Lacy?"

"No, no, moron – well yeah, maybe – but no. Follow along – she is giving us directions on how to proceed with the mission."

"Please spell it out for me; I'm lost."

"Basically, I think it says we are not supposed to do it," I say aloud for the first time.

"Not supposed to do what?"

"We are not supposed to go back in time – to lose our humanity in order to send the message."

He stands there with a confused look on his face, his eyes looking upward as if he is trying to determine if my story is plausible. "Really? You think so? Then what are we doing out here?"

"I don't think the mission has changed. I still think we are to make contact with the past."

"So maybe just send a note or something instead of sending us?"

"I don't know, maybe?" I let that scenario play out in my mind. What would we write in the letter? To whom would we send it? "Maybe Dr. Pergo could give us some insight?"

We walk to the front of the plane where he is heatedly pressing buttons next to a small computer screen.

"Everything alright?" I ask, as he turns suddenly toward us.

"Sorry, I did not see you approaching. I was trying to figure out what is wrong with the navigation screen. It went on the fritz a moment ago." He points to a small screen where alternating black and white patterns are flashing. "Other than that, we are making good time."

"Excellent," I say quickly, not paying attention to a word he just said. "We have something we want to run by you, to get your opinion."

"Great, what can I assist with?" he states cordially, as the screen goes completely black, except for the gold "Emblem of Unity" in the center of it.

"We read the letter again, and we think Myrna was writing direct instructions for the mission, specifically not to give away our humanity —" A loud siren emanating from a speaker next to the navigation screen, interrupts my explanation.

"Attention!" a voice shouts as the siren stops. The screen lights up and an I-Mort dressed in a red Dragon uniform appears, staring straight at us.

"That is the emergency channel!" Dr. Pergo exclaims and rises anxiously out of his chair.

"This is a special message to those who feel they are above the law. Your actions are treacherous and treasonous, the results of which are imprisonment for life if you cooperate immediately or death if you do not. The time for peaceful diplomacy has passed." The Serpent turns and walks away from the camera,

162

revealing a row of people standing behind him with hoods over their faces and binds on their wrists. "Additionally, every hour that passes before you turn yourselves over to authorities, one of these co-conspirators will be killed." He yanks the hood off the first hostage. "Beginning with this one." He pulls a gun from his pocket and fires a bullet through the skull of Governor Lloyd. His body crumples lifelessly to the ground as the computer screen goes black.

"No!" Lacy screams as I stare at the blank screen. "Governor Lloyd!" she cries and bends over at the waist, dry heaving. I put my arm around her as she starts wailing uncontrollably and falls to her knees. "That's our family," she moans incomprehensibly.

I look at Phil – he has his hands on his head, his face in shock.

"Listen, Listen!" Dr. Pergo shouts over the hysterical commotion. "We need to focus, please. Listen to me. Your families knew the consequences when they agreed to this. Please, listen!" I help Lacy to her feet as he continues, "We cannot stop now. Even if we turn ourselves in, they will still try us all for treason and sentence us to death. The only way to save them is to complete the mission. Listen!

"If the message this time is successful, then the instant it is sent, the future will be no more. Christ will have come sometime in the past, raptured our forefathers, and judged the earth. Your families will no longer be in harm's way, in fact, they will never even have been born."

"I do not buy that," Phil scoffs heatedly. "Then how are we here? We must have failed!"

"You must take a step back and look at this from God's perspective. You are looking at this linearly, the only way our human brains can fathom time, but He is not bound by time as we are. He is omnipresent, existing at all times and in all places."

"But Gold City is still over a day away! They will all be dead before we get there!" I yell back at him. "There has to be something else we can do!"

"It is all shadows, Sardis; don't you see? If we succeed, this very moment will be as if it never existed."

I pull the laser cannon from my pocket and point it at his head. "Now you listen to me. I don't care what you are talking about. This is what I know. Those are the people I love waiting to be executed. We have one hour to figure out how to save them. Unless you are on board with that, I can't follow you."

"Sardis, please, settle down," he pleads as I continue to hold the gun to his head.

"Now, as I was saying earlier. The letter Mom wrote me is telling us we are not to lose our souls. How can we accomplish this without turning all of us into I-Morts? Send them a direct message?"

"Hmm," he huffs, still looking at the gun. "I do not know how that will work. Just a plain message is far too risky. It would have to first reach the scientists, and they would have to willingly pass the information along. Then the person we target would have to actually believe the letter enough to act upon it. I just do not see it as a viable alternative."

"We better think up something fast, because I will not allow us to give away our humanity."

"I am sorry, Sardis, it is the only way." He sits down abruptly into his seat. "Unless... no, that will not –"

"Unless what?" I bark.

"Well, there has always been this rumor of another machine," he answers tentatively. "It was allegedly created to transport actual humans back in time, but it was never completed."

"Where is this machine?" Phil asks impatiently.

"Please, this is a useless endeavor. A fairy tale —" I raise my gun again. He looks disgustedly at it and sighs. "Alright, fine. I will appease you. The story goes that at the same time the government launched the information time machine program, they also began a secret program that would actually send a living human back in time. The government claimed the project did exist, but it was cancelled due to ethical reasons before the machine was completed.

"Some have always wondered if they truly cancelled the project before it was finished, or if some initial testing was done. But, friends, honestly this was over a hundred years ago. Even if the machine were operational at one point, there is no reasonable chance to think it would be of any use to us now."

"Where was this machine located?" I implore, ignoring his concerns. "Is it also in Gold City?"

"No, it was in Jasper City – which actually," he replies looking at his now functioning navigation screen, "is not far from our present location – only about fifty miles south."

"That is where we need to go," Phil states adamantly.

"I think Phil is right. We need to try," Lacy says.

"I am right. I can feel it in my gut. This is what God wants us to do."

Dr. Pergo groans disappointedly and shakes his head. "Please, I will not allow this pipe dream to persist any longer. Our time is precious and we need to spend it on ideas that will benefit the mission."

"Look," I shout angrily at him, "I realize the Fifth Seal chose you to lead this mission, but what they had planned has fallen apart. The Establishment knows we are headed to Gold City and what we plan on doing when we get there. The first mission had the benefit of surprise. We would be sitting ducks. We are not going, period. And if you continue to insist on taking us, then I am afraid I will have to relieve you of our duties."

"Sardis, I am not the enemy here. We are both pulling in the same direction."

"Then follow us!" I shout. "I know Phil. And one thing I know about Phil is that he is the Godliest man I have ever met; and if he is telling me that God is speaking to him, then I believe him!"

He looks curiously at me, and then towards Phil for a long moment. "Please forgive me. I have made a terrible mistake."

His remorse takes me by surprise, and apparently Phil as well, as he relaxes his shoulders and leans weightily against the control panel.

"I'm listening," I grunt hesitantly.

"It is your spirit, your love; I have not experienced passion like that for a lifetime. These old bolts," he snickers, "well, I guess these new bolts, do not have the capacity for it. You see, faith and understanding are a brain function, which is why I am here fighting for my God; but passion and trust, those are heart functions connected to your very soul. I have longed for that connection. To be plugged back in to the everlasting power source and feel His love flow through me again, where the irrational becomes surprisingly welcomed and the pragmatic melts to beautiful shades of gray. Thus, I humbly apologize for not appreciating this fact sooner. My service is always unto the Lord, and I can see Him alive and well inside each of you."

"Good," I say assertively, as a hint of a smile appears on Phil's face. "Then we head for Jasper City, immediately."

"Alright, we will go. The sooner we get there, the fewer martyrs the rogue will create."

I clap my hands loudly and give Lacy and Phil each a strong hug. "It is going to be okay." Phil eagerly returns my optimism while Lacy smiles and walks slowly back toward the cabin seats.

"I don't understand how the government would allow such violence," I hear her mumble as she grabs her pillow and drops into her seat. Through the chaos, that truth had not struck me until now. The Establishment was built on equality and justice, not on senseless violence. How could they move from shooting non-lethal bullets at me twelve hours ago to executing the governor of our territory on a live broadcast throughout the world?

"He went rogue," Dr. Pergo answers when I pose the question to him. "He is undoubtedly acting outside the wishes of the government. The emergency channel on these aircraft is a specific bandwidth, so all he would have to do is broadcast his message on that channel. The public as a whole would not see it. Surely other government officials are aware by now, but they will not act quickly enough to stop him."

"Why not!" I cry, outraged. "If he can get to Shiloh in a few short hours, then why couldn't they get there and stop him?"

"The government, as it is presently constituted, is not set up for such immediate military action. That is why the Dragons were created. Remember, there has been no unrest for years. There is no violence, no need for any other militia or police force. Citizens are locked away in their homes all day, immersed in their virtual reality chambers.

"The best case scenario is they rally some sort of rag-tag group together and send them to Shiloh, but it will be at least twenty-four hours before they arrive."

"And everyone will be dead by then." I shake my head in disgust. "I can't believe how that is possible —"

Another loud siren from the navigation system cuts my sentence short. The screen flickers violently before settling on the dreadful scene in Shiloh's town square. The Serpent is grasping a hooded prisoner by the shoulder and shoving him to the ground at his feet. Behind him is a makeshift gallows with three dangling nooses.

"I have changed my mind. I do not think you realize the severity of the situation you have found yourselves in and the fragility of my patience. I will now kill one co-conspirator every fifteen minutes until you are captured." He walks quickly toward the other kneeling captives and grabs the closest one by the arm and raises him to his feet. He drags him to the gallows and lifts him onto a stool before placing a noose around his neck. He walks back over to the prisoner on the ground and kicks him in the ribs, causing him to fall moaning on his side.

"To prove to you I am also a compassionate man who will honor your insolent surrender, I will allow this worthless slug to survive, since he did manage to do something right with his meager existence." He snatches the hood off the man on the ground. It is Ephie. The Serpent yanks him violently to his feet and pushes his face to the camera. His eyes are clenched and his face is battered and bloodied.

"I will allow him to live if he can perform one simple task to prove he no longer wishes harm to those in authority." He grabs Ephie by the neck and drags him to the foot of the gallows.

"He will live if he will dole out the just punishment to this wretch," he snarls and rips the hood off the man in the noose.

"No!" I scream at the glowing screen as I see my father's broken face below the knot. I feel Phil pulling me, trying to pry me away from the carnage and protect me from this moment, but I will not allow it. "Stop!" I yell at him.

"No, no, you can't make me do this!" I hear Ephie plead to the Serpent as Phil lets me go. "He is my friend – I – I can't do this."

"If you value your own life, you will," the Serpent replies smugly. "It is your choice. He is going to die either way. It is only a matter of whether you want to live or not."

Ephie lowers his head and sobs heavily. Phil once again tugs on my shoulder. "Sardis, you do not need to see this." I brush his hand away as Ephie raises his head and looks at my father. Dad is standing tall on the stool, his hands tied behind his back. He should hate Ephie for what he did, but instead his face is calm. He nods confidently toward the traitor, in essence giving his blessing for what will happen next.

"Are there any last words you would like to say, professor?" the Serpent mocks and then spits in his face. Dad flinches, but quickly regains his composure and looks directly at the camera.

"Sardis," he says smiling. "Do not be afraid. Mom is here; I can see her. She is dressed in white. I will tell her that you love her." The Serpent growls something I cannot comprehend and slaps him viciously in the face before Dad can say anything further. He then takes a step back and motions angrily towards Ephie, who lowers his head in shame.

Ephie stands there for a moment, still, before taking a step toward the gallows. He looks up once more at Dad's bloodied face, before looking at the stool on which he is standing. He turns again toward the Serpent who kicks out his foot violently, simulating how to dislodge the stool and send my father home. Ephie turns back toward the gallows as the screen flickers off.

"No!" I shout as I pound on the blank image. I fall to my knees and place my head in my hands. I stare at an irregular shaped pattern on the floor of the cockpit until my eyes gloss over with tears, and I can no longer decipher what made that particular shape so abnormal. I fight to keep my eyes open as the tears begin to flow. I stare desperately at the floor. If they close, I will never see the strange pattern again. If they close, I will see Ephie kicking the stool from beneath my father's feet, just as I watched Dr. Pergo wheeling my mother away on a hospital bed every night.

"No!" I shout again, squeezing my eyes tightly closed. The trail of tears burns the wound on my cheek, washing away my resolve as it flows. I stand and pound on the computer screen. I taste the salty mixture of tears and blood trickle into the corners of my mouth. Defeated, I lay my forehead on the screen as it flickers back to life. I jump back and watch as Ephie takes a step toward my father, his back to us. The image pulsates, flickering between darkness and the nightmare scene. He takes one more step until he is right below him. He turns one last time toward the Serpent before walking past my father and climbing onto the stool next to him. He places a noose around his own neck as the screen goes black once more.

I feel an arm around my chest, and this time I do not fight it. I am pulled back to the cabin and forced into a seat. Lacy's head is on my chest and I pull her tightly to me. I bury my face in her hair as Phil embraces us both. No words are said. No words are needed. I close my eyes and watch as the final servant receives his white robe.

Chapter 14

"It's time." I kiss Lacy on the head and softly pat Phil's shoulder. I am numb, undoubtedly in shock. My two friends are all I have now in this existence. We each stand and walk confidently to the front of the aircraft, now emotionally ready for *what must soon take place*. We can thank the Serpent for that.

"I have changed our course. We will be in Jasper City in ten minutes. The machine will be somewhere in the main government building. We have the element of surprise, but that will only last a short while before the Dragons arrive. There is no use in stealth at this point." He presses a button on the control panel and motions with his eyes toward the back of the craft. I turn and watch as the back wall rotates open, revealing a secret compartment. "I brought along a few new toys. I think you may decide to retire your century-old cannon."

"Excellent!"

"There should be something there for everyone. When we arrive, I am going to land us directly outside the building. It is also at the center of the city, just like in Shiloh, so we will be right in the heart of everything. I do not anticipate any hostile resistance initially while they scramble to figure out why their perimeter alarm is sounding. Soon enough though, they will realize it is us and will send the cavalry. Once we are inside, we will make for the lower levels. I have never seen the machine, but I have been in this building. If it is truly there, it will have to be underground."

"Do you think we will be able to operate it?"

"No, I do not."

"Good, that makes two of us." I walk to the back of the craft and examine the secret cache. Phil and Lacy follow quickly behind. I pull out a large weapon that looks like an otherworldly assault rifle. I hold the front grip with my left hand and press the butt firmly into my shoulder, as my trigger hand slides effortlessly into ideal position. It feels comfortable as I swing it around, sizing up imaginary foes.

"What is this thing?" Phil asks, pointing to an oblong shimmering opaque orb.

"I have no idea," I reply as I pop it out of its protective foam case. I wave it in view of Dr. Pergo and shrug my shoulders.

"Be careful with that! It is an incendiary device!"

"Oh," I mouth, and place it carefully back into its secure location.

"That may be a bit too much firepower for this exercise," he hollers. "And make sure you grab a vest."

Lacy pulls down the smallest of the three black protective vests hanging inside the compartment and slides it onto her shoulders. I pull down the other two and hand the larger one to Phil. Whatever material they are made of is surprisingly thin and light weight. I slide my knife and laser cannon into the side pockets of the vest and sling the assault rifle over my shoulder. I grab a small laser gun and hand it to Lacy, while Phil grabs a larger pistol and slides it into his vest.

"Here, hold this," Lacy instructs, handing me the gun I gave her. She pulls her hair back and slides a tie around it so it falls down her back. She grabs the sheath from her bag and secures it to her belt, then slides her knife in. "No non-lethal weapons today," she says, grabbing the gun back from my hand. She selects a rifle similar to mine, slinging it over her shoulder and sliding it around to her back.

"Why don't you trade in your cannon for an upgrade?" she asks with a smile.

"I kind of like this thing. Here," I hand her a stun weapon, "take one of these just in case. They have saved us twice."

"Phil," Dr. Pergo yells from the cockpit. "Use that small black one. It has a homing setting on it."

Phil stands there for a moment with an offended look on his face. "I think he just ripped on me." We all laugh as he grabs the black gun and slips it into his vest.

"We are making our approach. Two minutes."

"What an awesome feeling to be walking in the will of God!" Phil shouts, adrenaline flowing through him as he bounces exuberantly.

"How are you feeling?"

"I have so much energy rushing through me right now, I don't feel anything else," Lacy answers staring eagerly back at me. She has no make-up on to cover the cuts and bruises, but she is glowing. Her eyes are alive, speaking to mine through channels I never realized existed. We do not need the Establishment's neural communicators to tell us what we are thinking. It is wide open before us.

"Come here," Phil yells pulling us close to him. "Before we do this, I want to let you two know that these last few days have been the worst – and the best of my life – and I am honored to spend them with the finest two people I have ever known." He begins to choke up, but quickly collects himself and flashes the Phil face. "And I better be the best man at your wedding when this is all said and done."

"Deal," I say as we both laugh. I look at Lacy and she innocently shrugs her shoulders.

"Let's pray," Phil instructs, and we bow our heads in the tight circle. "Precious God, Mighty Deliverer, Awesome Warrior, make Yourself known in this battle. Guide our actions with your steady Spirit."

"Twenty seconds!"

"We entrust this victory into your hands and praise You in advance for the great works about to be done in Your Name. Amen."

"Amen." Lacy and I echo. I look one last time at the eager faces of my two friends and feel the same passion in my veins. The aircraft begins to slow and we walk toward the closed bay door. We softly touch down and the doors begin to open as Dr. Pergo joins us.

"Not taking a weapon with you?" I ask.

"You just cover me. I will do my best to handle the technical stuff."

"Then follow me," I cry and jog down the door and out into the bright sunlight. I quickly scan the perimeter, but oddly enough the streets surrounding the government building are barren. The only movement I see is the sunlight reflecting off the shimmering glass panels of the surrounding buildings, each one looking similar to the government building back home.

"Clear," I yell back and the others follow quickly behind. I run toward the face of the government building, and the outside panels slide open, but quickly close as a red light begins flashing inside.

"Blow it," Dr. Pergo instructs.

"Gladly." I whip the rifle into my hands and hold the trigger down, sending aqua-blue pulses of energy into the glass panels, turning them red hot before they shatter into pieces. We wait a split-second for the shards to finish falling before sprinting inside. There are two holographic greeters in the lobby, extending their hands in a genial salutation as we run past. The front desk is empty, but the chair behind the glass is spinning slowly, indicating someone has left in a hurry.

"The stairs are this way!" Dr. Pergo yells as he takes off down a hall between the elevators and the desk. The others follow quickly and I bring up the rear. We reach the end of the hall and he throws open the stairwell door. I glance back down the hall and through the gaping hole in the front of the building and see two aircrafts landing.

"We've got company," I announce forebodingly, as I close the stairwell door behind me and follow them down the spiraling stairs. Our steps echo loudly as we travel downward three floors before reaching the bottom.

"I guess this is it," Dr. Pergo shouts as he plows through the door. We enter a sterile hallway: white tile on the floor and white painted metal paneling on the walls.

"Right or left?" Phil shouts as we stand at the stairwell entrance, waiting for Dr. Pergo to give us our next direction.

"I don't know. I have never been here before."

"Right it is," Phil says and we follow him down the empty hall. A door opens ahead. An I-Mort wearing a white lab coat walks out. He sees us and quickly ducks back into the room as we run by.

"Grab him!" Dr. Pergo shouts. I turn around and barrel my shoulder into the door, but it does not budge. I stand back and blast the handle off, then pound my weight into the door again, this time opening it easily. I tear through the room in search of the I-Mort scientist. I realize it is a laboratory as I turn over tables full of beakers and pipettes. I locate the target huddled underneath a desk at the back of the laboratory and yank him into the middle of the room.

"Where is the time machine?" I demand, my gun pointed to his head.

"Please, do not shoot! Please!"

"Where is it!"

"Please, I do not know what you are talking about!"

I growl angrily and grab him by the collar. I drag him with me into the hallway, throwing him at the feet of Dr. Pergo.

"James?" Dr. Pergo asks surprised, reaching out his hand.

"We need to move!" I command as I see a soldier move through the small window in the stairwell door.

"Hold on a minute," Dr. Pergo says and fumbles with something in his pocket. He pulls out a small silver remote and presses a button. I hear a low rumbling noise emanating from outside. He grabs another remote and presses a series of buttons on it as well. "There. That should slow them down."

"What did you just do?"

"Remember that incendiary device? Well, I think it just leveled half a city block around our ship," he replies smugly. "I also dropped a few electron bombs in the stairwell on our way through. Any I-Mort on those stairs is sufficiently scrambled."

"Who are you?" the scientist asks.

"Dr. William Pergamum."

"Pergo?" the man shouts, astounded. "We worked together in San Francisco eons ago! You must have had a recent facelift. What in the world are you doing down here? And with these humans?"

"We are looking for H.E.2311."

"Oh," he huffs. "That project was cancelled decades ago."

"Yes. I am aware, but we need access to the machine. I know the rumors and the back story. I know it is real."

"I am afraid I cannot allow that," he replies, agitated.

"Oh yes you can," I counter and throw him to the floor. I point the gun once more at his face. "You will tell me or I will –"

"Or you will blow my head off? Be my guest. I have been in need of an upgrade, and I think the government will pay for this one, especially if I heroically impede the progress of the human traitors."

"Sardis, please. Let me handle this," Dr. Pergo interjects. He extends his hand down and helps James to his feet. "Why will you not take us to it?"

"I am not at liberty to discuss matters of national security. You are aware of my allegiance."

"That is what I thought," Dr. Pergo answers and looks around the hall. "Quick, follow me. Bring this prisoner with us."

I grab him under the arm and follow Dr. Pergo further down the hall. He tries a door, and then another, before finding one that is unlocked. He throws it open and we follow him inside. He looks around the room until he locates the security camera. He motions his head towards it, and I shoot it out. He grabs another device from his vest, places it in the center of the room, and turns it on. It makes a low buzzing noise.

"James," he says smiling. "I knew you were one of us! 'You are aware of my allegiance,'" he mimics and shakes his head. "I had not heard that since the war." The scientist looks wearily at him and then down at the device.

"Oh, yes. That will conceal our conversation. We are as good as invisible..."

"Wait, you are on our side?" Lacy asks the scientist.

He smiles and places his hand on his chest. "Always faithful to the Cause, until the Savior comes again."

"So you are going to help us?" Phil cautiously asks.

He nods. "Why do you want to find H.E.2311?"

"We wish to use it," Phil answers.

James laughs, and then looks at Phil strangely. "Wait, you are serious? It really is not operational."

"Please, we only ask for direction on its location," Dr. Pergo says. "And any pertinent information you may have. You do not need to accompany us."

"You have the right city but the wrong building. It is in the basement of the Government Technology Center. I have personally never been there, but I do have upper level security clearance." He unpins his I.D. from his coat pocket and hands it to Dr. Pergo. "This should get you into anywhere you wish to go."

"I stole it from you by force."

"Good." James answers. "I'll turn off my nerve sensors and you can blast my arm off. I was serious about needing an upgrade."

I laugh loudly. That is something I would say. I like this guy.

"There is a back stairwell out of this basement. Take a right at the end of this hall. It is the second door on the left."

"Thank you," Dr. Pergo says and places his hand on his chest. James does the same. I contemplate doing it as well, but instead, I pull my laser cannon from my pocket and aim it at his left arm.

"Oh, good." He opens a compartment on the forearm of his right arm and slides a switch. "Proceed."

I pull the trigger and close my eyes.

"Excellent! Did not feel a thing."

I laugh again and we follow Dr. Pergo out the door and down the hall. The door to the back stairwell is locked, but he waves the I.D. in front of it and it opens. We reach the ground level, and he peers out the door.

"There are forces out here but they are moving toward the front of the building."

"Probably responding to the present you left them," Phil quips.

"Where is this building?" I ask.

"It is east, three blocks. There is no cover so we are going to have to make a run for it."

"I am turned around down here… Are we on the east side of the building now?"

"Yes, fortunately we are."

"Good. Then this is what we are going to do: I am going to lead; Lacy, you are last. We will run for it until they see us. Only fire after we are spotted, and shoot to kill; everyone we drop is one less we have to worry about. When we make it to the building, we will head for the basement and barricade ourselves in the time machine room." I look at them and can see they are unsure. "Are you guys ready for this?"

"Let's roll," Phil says.

"Why am I last?"

"Lacy, I trust you the most covering us. Mom was the best shot there was and she trusted your dad the most, out of everyone she knew, to cover her. I see his fire in you. I know you can do it." She still does not look completely convinced, but she swings the rifle from her back and turns it on.

"I'm ready."

"Good. Here we go."

I push the door open into the warm autumn air. The Dragons that were running through a moment ago are gone, and the immediate area is clear. I take off running away from the building in the direction of the east road. The others keep up, but we are quickly spotted once we clear the cover of the building. Fortunately, smoke is billowing from both of their aircrafts.

"Keep running! There is no one between us and the technology building!" I cry. We have a few hundred meter lead on them, so if we can keep our pace, we have a chance. The three-block section of road leading to the technology building is lined on both sides by tall mirrored glass buildings. I do not look back until we pass the first intersection. We have kept in a tight group, but the Dragons are gaining on us. They have closed the gap so quickly that if I do not do something, they will overtake us. I hear a whizzing noise and see glass break in the building to my right. I turn back and see Lacy lying on the ground, scrambling to get back to her feet.

"Keep going! We will catch up!" I yell to Phil and Dr. Pergo, and sprint to protect Lacy.

"I'm okay, it just hit my shoulder." I help her to her feet. I see blood trickling down her fingers as a shot off my vest knocks me backwards. I prime my weapon and begin firing. Glowing metal shards explode through the air as each shot hits its target. Lacy opens fire as well. Soon the tall glass canyon walls are echoing with all out warfare. I turn toward the building next to me and blast out the mirrored window, and we duck quickly inside.

"We are going to have to take them all out. Hopefully by the time we catch up to Phil and Dr. Pergo, they will have located the machine and have it ready to go."

"Confound it!" a voice cries from behind us. I turn and see an I-Mort standing in the middle of the room we are in, smacking some sort of device off his leg. He is totally oblivious to the fact we are in here with him.

"I think we just crashed his virtual room," Lacy shouts.

"Yeah, his romance scene just turned into World War Four and he is pretty upset about it!"

I peer around the corner of the gaping hole in the mirrored glass.

"One hundred meters and about two dozen still upright," I relay and turn back into the room. "I'll sprint out and start firing. You blow the glass wall across the street, and I'll run straight into the building. We can cross fire until they are down."

"Got it!"

I turn to run, but stop, and give her a kiss. She winks and I run out from cover and begin firing. The scene is moving in slow motion as I repeatedly squeeze the trigger. Target after target flails and falls to the ground in pieces as I run. I do not feel the impacts of the bullets into the vest but only notice when my gait is interrupted. I make it across the canyon floor and into the far building without taking a direct hit to my flesh, and I easily dropped ten of their troops along the way. I hear Lacy open fire, and I move into position and take aim as well. Bullet fragments and laser rounds are shattering glass all around me, as one by one I pick off the advancing enemy. The one to the left, the three in the center – they are identical lifeless beings in my eyes. They do not garner the same respect the deer and the elk have in the natural order of things.

My eyes dart through the carnage for my next target, but I cannot find one. I creep out of my cover and take inventory of the grisly scene. No one is standing, only smoking and pulsating remnants of mechanical body parts strewn across the canyon floor.

"Come on!" I yell toward the far building. Lacy appears through the dark hole in the glass and runs my direction, her left arm hanging at her side. I look up the street and see Phil and Dr. Pergo nearing the technology building, apparently unscathed. The I-Mort in Lacy's building emerges from the dark hole and looks at us confused, and then disappears back into his room.

"I'm ok, just the shoulder," she explains as we meet in the center of the street and then take off toward the others. I turn back periodically as we run but do not see any further troops advancing.

"Hopefully we can make it before the next wave comes."

"Yes. And it will probably be the Serpent."

"Yeah," I grunt. "And they could show up anywhere. Keep your eyes open."

We reach the second intersection as the others disappear into the building. I turn once more and still see no sign of resistance. We continue through the last stretch of buildings and finally reach the steps of the technology building. We hurriedly climb the stone stairs as the drone of an approaching aircraft reverberates off the glass doors in front of us. I turn and see three ships approaching. Lacy throws the glass door open as I pull the laser cannon from my vest and hold down the trigger. I wait until the weapon fully charges before letting loose its powerful blast into the hull of the first aircraft, knocking it into the glass canyon wall. The explosion knocks the second craft sideways, causing it to bank hard left before crashing into the ground in an epic inferno. The third aircraft begins firing. I turn and dive into the building as the windows are blown out around me. I cover my head from the falling glass pieces, then quickly get to my feet and locate Lacy in an open elevator at the back of the lobby.

"Hurry!" she cries and raises her rifle, firing several rounds past me as I race through the open lobby. I reach the elevator and spin quickly. She lowers her rifle and frantically presses the button for the basement, as I raise mine and cover us. The Dragons have not reached the front of the building when the elevator doors close. The ten second ride is eerily quiet compared to the last few minutes of mayhem. When the doors open to the basement hallway, I expect to be greeted by more gunfire, but instead, Phil is standing a few meters ahead pointing his black gun at us.

He lowers his gun and waves his hand toward us. "Come on, this way!" He spins and takes off running further down the hall. We tear after him until we reach a closed double door at the far end. He waves the I.D. card in front of a keypad and they slide open. I look back over my shoulder as we move through, but the hall is still empty.

"Did you find it?" I huff out of breath.

"Yes! Dr. Pergo is working on it now. It's this way!"

We follow him down another long hallway until he slides his card again in front of a thick steel door. A light above the doorway turns green, and a loud 'thunk' emanates from the door lock. Phil grabs the handle and yanks it open, and we follow him into a dimly lit room, the only light coming from the screens of large computer-like machines along the side walls. Dr. Pergo is seated at one of them, frenziedly typing. The computer lights reflect off a large device in the back of the room. The outside appears to be framed in some sort of arch-shaped metal. I cannot make out what is inside the arch, but I imagine it must be the machine.

"I need the main power turned on down here," Dr. Pergo shouts. "Until we do, we will not be able to operate this. There should be an electric box somewhere. Find it and flip the power on."

"Phil, you and Lacy search for the box; I'll keep guard at the door."

They take off toward the back of the room, and I prime my weapon and walk to the door. It is too thick to hear if anything is going on in the hallway, so I stand there and wait. I imagine the Serpent standing outside, seething, wanting desperately to burst through the door and gain his revenge. Yet he is not the only one who would cherish the battle. My wound is fresh. He severed the final connection I had to this world, and I relish the thought to repay him in kind.

I hear an excited exchange coming from the back of the room as the lights flicker on. I turn back and Dr. Pergo is standing in front of the chair he was in, bending over the keyboard. He taps the keys twice more and walks quickly to the machine. Inside the metallic arch are two chairs with wires and cables stretched all around. He sits down in one and looks around, before standing up and fidgeting with some of the wires. I look back at the door but it has not moved, although I can feel we are almost out of time.

"I think it is ready," Dr. Pergo announces. "Unfortunately, it appears that only two of you will be able to go."

"No. We all are going," I heatedly reply. "The letter clearly states that we are all to go."

"Sardis, I understand your concerns, but there are only two seats. The machine can only transport two people."

"I don't care how many seats there are! The letter says –"

"I'll stay," Lacy cuts in. "The letter says for you to fall in love and never let that feeling go. It doesn't say to never let the one you love go."

"What? No. I won't allow it. If anyone stays it is me!" She walks toward me and grabs me by the hand, lifting it up to her face. Tears are now flowing down my cheeks as I brush the hair away from her eyes.

"Sardis, trust me. When I woke up in that prison cell, I was a lost and scared kid. I hated myself, the person I had become. I was stuck, unable to move, unable to get past the pain I felt every day. I was just floating through life, aimless. I lashed out at everyone, and worse yet, I treated people that loved me like dirt to make myself feel better. But now, I am alive again – now I have a purpose..."

"And you still have a purpose. You make your dad proud every day; you don't have to prove anything to him or anyone else."

"It is not about proving anything; it is about trusting. It is about trusting completely this feeling I have inside. It is about finally doing what I know I am supposed to do – what I was created for. And it is about loving." She puts her hand on my face as well. "Sardis, I love you. I didn't realize it until I finally stepped out of the lukewarm life I had been living." She smiles. "It was always you – from when we played together as kids, until your thoughts showed up inside my head the other day – it has always been you. Now, when I read the letter, I realize what it is telling me..."

"What is it?" I mouth, unable to utter a coherent sound.

She looks down and then back into my eyes. She starts to say something but stops. She leans forward and kisses me. I close my eyes as her arms wrap around me. I pull her close in a passionate embrace.

"I love you; I'll see you soon," she whispers in my ear as I feel a tingling sensation start in my side and radiate up my spine. I slouch into her arms, unable to move. She catches me as the base of the stun weapon falls from her hand and clangs on the laboratory floor.

"Take him," she yells to Dr. Pergo, who grabs me under the arms and slides me into the seat of the machine. I try to fight back, to scream for them to stop, but it is no use. I watch as they pull the vest and clothes from my body and tie me into the seat. Phil sits in the chair next to me, and Lacy straps him in.

"Clear," she yells and hurries back from the machine.

"God Speed," Dr. Pergo shouts as he presses a button. The outer metal frame begins to move, spinning slowly at first, before rapidly picking up speed. A strange sensation begins to overtake my body, as the door to the lab opens and the Serpent barges through. I futilely attempt to scream a warning as he barrels directly toward us. The last image I see through the spinning metal is Lacy pointing her gun with one arm and pulling the trigger.

End of Book 2

Book 3

Into the Light

Chapter 15

Beep...beep...beep...

What is that sound? I open my eyes and see fluorescent lights interspersed among white ceiling panels. I must be lying on my back. Where am I? Lacy!

I try to stand but I cannot. My arms appear to be constrained at my sides. My entire body feels weak, as if I were run over by a train. I roll my head to one side and feel tugging on my forehead and something strange in my nose. What is that incessant beeping!

"Hello, there." The voice is coming from my other side. I turn slowly toward the sound. It is an I-Mort in a white lab coat.

"He's awake," he says into a device on his wrist, and leans over me. He presses a stethoscope into my chest and neck. I want to say something, but for some reason I cannot.

"You caused quite the commotion in the technology building the other day." He sits upright and slides the stethoscope back around his neck. "Can you open your mouth?" I pry my jaws open, which is much harder than I expected it to be. "Good." He sticks his gloved finger into my mouth and pulls out a horseshoe-shaped plastic instrument.

"Ok. I think it should be easier to talk now. We were just making sure you could breathe on your own." He tosses the plastic object into a bin on the far wall.

"What is that beeping noise?" I ask, my words coming out slow and broken. My tongue feels dry and numb, and my throat is raw.

"That is just your heart monitor. You are in the hospital," he answers, using the same peaceful tone as the I-Mort at the hospital back home. I look closely at this face, thinking he may be the robot from Shiloh, but unfortunately he is not.

"Do you remember how you got here?"

"I think so." Two more I-Morts, wearing government uniforms, appear at the foot of my bed. Their presence makes me nervous. "Where is Phil?"

"Your friend is fine. He woke up yesterday and is in another location. You can see him later, but now we have some questions we would like to ask you."

"I want to see him."

"Is your name Sardis Alexander?" he asks, his peaceful tone now gone.

"Yes," I answer hesitantly. How could he know my name?

"Are you from a town named Shiloh?"

"Yes," I answer again, a bit more calm. Phil must have told them about us. I wonder what all he said.

"What is your purpose here?"

"I don't know. I don't know where I am," I answer glibly. My response seems to irritate him, and he stands up out of his chair. One of the others glides to the far side of my bed, so they are surrounding me. Normally I would feel threatened by their display of strength, but I have no concern for my well-being. My family is gone and the one I love is lost forever. What do I care if they kill me? I would welcome it.

"I will make this clear to you. You have violated immigration laws under the Articles of Human Peace and Equality. You will be sent to prison where you will spend the rest of your human life unless you cooperate with our investigation. We need to know who you are and what you are planning to do." He looks at the government official at the foot of my bed, then softens his tone. "We are also fair, so if your answers are deemed sufficient, you will be allowed some freedoms."

"*Some* freedoms? I will only talk when I know Phil is safe."

"You can trust us. He is perfectly healthy and happy in a secure location."

"I do not trust anyone, certainly not someone from the Establishment." The I-Mort looks at the official once more.

"The Establishment is a term the religious radicals are using to refer to someone outside of their mindless clan. He is one of them, one of the *Anti*-Establishment," the official answers.

"I am not here to cause any trouble," I respond hastily. "But yes, the town where I am from is entirely Christian."

"An entire town of one religion? Impossible."

"Where am I?" I ask again, irritated.

"You are in the hospital."

"What year is it?"

"What year do you think it is?"

"Well, it was 2420 when I left home, which happens to be exactly one hundred years since the Relocation Act was enacted that shipped all of us 'religious radicals' into tiny reservations all over the world. So since you have no idea about that, I guess it has to be sometime before 2320." They look at each other for a moment before the government official at the foot of my bed nods toward the one at my side with the lab coat.

"It is June 12th, 2312. You are in the hospital in Jasper City. What do you know about another time travel event from earlier this year? Inside of Gold City?"

I stare blankly back at him. "We acted alone. Any other event had nothing to do with our purposes."

"But you know about this event?"

I stare at them as I formulate a response. I think back to the many interrogations Dad put me through. I learned from them the best avenue to take was the truth, but that seems out of the question. Yet, the longer I stall, the guiltier I appear. I look toward the ceiling and close my eyes.

"I will talk, but you have to take me to Phil first."

He looks at the official once more. That one must be the leader. He nods in affirmation.

"That seems like a reasonable enough request. Once we determine you are stable, we will take you to him," the white coat replies. "My name is Dr. Andrew King. The nurses will take care of you. I will be back later to assess your improvement. Good day." The three of them glide from the room. A nurse walks in and taps on a screen next to my bed. For the first time I notice I am completely naked under the bed sheet, except for the wedding ring on my finger. I have wires connected to my head and chest and a small breathing device in my nose.

"Am I injured?" I ask the nurse. She smiles and grabs my hand gently, helping me to sit up.

"No, young sir. You appear to be in wonderful health. You do have a cut on your cheek, and we found a high level of some kinda' metal in both ya'll systems. Doesn't seem to affect ya'll health too much though."

"Wait, you are human?" I ask surprised. I have never seen a human from outside of Shiloh.

"Yes, sir. My name is Laura Ray. I will be your nurse today," she answers with a thick accent, as she fluffs a pillow and places it behind my back.

"Are you from Jasper City?" She pulls the sheet down and presses her stethoscope to my chest. She listens for a moment and then slides the stethoscope back around her neck.

"No, sir. I came to Jaspa' City a few years back. I am originally from a little town in the south."

"The south?"

"Oh, sir. It is just a term for the area I came from."

"Oh, ok," I answer still unsure. I like her though and feel comfortable in her presence. "Are you going to undo my arms?" I ask as she grabs my wrist.

"I'm just checkin' your blood pressure. Only the doctor can remove the restraints."

"They always had a machine to check that back home."

"Yes, sir. And they do here as well. I just like the old fashioned method betta'. It is more personable and I think more accurate."

"Good," I say smiling. "If you don't mind my asking, what is someone like you doing in a place like this? I would think your hometown would be much preferable to here."

"Oh I do miss it. That's for certain. You just have to go where the jobs are. People all over are leavin' home and headin' to the Great Cities. Soon there'll be nothin' left except them, I fear."

"How many cities are there?"

"You ask some mighty strange questions for someone who has been to the future," she laughs. "There are twenty. Five in our area."

"I am from outside Sapphire City."

"Is that so?" She leans in closer. "Now, if you don't mind me askin', what is a nice boy, like yourself, doin' in a mess-a trouble like this? There ain't no use in tryin' to fix it. We are just evolvin'."

"What do you mean?"

"I mean things ain't the same as they used to be, but that ain't always a bad thing. I know ya'll kind is against new technology and things like that, but people are just tryin' to help." She flattens my sheet with her hand and sits down on the side of my bed.

"What do you mean, 'my kind'?"

"You know, those who are against the new bodies. I heard ya'll go by the name: The Cause."

"Those bodies strip us from our connection to God, Laura."

"Now, Sir, I am a Christian, just like you. It's true, we ain't allowed to go to formal church in the City, but we get togetha' and sing praise and worship and study our Bibles. There are several I-Morts that attend, and we treat 'em the same as anyone else. Most of 'em feel guilty. They know they made a mistake."

"How can you say you are a Christian and willingly give up the soul God gave you?"

"I had a cousin," she starts and looks off toward the far wall. "Sonny was his name. He was a Baptist preacha'. A fine, God-fearin' man. He would get up in the pulpit on a Sunday mornin', and he would tell it like it was. And with passion – you would swear you was listenin' to Jesus himself." She smiles and shakes her head. "Mmm, mmm. He would talk about salvation and grace, and the promise of bein' *held*, as he would call it. Now, I don't quite rememba' the name of the verse, I think it's in Corinthians or Romans, but he would talk about how nothin' can come between you and God once you have been saved. 'No power on earth or in hell, or angels, or demons, or anything could separate you from the *love* of Jesus'," she quotes and looks at me in the eyes, with a loving expression. "Now, I understand what ya'll are thinkin' when you talk about losin' your soul, but everyone who is gonna be with Jesus in glory is still gonna be there with Him, and those who ain't, well, then they ain't. You are fightin' for the wrong thing. These new bodies ain't robbin' no one of their salvation, it is their choices they make beforehand."

"But people need to be warned of the consequences of their choice."

"Perhaps they do. But yellin' or fightin' a war won't fix nothin', it will only push people away – You gotta' show 'em the love of Jesus. You gotta' show 'em what they'll be missin'." She pats my knee. "That's all you can do. If people still don't wanna' listen, then there ain't nothin' more you can do for 'em."

"You say that, but you don't know the terrible things that are about to happen. Lots of people are going to die, Laura, and lots of people are going to choose I-Morts instead of allowing that to happen to them and their families."

"Now you know how God feels every day. He knows the choices we all make before we even do. He knows who is gonna' listen and who is gonna' try and do it on their own. People have always been tryin' to build their way to heaven. These new bodies are just the next step in that evolution." She stands slowly and straightens the spot on the sheet where she had been sitting. She taps the monitor one final time.

"You are lookin' fine. You should be able to see your friend soon. There are clothes for you on the desk next to your bed." She turns to walk out of the room.

"Wait, Laura."

"Yes, sir."

"What ever happened to your cousin, the pastor?"

"Well, sir – He passed away a few years back. His body just gave out. Some kinda' virus the doctors said. They took some blood and tissue samples, but they neva' did find out what it was. He was fine one day, then the next he was deathly ill."

"Oh, I am sorry to hear that."

"Thank you. He was a good man. The family wanted him to take a new body when he was dyin' but he wouldn't allow it." She winks. "Good day, sir." She walks out of the room, closing the door behind her.

I lay my head back and stare at the ceiling. I have never had a conversation like that before, and I am struggling with how to interpret what I just heard. I do not consider myself a devout person, not compared to Phil or others anyway, but I do consider myself a follower of Christ. Her faith seemed different from what I have experienced. It was more nonchalant, or maybe it was more personal; I cannot tell. She seemed more accepting of an I-Mort than someone from the Cause, which goes against common sense if one is a Christian. Yet, I do not get the impression she would end up giving in to the temptation to become one herself. Maybe she was straddling the fence? Or maybe she was actually on the right side of it?

I look at the desk and see the pile of clothes laying on it. They are nothing like what I would wear back home. The shirt is white with ornate gold and silver patterns on the front. It is collared and firmly pressed. The pants are the same material but gold and shiny. At least the socks and undergarments look similar.

The room is much larger than ones in our hospital and much different than how I imagined a room in the Establishment to look. The walls are white cement block and there are no windows. It actually looks like some sort of secure room: a glorified prison cell without the bars. The only way out is a door to my right. To the left is the desk and what looks like surgical machinery against the far wall. The only noise is the beeping from the monitor to my right, and, every once in a while, the sound of the bed vibrating.

In the quiet, I close my eyes and try to wrap my mind around everything. If it is truly the year 2312, then no one in my family is even born. If we are successful in ushering in the Second Coming, then the moment I left Lacy with her weapon pointed at the Serpent is now nothing more than an addendum to history. I think back to what Dr. Pergo said about God's being outside of time: being able to see all events in history at once. I never understood how that could be possible, but now it seems more real. If man could develop something to bend time, then it seems reasonable to believe that God would be able to do the same. He allowed Phil and me, mere men, to see the end of the story. No one will be able to claim injustice in His timing.

I can also see why I am strapped to this prison bed. What a powerful weapon our knowledge will be to those who are about to partake in a Global War they do not realize is even coming. Our knowledge would be catastrophic for the Establishment's planned Utopia; so if we ever hope to escape, then it is imperative they do not understand what we know. Hopefully Phil has figured this out.

My mind races a while longer before I doze off. I never feel as if I am fully asleep, but when I open my eyes and see Dr. King at the foot of my bed, I realize I must have slept for at least a little while.

"Your condition is stable enough to transport you to a secure facility. You will be able to see your friend there. Hopefully you will repay our respectful cooperation with some of your own. The guards will be in to escort you. Until we are satisfied you are not a security threat, you will be bound; and any time you are outside of a secure room, you will be blindfolded."

"Okay," I mutter, not knowing what else to say.

As he walks out of the room, three guards walk in and prepare me for the transport. One holds a stun weapon at the base of my skull while another begins undoing my restraints. The third is at the foot of the bed with another stun weapon pointed at me.

Once I am free, they quickly clothe me and bind my wrists behind my back. The thought of fighting runs through my mind, but at this point, I am without a weapon, outnumbered, and I do not know where Phil is. If we need to fight, there will be better times than this.

One grabs me by the shoulder and slides a metal halo around my head, covering my eyes. It is not tight to my face, but my vision is completely gone. I try to look above or below the metal ring, but all I can see is a blank white image. They grab me by the arms and lead me through the building until I am loaded into a vehicle. As we begin moving, the white image inside the halo begins pulsating and a low rumbling noise spews from the sides of the metal ring. The combination of the new image and the noise completely disorients me. I cannot tell if the ride lasts a few seconds or several minutes, but when it ends, I am ushered through a new building before being roughly shoved into a chair. They remove the device from my face. After a moment, my eyes adjust to the bright fluorescent lights, and I see Phil sitting across a table from me. He has a round glass ball around his head, but apparently he can see through it because there is a big smile on his face. His wrists are bound to the arms of his chair. An I-Mort guard stands behind him, a stun weapon in his hand.

"Are you okay?" I mouth. He nods his head in response. Another I-Mort walks in and places one of the glass balls over my head. Surprisingly, I can see and hear fine. The I-Mort then undoes the restraints from my arms and secures them to the arm of the chair, just as Phil's are. We sit looking at each other as the I-Morts leave the room. Suddenly the lights in the room go out and we are left in complete darkness. I yell to Phil, but hear no response. I frantically try and pry my arms out of the chair restraints, but it is no use. I scream again. No sound escapes the glass ball.

"Relax, Sardis," a voice instructs, as an image appears inside the ball. It is a peaceful rolling field of purple, yellow, and white wild flowers. There is a lake in the middle of the field with a deer drinking from the water. It lifts its head and its ears twitch as it looks at me. It flips its tail a few times and then lowers its head back into the serene blue water. I can feel a breeze on my face and can even smell the flowers.

"It will be your turn to speak with us soon," the voice says, causing the deer to lift its head once more. Instead of feeling relaxed, I am growing more and more incensed at their mind games. As if sensing this, a new scene appears in which the deer is lying on its side next to a small creek. I can see blood trickling down its neck and a red trail dispersing downstream. There is a "No Hunting" sign nailed to a tree directly behind the fallen animal that reads: *"Eye for an Eye. Tooth for a tooth. The penalty for treason is non-negotiable."*

I close my eyes, hoping to clear the image from my conscience and from being influenced any further by their methods. Phil must be going through the same mental torture. I know he will not crack. I must not either.

A different voice appears, "Mr. Alexander, it is your time to answer a few questions." I open my eyes and see a new vision: a panel of government officials sitting around a long table. One is the official that was at the foot of my bed when I awoke; the others I have never seen before.

The official in the center of the group begins speaking, "Mr. Conner explained to us the purpose of your mission. Now I would like you to explain it to us as well. If your stories do not match, or it is determined that you or both are lying to us, you both will be tried for treason." A smug grin forms at the corner of his mouth as he folds his hands on the table in front of him. "You may proceed."

I do not know what to say. I do not believe Phil would lie, but I also think he realizes the magnitude of the problems telling the truth would bring. Though I cannot move my arms, the *virtual me* sitting at the inquisition table can. I run my hands nervously through my hair as I determine what to tell them. Then, the solution hits me…

"Could I have a paper and a pen?" My request brings a furrow to the brow of the official, but he nods and a white sheet and black pen appear on the desk in front of me. I pick up the pen and begin writing. When I am finished, I slowly slide the paper to the middle of the table and the center official picks it up and begins reading.

"What does this have to do with your purposes?" he asks, handing the paper to the official to his left.

"That letter is the reason why I am here. If Phil told you the whole story, then you will realize this is the only piece of information you do not already have. We are here to try and stop a coming war, not to cause one."

"If it is true that your purposes are religious in nature, why would we believe your allegiance would be to our side?"

"Our allegiance is only to our God."

He looks intently at the table in front of him, as if deciding how to interpret my response. He sits back in his chair and looks at the official to his left when the deer in the meadow reappears.

"Ahh," I groan loudly, beyond frustrated with their interrogation methods. Another deer slowly trots into view, and I begin to wonder what the meaning of this new deer could be. I quickly shake my head and close my eyes. There is no hidden meaning; the only purpose is to break my mental fortitude. As if they knew my eyes were closed, a child's voice begins singing a slow lullaby. I listen to two mind-numbing verses before I open my eyes and stare blankly at the deer. At least with the deer I can imagine I am back home on a hunt; the lullaby is just too much to take.

"Is it true that you have nightmares?" the first voice asks. Not knowing if it is another trick, I do not respond.

"Is it true? I have reason to believe that it is," it asks again. Again I say nothing, only stare blindly at the two deer.

"Mr. Alexander, please answer the question," the voice from the government official booms into the peaceful scene. The deer lift their tails and trot quickly out of view.

"Yes. I often have nightmares."

"When was the last time you had a nightmare?" the first voice asks.

"I guess it was the night before we left on our journey – No I had one the first night we were gone," I answer, remembering the red haired girl.

"Was this nightmare different from the others?"

"What is the purpose of this line of questioning?" I growl.

"Please answer the question, Mr. Alexander."

"Yes, it was different. It was different from any I had experienced before."

"Please elaborate," the first voice asks.

"Ahh, fine," I moan. "There was a girl about my age, red hair and green eyes, who was running through a field. She seemed like she needed help, but I couldn't reach her in time and she fell off a cliff. That was it."

"Someone like this," the voice of Dr. King asks from outside the glass ball. He pulls it off my head, and I see the girl from my dream standing next to him.

"It can't be!" I utter loudly before regaining my senses. "No, this is some trick. I am not falling for this." A confused expression appears on the girl's face. Phil is no longer sitting across the table from me. This has to be some sort of mirage. Phil must have told them about the dream and they are testing me.

"Myrna, could you please bring in the friend you met the other day," he asks the girl. She nods and walks to the door, motioning toward someone in the hall. She smiles and opens the door wider allowing a female I-Mort to glide in.

"This is Eve," the girl announces proudly. "She was homeless... just wandering through town. I saw her and took her in."

I do not recognize who it is until she begins to speak. "Hello, Sardis. I do say you look rather familiar. Have we met before?"

"What is going on here? I agreed to cooperate peacefully but this charade has gone too far."

"Mr. Alexander, I assure you my daughter is no charade," Dr. King replies soberly. "Frankly, I am just as overwhelmed by all of this as you are." I stare at him dumbfounded, my mind a blur. They are real? Impossible. Yet I know that could be my mother. But Myrna – she is only a figment of Phil's imagination. Well, I suppose she is part of mine as well....

A smile creeps across my face as I begin to see how God has skillfully crafted history to create this moment. I am the one with the power here. Like the elk about to step into the arrow's flight, they are blind to the events about to take place. They are barren of faith, but desperate for the evidence of things not seen.

"Dr. King, I *have* met Eve before. In fact, I believe I have information that would be of great interest to you."

Chapter 16

He motions to one of the I-Mort guards who strolls toward me and releases my arms from their restraints. An image appears on the wall to my right: the same table surrounded by government officials that was used during my interrogation. I hear the door behind me open and turn to see Phil enter the room.

"Please, everyone, have a seat," the center government official instructs. "My name is Dr. Brandon Donovan. I am the United Elect of Jasper City. The others are on our Board." Phil walks over to the seat next to me, and I grab his shoulder with one arm and pull him close. He flashes his grin as we both sit down.

"Can I call you Tira?" I whisper to my mother as she sits next to Myrna, across the table from Phil and me.

"That is an odd name. Can I ask why?"

"Let's just say that throughout history you have acquired many names, but I happen to like this one the best."

She looks at Myrna who shrugs her shoulders. "Alright. I see no problem with that."

I glance at Phil; he is staring at Myrna. She notices the gawking and gives him an annoyed glare. "Do you have a problem?"

Phil shakes his head. "No, sorry. I just can't believe it's you."

She gives a disgusted huff and turns toward the projected image on the wall, slouching with her elbow on the table and blocking her view of Phil with her hand.

"Let's begin," Dr. Donovan states. "I want to gain a better understanding of the situation we have before us. We are hesitant to believe your motives are favorable – yet, we would be remiss not to recognize the depth of the opportunity your presence would create for our purposes."

"What are your purposes?" I ask coldly.

"They are very simple. We wish to create the best possible atmosphere for human equality. That means every living person on this earth has the same access to health, happiness, and security. That has been the goal of every respectable civilization throughout human history. The resources for that dream have never been possible until now. It is our responsibility to make sure we use these resources swiftly and justly to save mankind from the perils of disease, poverty, and prejudice."

"To create Heaven on earth."

"No, to fix the scrap heap we were given," he brashly counters, his voice reverberating in the small room. I look at Phil; he does not need to utter a word to show his disdain for that last comment, yet he keeps his cool. He gives me a look that says I should keep mine as well. He is right; if we hope to get out of here, we will need diplomacy.

"So what are you suggesting we do?" I carefully ask, changing the direction of the conversation.

"That is why we have brought everyone together. We want to better understand what you know. Now, we would be hesitant to believe one of your testimonies individually, but all of your stories seem to collaborate. Even Tira, as you call her, has given some spotty information that is in line with what you have claimed. Thus, we are interested in learning about the coming events of our history, especially concerning the upcoming war and subsequent Relocation Act, as you call it."

"You take this one," I say to Phil. "You are better with words and I think you stayed awake in history class."

He shoots me a dirty look. "From what I know from our history classes – a war erupts between those in the Cause and those in the Establishment."

"Please, clarify those terms for the benefit of the group."

"Oh. The Establishment is what we call anyone outside of our territories. Well, I guess there are no territories yet; I'll get to that later," he stumbles awkwardly. "They are basically anyone who is philosophically and civically opposed to God's being the Creator and Sustainer of the Universe. The Cause is a group of Christians who are fighting against the onslaught of our religious freedoms, or more precisely, an attack on the fabric of humanity as a whole."

He looks at Dr. Donovan for approval before proceeding. "The war begins in the year 2312 and lasts until 2320. At that point, the Cause has become a fractured entity, incapable of producing a viable resistance. The government decides to remedy the lingering hostility by segregating those who wanted to remain tied to their religious practices from those who did not. Territories around the globe were created to house the religious, while everyone else was forced to live in one of the twenty Great Cities. All other areas were deemed natural preserves, where no human development was permitted."

"So mankind is essentially divided?"

"More or less. Although the majority of those in the Cities were already I-Morts – but there was a decent percentage of humans. I would think roughly twenty percent."

"I do not understand how the human population could then become extinct in one hundred years?"

"It was the viruses."

"Please – explain."

"Sometime after the territories were settled, a deadly virus spread throughout the human population. The vector was never discovered, so there was no way to effectively prevent the outbreak. The population was already essentially quarantined, but still the virus continued to spread. The onset of the disease happened extremely fast. After the host was infected, symptoms were seen in twenty-four hours and within thirty-six the victim was dead.

"Eventually a vaccine was created. It was mandated for children under eighteen and all newborns, as well as anyone who wanted to live in a Great City. Unfortunately, the vaccine was rushed into use before adequate testing could be done; and several months into distribution, scientists discovered the antigen used to create the vaccine was also causing host's immune systems to attack healthy reproductive cells. In most cases, the person was rendered sterile."

"There must have been some who refused the vaccine," Dr. Donovan states in disbelief.

"Yes, there were some who abstained. They banded together in a territory outside of Gold City when the second virus hit."

"And only your community was spared?"

"Yes. Though our numbers dwindled – due primarily to government-levied reproduction regulations as well as many who deserted for the Establishment. There were about three thousand people when we left."

"Why do you think you were spared?"

"Our location – we were surrounded on all sides by natural boundaries. But I believe it was God's purpose for us to be spared. We were chosen to save humanity from itself."

"I see," Dr. Donovan says skeptically.

"So you are saying there were two viruses?" Dr. King asks.

"Yes, we were unaware of the second virus until recently. It evidently was deadly enough to eliminate the colony outside Gold City."

"I do not understand how the government would allow the human population to be so vulnerable to extinction. Any species that becomes endangered is protected. I would believe protecting the human species would be at the top of that list."

"Yes, I suppose that does make sense. I never really thought about it like that before – Although, now that you say that, they did start bringing shipments of food and supplies to our town roughly six years ago, well six years before we left. That was approximately the same time the colony at Gold City was wiped out."

"Interesting," Dr. King replies. "So it seems one of our primary concerns should be to prepare the human population for an upcoming pandemic."

"And be diligent to monitor the composition of the vaccine," Dr. Donovan adds. "Good, very good. Now, the next item we need to discuss is your purpose for using the time travel machine to be with us here today. Mr. Conner, you said in your statement that you came to usher in the end of civilization. This seems like a threatening scenario to me," he mocks. "Could you explain to the board what you mean by that comment and why we should be lenient in our judgment of your motives."

Phil clears his throat and begins assertively, "Well, sir, first of all, I did not say 'the end of civilization.' That is a misrepresentation of my testimony. What I did say was that we were coming to help bring about the Second Coming of Christ, something that has been prophesized and speculated about for almost twenty-five hundred years.

"You see, through cross referencing different prophesies in scripture with the current state of humanity, we realized the expiration date for this Promise had passed. When we learned of the ability to transfer information through time, we took that opportunity to send Tira here," he motions toward her with his hand, "to warn this generation of the calamities that were about to come.

"You can see that when her information was downloaded in to this body, she lost the ability to associate her memories with the purposes of them. Through time, she remembers more bits and pieces, but not before the war has ended and the fate of humanity is sealed.

"Fast forward one hundred years and the same group from Shiloh decides to try again, guided by the timing of the letter that Tira writes. Our purposes are the same now as they were then. We are only here to stop a war and help save humanity."

"How can you say you are going to save humanity when you intend for it to no longer exist?" Dr. Donovan demands. "I see those as incongruent statements, dangerous when espoused to the wrong ears."

"We have seen the result of history. Mankind chooses your path and look where it leads. Stopping the virus or coming up with a suitable vaccine is only delaying the inevitable. Instead of the bandage being ripped off, mankind will sludge through who knows how more years of steady decline until the result is the same."

"But at least we have a chance for life to exist! You are proposing suicide for an entire species."

"I am proposing nothing of the sort. Actually, I am saying the exact opposite. Christ came to give us life, and give it to us in abundance. This life you are referring to is a minute fraction of what He promises and what we should strive to achieve. The battle for the souls of mankind has already been waged and won. All that is left are the details and the timing of our Lord's return."

"We are all just pawns in a cosmic game? Just a civilization of lifeless robots waiting for the end to come?"

"With all due respect, Dr. Donovan, God did not create the civilization of lifeless robots."

A half sarcastic smile slides across the official's face. "I see we are at a philosophical standstill; so I will try from this angle. Suppose you are right – mankind had become morally bankrupt and emotionally stagnant. Are you saying there is no hope for a revival?"

"Not when they are no longer connected to the source of the revival. That is the core of the issue. We are sacrificing our souls for more meaningless time on earth."

"I take offense to the term, 'meaningless,' but I understand the point you are trying to make from your perspective." He looks at Dr. King, who nods. "So if we were to let you go, what do you intend to do? How do you plan to stop the coming war?"

"Honestly, I am not sure." Phil looks at me to see if I have something to add.

"We have not discussed our plan of action yet," I answer. "We were hoping to speak with leaders of each side and try to formulate a plan to end the hostility."

"Yes," Phil agrees. "We have no idea how to bring about Christ's coming, nor should we. The Scripture clearly states the hour and time is unknown."

"Very well, we appreciate your candor. Do you have anything to add, Dr. King, before we adjourn?"

That's it? No remorse for the war or the coming segregation of humanity? No questions about Myrna?

"I do have one more question," Dr. King responds. "Sardis, you said you had information for me. Have we covered it, or is there something else you would like to divulge?"

"Yes, you did not ask about Myrna and the dreams—"

"If you don't mind," Phil interrupts. "I would like to speak with Myrna alone before we openly discuss this."

"I do not trust my daughter alone with either of you," Dr. King growls emphatically.

"What do you mean dreams?" Myrna asks.

"Wait?" I say. "You were in here when we were being questioned about our nightmares."

"All I saw was someone sitting at a table with a glass ball on his head." She glares furiously at her father. "You told me they just wanted to see Eve!" She angrily shakes her head and stands abruptly, looking directly at Phil. "Yes, I will go with you."

"Myrna, please," Dr. King pleads and grabs her hand.

"No, Father!" she yells, yanking it away as tears begin to fall down her face. "I am through with your lies! You treat me like a baby one moment and then expect me to be this perfect citizen the next. I can't live with this constant pressure to be someone I am not, some perfect little accessory to your perfect little life. I can't take it anymore!" She runs from the room. Dr. King sighs heavily and looks down at the table.

"I will let you handle this one, Andrew. Good day all, and thank you for this discussion. We will be in constant contact," Dr. Donovan states as the screen on the wall goes black. I look at Phil, not knowing what to do.

"If you do not mind, Dr. King, I would like to speak with Myrna," he says with the pastoral tone I have heard countless times when I was the one running away. "I know you have no reason to trust me, especially in regards to your own daughter, but I ask you to listen to what I am about to tell you with an open mind."

"Go on."

"Dr. King, your daughter is a very troubled girl, a wonderful, vibrant, beautiful girl, but also woefully tormented and depressed. She tries desperately to please you, only to be disappointed."

"How dare you say that! You have no clue what you are talking about. I love my daughter."

"Sir, we have information that would lead us to believe differently."

"Oh, yeah?" he threateningly responds.

Phil does not flinch; rather, he leans in closer. "Have you ever heard of the Apostle Peter from scripture?"

Taken aback by the question, Dr. King softens his steely expression. "I am not very familiar with religious writings, but I have heard of Peter, yes."

"Good. Peter was Jesus' most trusted disciple. Jesus even gave him the name 'Rock' and claimed he would be the person upon whom He would build His church," Phil speaks, his voice strong and inviting. "So undeniably he is a good, honorable person, not unlike yourself. However, during their final meal together before Christ was crucified, Jesus tells Peter he is going to deny knowing him: choosing to sacrifice their relationship for a respite of safety, not once, but three times before morning. You can imagine what Peter must have felt. This was the person whom he loved. He had sacrificed his time, his livelihood, to follow him. There is no possible way he would do such a thing!

"If you know the story then you realize Peter does just that. He denies knowing Christ three times before the rooster crows in the morning. Ashamed for what he has done, Peter runs off and sulks in *Jesus' most desperate moment*. He picks up his net and goes fishing as Jesus is executed. Think about that. This is the person whom God willingly chooses to build His church upon, and he is so self-absorbed in his own pity, that he is not even around when the person he loves more than any other is taken from him."

As Phil pauses, I look at Dr. King. It is sometimes hard to determine what an I-Mort is feeling by its expression, but at this instant his face is frozen, his eyes no longer reflecting the anger that was present a moment before. He appears to be anxiously waiting, or maybe even afraid to hear what Phil is about to say.

"Dr. King," Phil continues boldly, "this I-Mort sitting next to you will soon take the name, Myrna, to honor the memory of a girl she loved, a girl who took her in and gave her a home while the girl's own family turned their back on her in *her most desperate time of need*, and a girl who then takes her life because she does not understand how valuable and loved she truly is. I am asking you. Please – Please allow me to speak with your daughter and share with her the truth about this love: the truth that before the world was created, God knew her. He knew her and loved her more deeply and more richly than you or anyone else could ever dream to. Please. This is why *I* am here. This is why *God* sent me."

Dr. King sits there for a moment, staring blankly at the table. There are synthetic tears rolling down his desolate façade. He is Peter, running away from his beloved, and he knows it. His world is shaken, his purpose cracked. He looks at Phil as if he is going to speak, but lowers his head, nodding weakly. I then nod to both Phil and Tira, and we stand.

"I was given the authority to release you if I deemed you were not a threat to society," he states and looks Phil directly in the eye. "It is my opinion that society would be worse off without you in it. You are free to go."

"Thank you, Dr. King," Phil humbly replies. "I will speak with Sardis, but I was hoping I could spend some time with you and your family." He catches me off guard. I am about to say something when he continues. "We have no place to stay, no food to eat, and no resources to buy anything." He looks hesitantly at me, apparently aware of my angst, but I am glad I did not interrupt. I had not given our situation much thought; I was only eager to get out of here.

"No need for a conversation. This sounds good to me," I reply and look at Dr. King. "As long as you are agreeable."

"I would be much obliged. I also feel the board would like that arrangement. Tira, see to it these gentlemen find their way home. Thank you." She nods and motions with her hand toward the door, and I follow Phil into the hall.

"That was great, Bud," I whisper to Phil as we walk down the hall and into a lobby area. He smiles and subtly nods his head, though his focus is on something else. I look and see Myrna sitting on a bench in the far side of the lobby. She is just as I remember her from my dream, down to the forlorn expression on her face. I can tell Phil is overwhelmed emotionally. He has waited his whole life for this moment, and though I would like to go and meet her, I decide to let Phil have this time alone.

"Tira, would you like to show me where you have been staying? We have so much to talk about," I say and give Phil a wink. I expect to get the Phil face, but instead he simply nods and walks across the lobby. I cannot help but think back to the moment in the forest shortly after he was attacked by the bear. There was no joyous Phil face, no kidding around and making light of the moment. He was filled with something then, just as he is now. He is alive, completely trusting in what he knows to be true, at the most critical junction of his life. I watch as he walks completely across the water, about to defend ardently his relationship with Jesus, with no crowing rooster in sight.

"Your friend is very passionate about what he believes," Tira remarks as we walk away from the building.

"Yes – Yes he is."

Chapter 17

"Wow," I say aloud as I sink into my favorite chair, exhaling heavily, taking in the beautiful scene around me. Phil and Myrna are sitting at the kitchen table, laughing hysterically at a picture they took of themselves, while Tira is bustling around the kitchen, cooking something that has my mouth watering. I nestle into the cushions and close my eyes, reliving the events of the past few joyous weeks. Phil and Myrna have been inseparable. That first night he explained to her how much she was loved, just as he had told Dr. King he would. It was something she had never known and she accepted this Love with open arms. I had never seen someone whose life had been changed by the love of Christ; I had only read about how it was a common practice before the Relocation. Stories in Scripture like the Prodigal Son or the Lost Sheep, they make sense now. The purpose for our mission – it makes sense now. This was missing from the world I knew and even from Shiloh. This is a deeper kind of love, a more impactful passion. Scripture states there is rejoicing in Heaven over each sinner who comes home, and now I can see why.

Somehow Phil managed to get his Bible from home safely through the time travel event, and he and Myrna have been pouring through the Scriptures at night. He says it is as if he has been reunited with a friend he has not seen in many years, someone he knows everything about and has so much in common. One would not think so, looking at the two of them. He is a clean-cut regular Joe while she is beautifully different. Her arms and legs are covered with tattoos, and she explained her hair is naturally red, but not *that red*. Her personality is outgoing and adventurous, but she is also extremely humble. When she enters a room, one cannot take his eyes off of her – awed by her beauty and drawn to her light. I joked with Phil that I had better be the best man at his wedding. He laughed, but insisted their relationship was not going in that direction.

"Don't get me wrong, Sardis," he said to me one night while we were lying awake in our shared bedroom, "I think she is the most amazing person I have ever met; I am drawn to her, and we are so comfortable together – but I feel like she was created for something more: as if she is more than just *one girl* from Jasper City. She is so dynamic – so – complex."

"You're in love, Philistine…"

"Maybe I am, but I know in my soul that I am not the one for her. She is too – *brilliant*."

"Nah. Don't sell yourself short, Bud. You are the greatest guy I have ever met. Any girl would be fortunate to have you as her man." He just chuckled at my attempt to make him feel better and rolled over and went to sleep. I can tell he is in love, but I can see what he is saying about Myrna. When she is near, I feel as if I am in the presence of something extraordinary, yet fleeting – As if when I close my eyes, she will not be there when I open them, and all that will be left is a warm feeling reminding me I had been touched by something greater than myself.

Tira has been blooming as well. For me, it has been immensely gratifying to see her experiencing the meaning of her memories again, each connection rekindling a piece of her spirit. She loves hearing me tell stories from when I was growing up and seeing if she can match them to her recollections of the event. Most of the time, my version tends to be on a slightly grander scale.

"Wow, I don't remember that twelve-point buck you got in the Pine Glen," she would say, "I remember a pretty nice size eight point, but not a twelve…"

"Oh yeah, it was a twelve, I remember," I would insist, and she would laugh. Her laugh was almost the same as I remember, big and bold. It could just be the way most I-Morts laugh, though, because I never remember hearing one genuinely laugh before. Either way, it is a welcomed event.

I told her about the letter and that version of her I-Mort self, about Dr. Pergo and the second mission. We discussed great-grandpa Isaac and the upcoming war. Most of all, we enjoyed talking about Dad. She obviously has many memories I cannot help her with, but filling her in on some of the details I can remember seems to have helped. We talk about what it was like after she was gone; how hard it was for Dad and me to reconnect, and how we secretly blamed the other person for what we were feeling, even though in our hearts we knew neither was to blame. I told her how the last few days before we left we had begun to mend our relationship, and how much I learned about his love for her.

I also told her about Dad's last moment before he went home. How proud she would have been at his confidently standing before the Serpent. She was overjoyed to realize both of their souls are now rejoicing together in Heaven.

The most difficult times are at night. I lie awake, thinking of Lacy. When I finally fall asleep, I dream about her bobbing ponytail or her sparkling eyes. I can feel her embrace or her warm breath on my cheek. I dream about our wedding day. She is dressed in white, a gorgeous gown with a simple leafy tiara in her hair. I watch her gliding down the aisle, a bouquet of white flowers in her hand, her eyes fixed on the ground in front of her until she is a few steps away. She looks up, her face glowing, her hair gently being moved by an unknown breeze. A smile breaks across her face as our eyes meet. Phil, my best man, winks as he takes the bouquet from her hand. I reach for her and feel her touch. A single tear rolls down her cheek as I squeeze her hands in mine. I want never to wake, merely to live here in this moment. I grip her hands so tightly....

When I wake, I am empty, homesick. I know I will see her again someday, but that is little comfort. I miss her now.

"Sardis, come here!" Phil shouts, and I pry my eyes open to see him and Myrna still sitting at the kitchen table. "We just received an urgent message from the Council of the United Elect!" He lifts a sealed letter from the table and waves it.

"Oh, yeah? Which City?" I reply, having learned a little about the structure of the current government. Each Great City is led by a single individual called the United Elect, who in turn is governed by a small board of other elected officials.

"Not a city, Sardis, this is a letter from the Council itself. You know, all twenty of the United Elects get together in a Council every so often? Ring a bell? No? Did you really sleep through all of history class?"

"Not all of it. I remember the time you tripped walking to the front of the class to give your semester presentation."

"Good. At least that year wasn't a total waste." He slides his finger underneath the seal and pops the envelope open. He pulls out an ornate looking card and looks strangely at the front and the back of it before holding it up so I can see.

"What does it say?" I ask, now intrigued. I drag myself out of my favorite chair and join them at the table.

"It is an invitation for me to come and speak at the Council. They are having a week long globally broadcasted debate among leaders of several different societal groups, and I was nominated to represent the Human-Christian group."

"Really?" Myrna beams. "That is a big deal!"

"Yeah – I wonder why they would choose me?"

"Probably your dad had something to do with it," I reply, nodding at Myrna. "And probably Dr. Donovan."

"Are you going to do it?" she asks.

"I will have to pray about it, but we have been waiting for some sort of direction on what to do next…"

"I would say this counts as a positive direction!" I remark. "Brush me up on my history. Where does the Council meet?"

"They meet in Crystal City." He is still staring at the letter as if not yet allowing the information to sink in.

"That is just outside of Jerusalem!" Myrna gushes. "We were just talking about how we would love to go there and see the Biblical sites!"

"Yes, I know –" He puts his hand to his brow and leans on the table with his elbow, as if he was somehow bothered by that fact.

"What's wrong, Bud?"

"Just taking this all in; that's all," he answers softly. "The Council is in three days; I would need to leave tomorrow."

"Tomorrow?"

"Wow, that does not leave us much time – though I guess we are getting pretty good at making rash decisions." I watch his face for a reaction to my witty remark, but he is oddly still, until he slowly slides his hand down his face, wringing the end of his chin.

"Sardis, could I speak with you alone, please?"

"Yeah, sure," I answer, confused. He motions toward the bedroom we have been sharing, and I walk in as he follows and closes the door.

"I want to ask you something," he begins, a concerned look in his eyes. "You know I love you like a brother..." He hesitantly looks down at the ground as if searching for the correct word to say.

"What's wrong?" I ask, a pit beginning to form in my gut.

"Have you burnt your boat?"

"What?"

He frowns and rubs his arm before leaning heavily against the closed door. "When Jesus called Peter, he left his boat and all his stuff, and followed after Him."

"Yeah, okay...."

"The problem was, Peter did not truly understand what it was going to cost to follow. When the Lord needed him on that Day, Peter ran. He went back to what was comfortable. He climbed back into his boat and –"

"Please, just spit it out."

"Fine. I am concerned you are not devoted to this anymore and maybe never have been."

"What? What are you talking about?"

"I feel like you have given up – like you are content with where we are at. Like you were only doing this to impress Lacy, and now that she is gone, you don't care anymore."

I can feel the rage beginning to boil. I shake my head repeatedly and close my eyes to try and quell the fury, but the feeling continues to rise. I open my mouth to blast him, but a brief sensation of dread catches me off guard. Is he right? Instead of lashing out angrily, I get defensive.

"That is ridiculous. I can't believe you would insult me like that, after all we have been through!"

"Look, the invitation states that I can only take one person with me. Obviously I want it to be you, but I have to know where you stand. I have to know if you are willing to do what it takes if things get hard. This could be the most important event of –"

"I can't believe you would doubt me!" I am no longer defensive; now, I am only blinded with anger. "Go ahead, take your sweetie. I know that is what you want – As if I am the one who has lost their desire to do this!"

"Sardis, please. Settle down and listen to me."

"I've heard all I want to hear. You go ahead and take her. Tira and I are going to find Colonel Justice."

"What are you going to do when you find him?"

"Something! We have done nothing since we got here. We know this war is coming; we need to start doing something to prevent it."

He sighs heavily and shakes his head. I storm out of the room and past the kitchen, not making eye contact with anyone. I head down the stairs, out of the apartment, and into the street, not knowing where I am going. I just need to clear my head. I cannot believe after everything we have been through, he would think I was doing this for some selfish reasons. Sure, I have been out of it lately, but, come on, I just watched my father be executed and lost the love of my life in the matter of a few hours. Excuse me for being human!

"Sir," I hear from behind me. I quickly turn and see my nurse from the first day. She has a long coat pulled around her and a scarf covering most of her face, even though it is fairly warm. She hands me an envelope and quickly walks away. I look down and see *"Open in Private"* scribbled on it. I glance back to where she was, but she is gone. I scan the street and sidewalks but see no sign of her. I slide the envelope into my pocket. Instantly I feel as if I am being watched, so I quickly duck back into the entryway of our apartment. I have no desire to go back upstairs and face Phil, but I also do not feel I am clear of the government's gaze. I swallow my pride and march up the stairs. They are all sitting at the kitchen table as I walk by and enter the bathroom. I shut the door behind me and search for any place that may have a camera hidden, but see nothing suspicious. Still, I am not convinced, so I crawl into the shower and place a towel over my head before pulling out the letter.

Mr. Alexander,

Ever since we spoke I have had an overwhelming sense of connection to you, as if our lives are somehow intertwined. I also saw your leadership qualities and knew that soon you were going to do very important things for this world. With this in mind, I learned something that has shaken me. I knew I needed to tell someone and you are the only one I knew I could trust.

I was walking past Dr. King and a group of other scientists, when I heard one of them speak my cousin's name, the one who was a preacher. I was intrigued, so I stayed within ear shot and realized they were talking about a drug they were calling Sonny Ray, his name. At first I thought maybe they had found a diagnosis for his disease, so I tried to research the name but found nothing. I began to become suspicious, so I did some more investigating. One night, after Dr. King had gone home for the day, I went into his office and accessed his computer. I located a file that had my cousin's name on it. When I opened it, I found something terrible. The virus my cousin had was something they could not

*identify and could not treat. They decided that instead
of curing him, they would harvest his blood and create
a stockpile of the virus. I saw drawings of some sort
of dispersion device and a population chart. I was so
frightened by what I saw that I closed the file and left
as fast as I could.*

*I knew what I saw was important, so I prayed for
God to give me wisdom on what to do. Every time I
closed my eyes, I saw your face.*

A wave of nausea sweeps over me as I realize the meaning of Laura's letter. The virus that wiped out most of the human population was not a random act of God; it was a biological attack by our own government and Dr. King was somehow involved. I have been living in the same home as this man, talking with him every evening. Has he been using the information I tell him to help develop his plan? Has he been monitoring every movement we make? Is he somehow watching me now? The thought sends a chill down my spine, and I hastily slide the letter into my pocket and throw the towel off my head. My only thought is to tell Phil; we have to get out of here and warn the Cause – his speaking engagement will have to wait. I open the bathroom door and Dr. King is standing directly outside.

"Sardis, there you are," he says with a smile on his robotic face. I stare at him, terrified. I hope he cannot see the fear in my eyes. "What do you think of this opportunity that Phil has?"

"Oh – I think it is wonderful." I force a fake smile. I feel as if he is staring directly through my skull and into my mind, as if he is searching through my memory to see if I know his awful secret.

He leans in close and lowers his voice, "I understand you want Myrna to go with him on this trip. I realize you are just being overly nice. You will go tell them that it is best for you to go with him. Right?" He has a smile on his face, though the tone of his voice is much more ominous; yet, I am partly relieved that he seems to be more concerned about his daughter's going off alone with Phil than he is about my knowing his secret.

"Yes, well, I will have to talk with Phil about what he thinks is best," I evade. "I think I'll go and ask him now, if you don't mind."

"That is a great idea, Mr. Alexander. I will come with you."

"Oh. Okay."

He escorts me to the table where Phil and Myrna are eating the meal Tira had prepared. Phil gives me a half smile. I had forgotten about our heated argument just a few minutes before.

"Phil…" He swallows the food he has in his mouth and takes a drink.

"What is on your mind?" he formally replies, as he sets his glass back down on the table. I can feel Dr. King staring at me, waiting for me to broach the topic. I do not know what to say. I obviously cannot bring up Laura's letter now.

"It is about the Council…."

"I was thinking about the Council, too, and what we were talking about earlier. I think we should all go: the three of us."

"Oh? I thought there were only two tickets to the event."

"There are, but I would love it if you would come with us. I think it is a good idea if we stay together. We will only be in the Council for a short while. I would love the moral support."

I look at Dr. King and he has a scowl on his face. He motions to me with his eyes, wanting me to say something in rebuttal.

"I don't know if this whole thing is a good idea or not…"

Phil's brow furrows as he looks at me. I have seen the look on his face before; it is not one of confusion, but rather it is as if he is trying to decipher something deeper in my response. Maybe he can read some sort of cue from my face as well, because he does not ask the obvious question.

"I see. What do you think Dr. King?"

"Oh, me?" he asks surprised. Relief flows over me. Now if Dr. King wants his displeasure shown, he will have to do it himself.

"I think it is a wonderful honor," he replies heartily. He looks at me and then at Myrna. "But I also think it is something you and Sardis should do on your own."

"What?" Myrna fires indignantly.

"I am sorry, dear, but I do not feel this is a good idea."

"I can't believe this," she mutters repeatedly, forcing him to talk louder.

"Your mother and I have been discussing your sudden – change – and we are concerned for you."

"Concerned for me! Are you kidding me, Dad? I have never felt more right than I do now!"

"Myrna, come on. This religious stuff is a bit ridiculous. I think it is about time these two move on to bigger and better things. Right?" He points at me and glares hostilely. I do not know how to answer. I want to get out of here as well, but to meet up with the Cause, not with more of the enemy. Is it really his daughter he is concerned about, or is it something else?

"I feel strongly that Myrna and I are supposed to go to Crystal City," Phil answers and looks at Dr. King. "If you would feel more comfortable, you could come with us as well."

No Phil! I think as I subtly wince. That is the worst case scenario!

"No, I cannot spare the time away from the hospital." Thank God!

"I will need to speak with your mother. Maybe we can find a suitable solution," he adds, agitated. "I will go find her now. I

225

think she is at the market." He glides briskly out of the apartment. As soon as the door closes behind him, I let out a large sigh.

"Phil, I need to speak with you."

"What is it?" he replies wearily.

"In private."

"You can say anything here. Please, I do not want to go through another shouting match with you."

"No. You don't understand. *I need to speak with you in private.*" He gives me an irritated look but then nods towards our bedroom. I shake my head and grab him by the arm and lead him into the bathroom. This has to be safest room in the house....

"Just one minute," I mouth to Myrna through the crack in the bathroom door, just before I close it.

"What are you doing?" Phil remarks, as I usher him into the bathtub.

"Here; read this," I whisper and hold out the letter. He groans, but takes it from my hand and begins reading.

"Who wrote this?" he asks as his eyes move back to the top of the paper, and he scans the words once more.

"My nurse from the first day," I whisper. "We have to get out of here and alert the Cause."

"I don't believe this. Dr. King is not the type of person who would sign off on something like this."

"Come on. Open your eyes, Phil. He has been playing us this whole time."

He shakes his head and hands me back the letter. "I have prayed about this Council, Sardis, and I know I am supposed to go and Myrna is supposed to come with me."

"Phil? Do you understand the ramifications of this letter? Our own government is responsible for the spread of the virus! We

226

can't trust anyone in the Establishment, not Dr. King, not Dr. Donovan, not anyone."

"How do you know you can trust the Cause?"

"Don't you remember all the stories about Colonel Justice from when we were growing up? What he did to try and save humanity? How much of a Godly man he was? He is the only one here we can trust...."

"Sardis, I trust God, and he is telling me to go to Crystal City."

"Ahh," I groan, frustrated with his stubbornness. I cannot believe he is blowing this off. Think of the grave danger this is going to be to our mission. We have to do something about this!

"Fine, you go – But Tira and I are going to meet Colonel Justice," I angrily conclude.

"Sardis, I think you should come with us. Please, trust me on this."

"Phil, I love you, buddy, but you are wrong on this one." I fold the letter and slide it back into my pants pocket, so I can show the Cause when we meet up with them.

"Come on," I say to Tira as I walk back into the kitchen. She walks over toward me and I put my arm around her. "We are going to go meet great-grandpa Isaac."

She gives me a strange look. "I thought you were going to Crystal City? With Phil – for the Council?"

"No, we will let those two go. Besides, we will be able to watch Phil and Myrna on the broadcast." Phil emerges from the bathroom and walks straight toward me, grabbing me by the arm, and pulling me close for a strong hug.

"I love you, Sardis. I will see you soon." He pats my back a few times and gives one final squeeze. "And there is one more letter you need to read. It is yours," he whispers into my ear. "But not now. God will show you when you are ready." I stand back and am about to ask him what he is talking about, when he nods toward Tira. "Go. It is time. I will deal with Dr. King when he returns."

"What?" I say confused. Tira grabs my hand and pulls me toward the door. What does Phil know that he is not telling me?

He hurries by and opens the door for us. "Remember when I caught that fish in the river – bumbling and clumsy me of all people?" I shrug my shoulders, dumbfounded by his actions.

"I can still see the expression on your face," he chuckles, as Tira pulls me through the doorway to the top of the apartment stairs. "I'm not sure who was more surprised there was a fish in that net – you – me – or the fish!" I unexpectedly *laugh*. He gives a knowing wink before shutting and locking the door.

Chapter 18

"Believe it or not, that was the second aircraft ride we have shared in this part of the world," I remark to Tira as we step off the Great Cities Airtaxi into the Air Depot outside of Sapphire City. It is refreshing to be back in familiar terrain and hard to believe that twenty-four hours ago I was relaxing in my favorite chair.

"I remember your story," she replies as we scan the bustling terminal to get our bearings. "It would be nice if I had a few more of those memories now."

"No kidding. It would make finding great-grandpa Isaac a lot easier; that's for sure." I hear a drone from behind me as the aircraft we just exited lifts straight into the air and disappears through the same hatch in the roof of the Air Depot that we used to enter. The hatch closes, and then quickly opens again, as another craft floats down and lands behind us. These unmanned taxis travel between each of the Great Cities – free public transportation for those who call one of the Great Cities their home. I shake my head in awe and begin walking away from the landing zone. I have never seen a place like this before. The only thing I can compare it to is the lobby of the government building back home, but on a much grander scale. It is enormous. Like bees in a hive, aircraft are buzzing in and out of dozens of hatches in the high domed roof. There are humans and I-Morts everywhere, racing to and fro, talking and smiling, seeming to enjoy the chaos. I am completely overwhelmed by the flashing lights and strong aromas; so much so that I can feel my head begin to ache. I guess one has to be inoculated to this atmosphere before he can begin to enjoy it.

"Although... I think it may be easier to find Colonel Justice first. I researched his location and at least I have an address for him. Grandpa could be anywhere."

"Oh, good! What is the location?"

I reach into my pocket and pull out a scrap of paper. "193 West Jewel Street."

She opens her hand and begins pressing her palm. "He is about eight blocks from the depot. West," she instructs, pointing towards the far exit.

"I didn't know you could do that!"

"Yes, it is a new innovation for this particular model. It has been quite helpful in my travels."

"Lead the way then!" She grins and begins for the exit.

I lift my hand to shield my eyes from the bright sunlight as we enter the street. The fresh air feels and smells amazing. It reminds me of a bright sunlit afternoon in the forest, Mom guiding us through some new terrain on the trail of a trophy buck. She skillfully navigates the uneven ground, sliding through brush, deliberately placing each step so as not to disrupt the atmosphere of the forest. I look at Tira and she is holding her hand close to her face in an attempt to see the digital map on her palm through the glare. I enjoy her company, and it is wonderful when I do see glimpses of Mom's charm and wit, but she does not hold a candle to my mother.

"That way," she points, apparently satisfied with what her hand is telling her. I follow her through the glass canyons for several blocks, until she stops at the base of one of the tall buildings.

"I think this is it," she says, looking up at the towering structure. I nod in agreement. We walk to the front of building expecting the glass panels to fold open allowing us to enter, but they do not; instead an alarm begins to blare. An I-Mort security guard appears from behind us with a stun weapon in his hand.

"We are here to see Colonel Luke Justice," I explain as he begins to move closer, weapon raised and pointed directly at me.

"You have triggered a security alert. I cannot let you enter," he answers firmly.

I raise my hands slowly into the air. "We are from Jasper City."

The guard presses a button on his forearm and then quickly grabs the stun weapon again with both hands. "You must leave the premises at once!"

"You have no traceable signature," Tira whispers into my ear. Of course! How stupid of me. It will be another hundred years before my tracking dye is logged into the government's database. I am about to explain our circumstances, when the doors to the building open and a tall man in dark clothing appears.

"You are here to see me?" he authoritatively asks.

"Are you Colonel Justice?"

"Yes, I am Colonel Luke Justice. What business do you have with me?" He waves at the guard, who lowers his weapon but remains standing where he is.

"Could we speak with you in private, Colonel? We have important information –"

"Why would you assume I would speak with you?" he rebuffs and turns back toward the open lobby. I do not know what to say. If only Phil were here – or even Dr. Pergo. That's it!

"You are aware of my allegiance," I yell and place my hand on my chest. He stops and slowly turns toward us. He peers intently at me.

"That's what I thought." He gestures toward the security guard. The guard grabs my arm and escorts us into the building. We are lead through the lobby and into an elevator where Colonel Justice is standing, his shoulders back and his hands folded behind him. His jaw is clenched and his lips are pursed in an angry manner, exacerbating an already protruding chin. His eyes, set high on a chiseled face, are staring straight ahead at snow falling in a peaceful winter meadow scene on the elevator walls, so real I can feel a chill running down my spine.

"This way," he instructs as the elevator stops. We follow him down a hall and into a large conference room. There is a long parquet patterned table at the center, around which is at least a dozen chairs.

"Wait here." He walks across the hall to a room where several elderly people are standing inside. They seem to have been waiting a long while to see him, because as soon as he opens the door, they flock eagerly around him. He smiles warmly, embracing and speaking with each. His demeanor is markedly different from the strong indifferent leader we saw in the elevator. He holds each by the hand and prays over them, tears flowing freely as he does so. After about fifteen minutes and at least twice as many prayers, he rejoins us in the room and closes the door behind him.

"A good shepherd always tends to his flock," he states jovially. "Please, take a seat. Now, what is it that I can help *you* with?" He motions toward the parquet table, and Tira and I sit on one side while he walks around and sits directly across from us.

"I have very important information to share with you," I say, as he adjusts his slightly overweight body in his chair in an attempt to get comfortable. "But in order for you to fully comprehend what I am about say, I need to explain who we are."

"I know who you are. What is it that you want to tell me?"

"Oh?" I say, caught off guard. "Well – ok – well – read this letter." I dig into my pants pocket for Laura's letter, only to discover it is not there. Frantically, I shove my hand into the other pocket but also find nothing.

"I know it is here somewhere," I mumble as I feel the weight of his steely gaze on my face. I reach into my jacket pocket and luckily find it folded inside.

"Here," I grunt, reaching the sheet of paper across the table with a noticeably shaking hand. He grabs it, pulls a pair of glasses from his pocket, and holds the letter close to his face.

"I am not sure what all you know about the future of humanity –"

"Mr. Alexander, I have friends in very high places," he interrupts, glaring over the tops of his glasses. "I have heard your testimony before the United Elect in Jasper City. It was very interesting indeed," he looks back down at the letter before peering over the top and finishing his thought, "and it gives us even more reason to focus our efforts on freeing our people from their bondage, no matter the cost. Our race depends on it."

"Yes, but if you heard our testimony, then you must realize the outcome of the war is not in our favor. All it does is fray the already tenuous relationship between us and the Establishment."

He huffs and looks back at the letter. "Great. An idealist."

Frustrated, I lean back in my seat. Tira is sitting forward, her hands crossed on the table, looking keenly at Colonel Justice. I watch his face as he reads. His angry glare returns and he slams the paper down on the table.

"This is an outrage!" he growls, standing and walking to the wall where he presses an intercom button. "Code White. I repeat. Code White." He releases the button and storms out of the room.

"I think we found our man," I whisper to Tira. She sits up in her chair and places her hands on her lap, her expression unchanged. "Do you not agree?"

Before she can answer, Colonel Justice walks back into the room and takes a seat across from us once more. He leans over the table, his face now calm.

"Don't worry. We will take care of this." He flashes a confident smirk, his emotional outburst seemingly a thing of the past. He presses another button on the side of the table. One of the parquet squares opens and a bowl of fruit and a plate with bread and cheeses rises out of the hole. He grabs a few grapes and pops one into his mouth. He motions toward the food, "Don't be shy."

"Thank you, sir." I eagerly grab a banana and a hunk of bread. I am starving. As I quickly peel the banana, an I-Mort walks into the room holding a tray with a pitcher of water and several glasses. It pours two and sets them in front of both Colonel Justice and me.

"Tell me about this friend of yours. I am fascinated to hear what he is going to say at the Council Debate."

"Who, Phil?" I ask startled. How does he know so much about us? We just found out about the Council yesterday.

"Well, Phil – Phil is my best friend. I have known him since we were kids. He is the most genuine person I know. He is loving, kind, very spiritual –"

He slaps the table joyously when I briefly pause my description. "That is great! Good to hear! I am glad someone with impeccable moral character is going to represent our causes at the debate. I am curious though; what do you think he will say? What points will he champion?"

I awkwardly swallow the piece of bread I have in my mouth and have to take a long drink of water to get it to go down. I believe Colonel Justice is on our side, but I also realize his intentions are for war. I decide to proceed with caution until I can trust he will acquiesce to our peaceful resolution.

"I am not sure what he will say."

"I was just curious for my own benefit," he replies heartily with a large smile, evidently sensing the trepidation in my response.

"I thought maybe I could get the inside scoop as to what he was going to say tomorrow; that's all. I like to be in the loop," he adds, fidgeting with a neural transmitter on his wrist, identical to the ones Phil and I had.

"Have you ever seen one of these before?"

"Yes, actually. Phil and I had a pair of them."

"Oh, really? I figured these would have been ancient technology by the time you came around, as fast as things go out of style these days."

"We were behind the times in Shiloh. Technology was not our thing," I answer dryly.

"Is that so? What was your thing?"

"Faith, I suppose – and family – community. We all helped each other and did our own part, so no one was ever in need."

"Sounds like heaven." He leans comfortably back in his chair. "At least much more so than this Utopia the Establishment is championing."

"For everyone's sake, I hope it wasn't," I mumble under my breath. He pulls another grape off the bunch and pops it into his mouth. We sit there for a few moments. I want to find out why he is so interested in Phil, but I realize I am too intimidated by him to ask. I look at Tira. She is sitting quietly, evidently content with letting me do all the talking. Instead of striking up conversation though, I find myself staring at the neurotransmitter on his wrist in an attempt to avoid his gaze.

"Here," he says pulling off the device and handing it to me. "Maybe this memento will remind you of home."

"I can't take that, sir."

"Don't worry about it. I have a dozen more. Besides, I am sure a small reminder of simpler times would be a welcomed change. I can't imagine all you have gone through recently."

"Thank you," I answer humbly, turning it over in my hands. I think of the first time I put it on. I can still see Lacy's face and feel the pit in my stomach when she approached me on the road. I can see her eyes and smell her perfume; I can see her ponytail bobbing back and forth as she walked away –

The door to the room opens abruptly, splintering my pleasant thought. Several men, dressed in similar dark clothing to Colonel Justice, stroll in. He stands and shakes the hand of each one. Tira and I stand as well.

"These are our time-travelling friends, Sardis and Tira the I-Mort. They will be staying with us for the foreseeable future." We both nod politely. They shake our hands and tell us their names.

"It was very enjoyable to meet you two," Colonel Justice says to Tira and me, as the others sit around the table. "I will be in contact with you after our board meeting; and tomorrow we will watch this debate together. Ok? Good. My servant will see you to your room."

"Wait –"

"If we need further information, Mr. Alexander, we will call for you. We value your knowledge, but our decisions will be made by this group of trusted officials."

He nods toward the I-Mort Servant who taps me on the shoulder and gestures toward the open door. Reluctantly, I concede and follow the Servant through the building to our sleeping quarters. It is a beautiful suite with a bathroom, kitchen, living area, and two bedrooms. Before the Servant leaves, he shows us how to use the many amenities and gives us a menu with a list of food items the kitchen staff will prepare for us at our convenience. I sit on the couch as Tira pours me a glass of orange juice.

"To answer your remark from earlier," she begins and hands me the juice, "I am not sure what to think of our new friend. His demeanor makes me uneasy. I think we should be careful with what we tell him."

"There is pulp in this," I groan. Mom knew I hated the pulp.

"Oh! I am sorry. I will strain it out for you."

"No, no. I am sorry," I mumble, embarrassed. "Thank you for the juice, I appreciate you doing that for me. I am just beyond stressed out. I am sorry. And yes, I do agree with you, we need to be cautious with Colonel Justice."

"I understand, Sardis. It has been a long eventful day."

"Day? I have been running on empty since I found your letter." I set the juice down and lie back on the couch staring at the ornate gold patterns on the ceiling. For someone who is so opposed to the Establishment, he sure seems to enjoy many of their perks.

"Why don't you go to bed?" Tira asks softly. "You seem tired, dear."

"Thanks, Mom, maybe I will do that," I answer thoughtlessly, as I have done a million times before. I open my mouth to correct my mistake, but she is smiling so I decide against it.

"Thanks again for the juice. Goodnight. I'll see you in the morning." She nods contentedly. Somehow I feel almost normal as I crawl into bed.

When I awake, I am completely disoriented. I anxiously scan the room until the pile of my clothes, lying on the chair next to the bed, jogs my memory as to where I am. I stumble into the living area. Tira is sitting on the couch, gazing at the screen on the wall. I sit next to her and realize she is watching the preliminary portion of the Council Debate. The moderator is explaining what is going to happen over the next few days. Tonight each group is going to give its opening remarks.

"What time is it?"

"It is ten, Sardis."

"I thought this thing was sometime this evening?"

"It is in the evening – in Crystal City, but they are ten hours ahead of us."

"Oh. I guess I slept through that history class as well."

"Remind me to ground you in about a hundred years for that comment," she jokes, showing a glimpse of Mom's humor.

I smile and nestle into the cushions. "Has Phil been on yet?" The cobwebs are beginning to clear and I feel a twinge of excitement.

"No, it is just starting." She presses a button on the armrest of the couch and the image becomes larger, almost filling the entire wall. "Wait – There they are now. Look – Standing in the center there!"

"Philistine!" He and Myrna are standing behind a podium on a stage in the center of a large auditorium. There are three podiums on either side of theirs, with two people standing at each. Phil has his silly grin on his heavily makeup-caked face, while Myrna looks stunning in a gorgeous long sleeved white gown, her hair falling in beautiful red streaks across her face and onto her shoulders.

"Those must be hair extensions. She looks beautiful!" Tira coos.

"Wow. Yes, she does. And Phil doesn't have his glasses on; he almost looks presentable. By the way, have you heard anything from Colonel Justice? He said he was going to watch the debate with us."

"No, I have not seen anyone today. I will call the Servant." She presses a different button on the armrest, and a hologram appears next to us.

"How may I assist you?" the I-Mort Servant asks.

"Could we speak with Colonel Justice? The debate is about to begin, and we would like to watch it with him," Tira replies.

"I am sorry; Colonel Justice has gone out of town. He sends his deepest apologies on backing out of his commitment."

"What?" I cry. "We just saw him yesterday evening."

"Again, I am sorry to inform you that Colonel Justice is not available at this time. I would be glad to assist you in any way."

"No. Never mind," I mutter, disappointed.

"Thank you for understanding."

"Wait!" I yell as the image disappears. Tira pushes the button once more, and the hologram zaps back into view.

"How may I assist you?" he asks pleasantly.

"Sorry, I forgot to ask where the kitchen is located. I would like to get some breakfast before the debate gets started."

"No need to leave your room, Sir. Just tell me whatever it is you would like, and I will bring it up to you."

"If it is alright, I would like to walk down and get it. I hate being cooped up inside all day. I want to stretch my legs before our friends come on."

"I am sorry, but Colonel Justice gave orders that you are not permitted to leave your room until he returns."

"What?" I shout alarmed.

"I will inform you when he returns. Until then, enjoy our hospitality. What is it that you would like for breakfast?"

"Wait! Where is he going? When will he be back?"

"I am not at liberty to divulge that information. I would be glad to assist you in any way, so your stay will be as pleasing as possible."

"What is going on here?" I demand angrily, slamming my fist into my leg.

"Whenever you are prepared to order, press your call button and I will return. Have a wonderful day," he says joyfully and disappears once more.

I stand and walk to the door. I try the knob but it will not turn. I bang my shoulder against it, and it does not budge. Panicked, I look around the suite and realize there are no windows and no other ways out. We are trapped. My mind is spinning trying to decipher what is happening. Why would he lock us in our room? What threat would we pose? Why can't I speak with him? I just want to know what is going on – The neurotransmitter! I slide it on to my wrist and turn it on. Immediately I hear his voice inside my head.

"*Alright, gentlemen, we will land in Crystal City in three hours. This is the opportunity we have been waiting for. Are you ready?*

"*Good...*"

"What is going on?" Tira inquires anxiously. I wave my hands at her and place my finger to my lips. If I speak, he will hear me, and I also do not want him to somehow hear her speaking. For the moment Colonel Justice is silent, as Phil begins speaking nervously on the screen.

"Thank you, Elect Donovan, for that kind introduction. My friend Myrna and I are extremely excited to be able to share our story with you this evening." He cracks a smile as the nervous energy leaves his face, replaced by the confidence I have seen so many times before.

"Most people seem to already know who I am. I guess I should thank the Council's Advertising Organization for that, but if you are one of the fortunate ones who have never seen my face before, my name is Phil Conner. This is my lovely friend, Myrna King, who will be sharing her story as the evening unfolds." He looks at Myrna and gives her a wink as respectful applause and some laughs echo through the auditorium.

"Before I begin, I would like to share some background information about myself. Believe it or not, I will not be born for another ninety years. You may be asking yourself how this is possible. Well, the answer lies in the amazing technology produced by a group of scientists from Jasper City. They created a machine that could transport humans through time –" he looks at his hands, "– and I guess I am living proof their invention works!" A slight wave of laughter rolls through the audience. He is about to continue speaking when Colonel Justice's voice reappears in my skull.

"Yes, I think the people will believe it. When the virus spreads, we will show the world the letter and have Sardis tell his story. When the virus wipes out a third of the population by next week, I will swoop in with the antidote. I am a miracle worker, you know..."

The only sound I can hear now is the pounding of my heart in my ears. My face must convey my panic, because Tira rushes over to my side as his voice sounds once more.

"So what if they send their pathetic army. The government is spineless. They will probably have their soldiers equipped with non-lethal weapons. Plus, the populace will already be on our side. They won't stand a chance."

Tira impatiently waves her arms, trying to pry some information from me, but I am petrified, unable to move. If he finds out I am listening into this conversation, we are all dead, including Phil and Myrna. All I can do is close my eyes in an attempt to process what this means. I stand, motionless, as Phil speaks in the background.

"That is the reason why being human is so vital to life as we know it. What good is it to be happy all the time if you cannot feel the joy that is the root of the happiness? What good is it to have all the pleasures you could ever want at your fingertips but never be able to love again? What gain do you have living forever if you have no loved ones with which to share your daily triumphs?

"You see, man was reactionary in the creation of these new bodies. We were afraid of dying, of cancer, or of being ill. These new bodies cured things, like disease and famine. They seemed to correct all the mistakes God had made – but is that truly the case? I argue it is not. When God made us, he was not concerned with making sure no one ever experienced an unfortunate circumstance. Rather, he focused on creating something beautiful and awe inspiring, something that could feel, that could love, that could make choices for itself; and in doing so, mankind is going to experience weakness and hurt. These deficiencies are not included in our being as a mistake; rather, they are put there so we can understand what we are enjoying now is only a shadow of what is to come when we are made perfect in His presence. So when we choose to hide our weaknesses, we are stripping God of His power to move through us, to show the world there is hope, there is something out there still worth striving for. We do not have to settle for an eternity of being comfortable robots, when we can be completely alive now; with the guarantee that when we finish our race here on Earth, we will be welcomed with open loving arms to an eternity of unspeakable joy, walking hand in hand with the Creator and Sustainer of it all." Phil finishes to a thunderous round of applause, which unfortunately is drowned out once more by the sinister and Lawless voice in my head.

"What are we going to do about Phil? It does not matter what Phil says. In fact, eliminating him may be the best option…."

"Thank you, Mr. Conner, for your opening statement," the moderator states, as I stare helplessly at my best friend, ten-thousand miles away.

"How will we kill him? We will let the people do it. We will lump his zealous faith in with the impotent promises of the Establishment, so when neither his praying nor their Utopian promises can cure their illness, they will turn on both of them. We will make a public display of it, when the debate finishes and the world is in chaos. It will be even more fuel for our Cause –

"Wait – hold on – What is that? Oh wonderful! Good news everyone; I just got word the initial dispersion of the virus was a success."

Chapter 19

I rip the transmitter from my wrist and throw it as hard as I can against the far wall. How could I be so stupid, to trust this man I had never met over my best friend? Phil knew this was going to happen. He was trying to tell me, but I wouldn't listen. He was right to doubt my motives. I am not following God's plan; I am following my own.

"Please, Sardis, what is going on?" Tira pleads.

"We have to find a way out of here. Phil is in trouble; something terrible is about to happen."

"Stop speaking in riddles! What is going on!"

I realize they may be able to hear me if I tell her, but at this point I do not care. I walk over and whisper into her ear. She tightly grabs my wrist as I relay the horrible information. She painfully looks at me for a moment, before releasing her grip as her gaze changes to one of a newfound determination.

"We are going to save them or die trying," she says and presses the button on the couch.

"How may I be of assistance?" the Servant graciously asks.

"Yes, could you bring us a ham and cheese sandwich, a bowl of tomato soup, a glass of milk, and fresh towels and linens, please?"

"It would be my pleasure. I will be there in two minutes and twelve seconds," he states and disappears.

Tira leans close and whispers into my ear, "When he arrives, his hands will be full. I will walk over to assist him, while you come up from behind and disable him. Take one of those kitchen knives and plunge it into the back of his neck at the base of his skull. It will disable the computer and we will be able to slip out the open door."

"Yes. Good... And when we reach the hall we will make a break for the elevator and then –"

"That is too risky. We could get trapped inside. We will need to jump."

"Jump? You may not die when you hit the ground, but I will."

"Trust me, please. And once we are in the street, we should be safe."

"Okay," I concede and scan the room for any final hindrances to our plan. I walk into the kitchen and grab a heavy knife from the block and slide it into the back of my pants. Tira sits nonchalantly on the couch while a female I-Mort on the screen speaks about ending world poverty.

"Oh, wait," Tira says and hurries toward her room, returning shortly with the small backpack she has been carrying since we left Jasper City.

"Are you sure you have everything?" she asks, as she returns to her seat.

"Yeah, I don't have anything. What do you have in there?"

"I will show you later," she answers as the door opens.

"Breakfast is served," he announces backing into the room, pulling a cart with our food and supplies. Tira nods, but I do not have time to make it to him before he turns and sees me coming. He falls to the ground and pulls a stun weapon from the bottom of the cart. I stop, holding the knife at my side, while Tira is standing next to the couch. We are all frozen, waiting for someone to make the first move. He only has one shot with the weapon, so I dive toward him, knowing if Tira were to be struck, she would be completely disabled. He slides backwards, pointing the weapon at me as I crash upon him, plunging my knife into the arm holding the weapon. My body tenses, preparing for the incapacitating feeling I have felt before, but it never comes. I wrestle him to the ground and put my knees into his back. I pull the knife from his arm and drive it into his neck, shooting sparks as his body goes limp. I turn excitedly toward Tira who is pulsating on the ground next to the couch.

"No!" I rush to her side and pull the remnants of the stun weapon's projectile from her chest. She stops convulsing and lies there motionless.

"Wake up!" I yell, shaking her, but it is no use. I slam my fist into the couch and lean my head against her chest. I feel the tears welling as the anger I have learned to control, begins to rage inside of me. I close my eyes and try to fight it back, but all I want is to take that knife and stab it into the heart of the man who did this. I am losing the battle. I stand up wildly, yank the knife from the neck of the servant, and head for the door. There is no one to save me this time but myself. I make my way down the hall toward the elevator. I remember what Tira said about its being a trap, but I do not care. I welcome the challenge. I press the button and wait for the doors to open. I see my eyes, ablaze with righteous anger, reflecting in the metal doors. I grip the handle of the knife tightly, preparing for whatever emerges.

"Sardis," I hear inside my head. I spin around but no one is there.

"Sardis," I hear again, this time louder. I have heard this voice before, but I cannot remember where or when. I race back toward our room. Tira is still lying motionless beside the couch and there is no one else around.

"Who is calling my name?" I bellow, my voice echoing in the large room. There is no response.

"Answer me!" I scream, spinning wildly in search of the voice. As I turn to leave, Tira's pack catches my eye. I grab it off the couch and unzip it. Inside are Phil's Bible and a small sheet of paper with something scribbled on it. I grab the paper.

"Revelation 3:1? What are you trying to tell me?" I shout, as I grab the Bible, flip to the verse, and begin reading:

To the angel of the church in Sardis write:

> *These are the words of him who holds the seven spirits of God and the seven stars. I know your deeds, you have a reputation of being alive, but you are dead. Wake up! Strengthen what remains and is about to die, for I have not found your deeds complete in the sight of my God. Remember, therefore, what you have received and heard; obey it, and repent.*

I fall weakly to my knees as the words shake me to my core. I feel dead, just as the Scripture says, but I have no desire to feel alive again. I have no one, nothing to live for. Everyone who was trusted into my care is gone. I have failed.

"Sardis..."

"I don't know how to fix this!" I scream to the voice in my head. "I don't know what to do! I cannot do this on my own!"

"Sardis..."

"What, Lord?" I cry, my voice as broken as my soul. "What, Lord?"

"You are not alone," the voice echoes inside my heart. "No matter how far you run, or how deep you fall, there I will be."

"Then help me now!" I cry with all my being. I lower my head and wait for a response, but there is none. The voice is gone.

"Show me what I am supposed to do!" I wail, pounding the arm of the couch as I begin to sob. "I don't know what I am supposed to do..." I kneel there, tears flowing freely as I stare at the text, the words meaningless through my blurry eyes. I wish Phil were here. He would know what to say, what to do next. He would grab me by the hand and say a prayer, and he would magically know where to go or what to do. Maybe that is why I loved him so much. He always made me feel better about myself. I felt safe in his presence, like his faith was a crutch for my own. The passage is right; I am a phony. My faith is hollow: strong and imposing on the outside, lost and scared below the surface.

I close my eyes tightly and release the heavy air in my chest. I rest there, quiet, my mind blank – until the tears have dried on my face and I have regained my composure. I sit up and place my hands on my knees, my chest aching slightly from the heavy sobs. I look down once more at Phil's Bible, and I am taken back to his sermon in the forest. I see him standing there, his soul on fire after defeating the bear. He is explaining to me how God was using me and I did not realize it. How I was unknowingly walking on the water, being held by the arm of Christ who was living and working in me. How I needed to trust that. I did not trust it then. Do I now? I don't know. I lower my head, defeated, and feel the tears beginning once more.

"No," I mouth defiantly, sitting up straight and pounding my fist on the floor. I have to trust. I have to – It is all I have left. I place my hands in my lap and humbly lower my head.

"Father," I whisper desperately, "I am yours. Completely."

I slowly open my eyes and see the text open again before me; the passage is the Seven Churches of Revelation. I did not notice this before, but Phil has several things underlined and notes written in the margins of the page. "Alexander," is written next to the church named "Sardis." Phil's voice from the last time I saw him echoes inside my head... *"This is your letter."*

Another note is circled, with an arrow pointing to a list of the other six church names. It reads, "Don't you see? You are *supposed* to be here." That is what Phil told me in the forest, I recall, as I read his list of names: Ephesus *Porter*... Smyrna *King*... Dr. Pergamum... Thyatira *Alexander*... Philadelphia *Conner*... Laodicea *Fair*....

"Whoa," I gasp as a feeling of panic and astonishment sweeps over my body. I cannot believe I had never made the connection between our names and the Churches. I quickly scan the passage written to each church, and my excitement grows with each new revelation: Ephesus – lost his first love; Smyrna – poor and afflicted, faithful until death; Pergamum – lives where Satan's throne is, yet did not renounce his faith –

"Incredible!" I shout, setting the Bible on my lap. I close it confidently and toss it back in the bag. I do not need to read the rest of the passage; I finally understand. I can feel it now – the trust. It is what Phil experienced after the bear and what Lacy found at the time machine. It guided Tira's hand to write the letter and now it is leading me to my final purpose. This is where I am supposed to be.

I walk to the Servant and separate his mechanical head from his body and slide it into the bag. Instead of heading toward the elevator I turn right, run full speed down the hall, and jump through the glass window. For a brief moment, as I free-fall through the warm summer air, I am complete. I can feel God's

Spirit. I exist wholly on faith and God's purpose is my unequivocal end. A smile breaks across my face as I feel an extreme blast of air on my body, slowing me to a stop just before I hit the ground. The air then tosses me upright before ceasing, and I land safely on my feet. I look down and see a metal grate extending completely around the perimeter of the building, underneath which are honeycomb-shaped metal cylinders with what appear to be large fan blades inside. I look at the surrounding buildings and they each have the same grate structures. A vague shadow of a history lesson emerges in the recesses of my memory as I sprint away from the building in the direction of the Air Depot. I seem to recall a lecture on Establishment propaganda; how they would install elaborate safety measures in new buildings in an effort to lure people to live in the Great Cities. No need to fear heights when you can accidently tumble out of the window of your twentieth-story apartment and land safely on the ground below.

I am out of breath when I reach the depot, but I have not been followed and no one seems alarmed at my presence. I hastily scan the terminal before locating a craft destined for Crystal City. At the entrance of each loading dock is a travel information screen depicting the number and nature of passengers aboard each vessel. Thankfully this one is empty, and I watch as the commuter tally increases by one I-Mort as I board the craft. After a few more minutes and no more passengers, the unmanned aircraft lifts straight into the air, and I watch the bustling scene disappear as we accelerate through the hatch in the roof.

"You will reach your destination in twelve hours and eleven minutes," a kind female voice states inside the cabin as a countdown clock appears on the wall above the closed bay door. It is two in the afternoon, so that will get me to Crystal City at noon their time tomorrow. I slide the pack off my shoulder and lean back in the comfortable seat. All I can do now is rest. I close my eyes and for once see nothing. I have a strong urge to pray, so I meditate on the day for a moment and open my heart to the Lord.

When I awake, the clock above the door reads five hours and seventeen minutes. It is dark outside, and what light I can see is reflecting off the Atlantic Ocean. I turn on the broadcast hoping to hear commentary on the debate, but, instead, a government official is sitting at a desk, speaking directly into the camera.

"The early estimates are that nearly two-thirds of Gold City, three-quarters of Ruby City, and almost all of Crystal City have been affected. Hundreds of thousands of people are dead this morning, and that number could soon rise to the millions. Government officials are working around the clock to find a diagnosis for the mysterious pandemic, but at this point, no official word has been issued to the cause or a possible cure. All humans around the globe are being instructed to stay in their homes until further notice." He pauses for a moment to collect himself before continuing.

"The conclusion of the Council Debate has been cancelled for this evening, though two of the presenters, the Human Religious contingent, are being made available for emotional support today at the Town Square in Crystal City. We will send you to that scene live and keep you updated on any further developments."

The newsroom cuts away and there are a few seconds of darkness before the image of the town square appears on the screen. I remember the last time I gazed upon a scene in a town square while riding in an aircraft. Thankfully, Phil and Myrna are standing on a makeshift stage and not before the gallows.

They are wearing protective garments that look like blankets wrapped around their head and body. Surrounding the stage is a sea of people, the humans all wearing dust masks. If the news report is correct, then all of them are infected. A government official hands Phil a microphone, and he begins to address the crowd.

"I have only been in your city for two days, but I feel as if I am one of you. The kindness you have shown my friend and me has been overwhelming and humbling." A loud murmur rolls through the crowd along with a few incomprehensible screaming voices. Phil takes a minute until the scene settles before continuing.

"I can see why God chose this place as the center of His earthly kingdom. Jesus cried over your ancient ancestors before He died in this very place. That is how much He loved this city and this people."

"Get on with it!" an angry voice from the crowd echoes into the microphone. Several more voices shout simultaneously, causing the official to step in front of the podium and fire a round into the air. He waves his hands and then presses his finger to his lips, before slowly returning to where he had been standing.

"The wonderful news is: He loves you as much now as He did then," Phil continues excitedly, oblivious to the growing dissent in the crowd. "He is here, weeping over us and longing to pull each and every one of us close to him, like a mother hen gathering her chicks."

"It is true!" Myrna shouts, as Phil moves to the side and she stands before the podium.

"You see, for all of my life, I had been running – searching for something to ease the aching I had inside. I had a yearning for something to hold onto – a dream I could be something more than just a girl from Jasper City – that I was meaningful – that my life had a purpose. I was lost and scared, just as you are now. I was literally hours from ending it all when Jesus found me. He told me He loved me..." Her voice breaks. "He loved *me*," She states firmly through tears. She wipes her eyes and takes a deep breath. "He loved me the way I was, for who I was. He tore away the fear that held my heart captive and allowed it to beat freely for the first time in my life. He healed me and made me whole, and He will do the same for you. Please, come now, and we will pray with you, or cry out to Him from where you are. He will hear you and heal your heart, just as He did mine." An angry murmur once again buzzes through the people as a new voice reverberates through the square.

"If you want true healing, do not listen to their religious babbling." The camera pans the crowd, then zooms in on Colonel Justice standing on the steps of the government building. "Come; let me place my hands on you. God has shown me how to heal you *now* of your sickness, no matter your spiritual state."

Another loud rumbling erupts as a flood of people rush the government building stairs. The camera pans out again, showing several people on the stage being held back by government officials. They are pointing and screaming angrily at Phil and Myrna, who are both standing still, heads bowed in prayer. The scene once again goes black before the news desk appears once more.

"A truly unprecedented day in our history," the official states solemnly. "There are now seven more cities reporting cases of the unknown illness. If you are a resident of Jasper, Emerald, Sapphire, Carnelian, Topaz, Amethyst, or Beryl Cities and their surrounding areas, please take refuge in your homes now."

"Alright Lord," I sigh. I bow my head to pray for Phil and Myrna's protection, but as I do, I suddenly realize all of this is my fault. My decision to trust Colonel Justice led him to the virus. The fate of millions of lives is on my head, and I am powerless to do anything about it. I slam my fist into the seat of the chair. "I can't do this," I sob, my eyes beginning to fill with tears, as a voice appears from behind me.

"Be still," it says as I turn and see a glowing figure dressed in a white robe. I am frozen, my heart beating so violently that I feel as if my ears are going to explode. It lifts its arm slowly toward me, and I instinctively fall down to my knees.

"There will be no more delay." The figure holds out his right hand and opens it, revealing a small metal object.

"Who are you?" I stammer.

"I am here to prepare you for what must soon take place." I reach out and grab the object from his hand. It is a military pin, similar to the one my great-grandfather gave Tira, only it is made of pure gold.

"What is going on?" I ask, holding the pin close to my chest, my body shaking heavily.

"Vengeance for those under the altar!"

"I don't understand."

He stares at me, his eyes inhumanly glowing. "Yes. You do. Close your eyes."

I look at him and then down at the pin in my hand. I have no idea what is going on or what he is talking about, but I decide to trust him. I close my eyes and see my father. He is dressed in a white robe, surrounded by others dressed the same. "Is this Heaven?" I ask Dad, but he shakes his head.

"You are ready, Sardy," he says with a smile. "I am so proud of you, and so is Mom." My thumb moves to their wedding ring, and I spin it on my finger. I remember how I put it on so I could be inspired by their love in my darkest moments, but now I feel a love that is infinitely more intense. It is so pure, so raw, that it pains my entire soul, yet excites it at the same moment.

"What is that?" I ask, wondering what that feeling is.

"It is He," he answers smiling.

I open my eyes. "You mean it is time? He is coming?" The figure nods his head. "But all these people – they are dying. I did that. I am the one responsible. We have to do something."

"You are no more responsible for their fate than God is. You understand what happens to man. The achievement they have strived for since the Garden is finally realized. They have become God and replaced his Presence with a shadow. Their hearts are hardened even now, as there are two who are witnessing, pleading for them to understand what must happen next. But they will not listen. Their fate is sealed. It has already happened; you can testify to that just as God can. He has shown you what would have happened so you will understand what must now take place.

"Come. Watch." He motions toward the broadcast screen. The town square is once again in view. Phil and Myrna are standing on the stage, while countless green-clad government soldiers are stationed between them and the overflowing crowd surrounding Colonel Justice.

"The preliminary reports are truly miraculous," the voice of the government official exclaims over the chaotic scene. "This man, the leader of the underground religious uprisings, seems to have discovered a cure for the spreading disease. Though unclear what his methods are, those who have been touched by him report that he possesses the power of God. As soon as one is in his presence, he begins to feel better. Within hours, he is completely healed." His last few words were almost entirely drowned out by deafening chants roaring from the joyous crowd.

"Justice! Justice!"

"Meanwhile, the government has brought in their Special Forces Unit to keep peace in the riotous scene. The two religious leaders have been continuing to present their views to the crowd during this time, but the reaction from the masses has grown increasingly more violent, and it is unclear why they are still permitted to speak. A few moments ago, a man tried to rush the stage and was fired upon by an unseen weapon, leaving him consumed in fire. Hopefully, the army will restore peace soon—" his voice abruptly trailing off as he watches in horror as a red-clad soldier walks onto the stage and begins viciously beating the two who had been witnessing.

"No!" I scream. The figure standing with me lowers his head and closes his eyes. The crowd cheers as the Serpent picks up each lifeless body and tosses them into the crowded street.

Chapter 20

A sharp pain in my finger jolts me back to the cabin of the aircraft. I have squeezed my fist so tightly that the pin has lodged itself there. I open my hand and pull it out. The blood begins to ooze out of the small hole in large drops.

"He knew," I utter inaudibly. "As soon as he read the invitation, he knew what was going to happen. I could see the weight of it on his face." The cabin is quiet. I stare at the blank screen. I can feel the stickiness of the blood between my fingers. In the past I would have been overcome with grief, paralyzed, unable to move forward, but in this moment *I am still*.

This is the feeling I have yearned for since Mom described it to me when I was young. I always thought my gift was my ability to feel things, but I was wrong. I experienced life through my own understanding of how I knew it to be, not how it truly was. My own understanding could only lead me to the edge of truth; I had to completely let go of myself in order to finally experience it. Phil would tell me these feelings were from God and I needed to learn how to trust them. I always thought he was shallow and closed-minded. I knew the chemicals racing through my body were why I experienced certain emotions. I could feel that. But now I realize I traded my faith in the mechanism for a true faith in the Creator of the experience. There is a purpose for the pain and there is a purpose for the anger; it is a deeper understanding – only found when one enters the stillness of God's presence.

"I'm ready." The words confidently leave my lips. I feel adrenaline begin to pump through my body, preparing me for the culmination of my faith.

"In three days there will be a Great War unlike any before seen by man," the figure begins solemnly. "It will begin as a conflict between the forces of the Serpent and those of the Lawless One. The two great armies will battle ferociously – hand to hand, sword to sword – each blow a retribution for their perceived depravity.

"It is at this time, those who have kept watch will be taken. It will begin with Phil and Myrna. They will have lain broken and mocked in the street, refused burial, and accused like the Father of propagating a testimony of hate. Each side will make an example of them for their own purposes." The figure shakes his head angrily. "Oh, how great their fall will be!" he bellows, causing me to take a step back. "When the two witnesses rise on the third day, the war will commence. It is then you will look to the eastern sky and command the Armies of the Lord into battle."

"Me?" I reply stunned. "But I thought –" I begin in rebuttal but the figure is gone. I spin around, my eyes wildly searching the small cabin, but he is nowhere to be found.

"Wait!" I shout, but the cabin is silent.

I look up at the countdown clock: three minutes? How can that be? It seems like only a few moments have passed since it was five hours. I put the gold pin in the bag with Phil's Bible and sling it over my shoulder. I look out the window of the craft and see brown desert engulfing pockets of green and ribbons of blue. For a brief moment, I am transfixed by the beauty. Even in the vast barren wilderness there is life and hope.

"Please prepare for landing," the kind female voice announces. I oblige and sit in one of the chairs, waiting for the craft to slow and begin its descent. When the bay doors open, I will be a marked man. I am a known ally of Phil's, so I will be seen as dangerous by the government. Conversely, Colonel Justice will be looking for me to corroborate his story that the virus was released by the Establishment.

I smile and bow my head. *"If my God is for me, who can be against me?"* I say aloud as a supreme feeling of confidence and power emanates through me. This is what Phil knew and what I finally understand. No matter what is waiting when those doors open, I have Someone living inside me who is greater.

The aircraft touches down softly. I hear a familiar voice as the bay door opens.

"How wonderful to see my servant –" his voice trails off when he sees *me* standing at the top of the stairs. I pull the head from my bag and toss it at his feet.

"Sardis!" he shockingly states, taking a step backward to dodge the rolling head. I can see panic on his face as his eyes frantically scan the cabin behind me for more foes. I walk deliberately down the stairs toward him, my eyes fixed on his.

"What is the meaning of this?" he blares pompously, in an attempt to gain control of the situation. "You repay my hospitality with this abomination?" I do not respond. Instead, I walk directly through the little group of Cause leaders who have gathered around him.

"How dare you disrespect me like that! Guards, seize this murderer!" I do not break stride. Each step is purposeful: led not by my intuition, but by an innate force dwelling in the depths of my being. The further I travel into the light, the more certain I am of what is about to take place.

I reach the town square. The scene is volatile, bubbling over with anger and fear. I wade through the crowd, searching the ground for my friends as people scream obscenities. My heart aches for them. They are desperately waiting for their savior to return, the one who will cure them of their virus; but they are blind to their true condition. An excited murmur races through the throng as Colonel Justice approaches.

"There he is!" he shouts. "Arrest that man!"

Angry faces in the crowd turn toward me as I pass, but I am oblivious to their looks of disdain. At the base of the makeshift stage, I find Phil and Myrna lying together in a heap. Their bodies are broken, lifeless. I run to them. I look at Phil's face. It is badly beaten – his features swollen and barely recognizable. I am overcome with emotion, not of anger or sadness, but of raw passion. I can feel my heart burning intensely in my chest, the words of promise that were drilled into my memory as a youth, now pouring out of me as I hold his face in my hands.

> "You are finally before the throne of the Lamb.
> And you will serve Him night and day.
> Never again will you be hungry, never again will you thirst!
> He will lead you to springs of living water.
> And He will wipe away every tear from your eyes."

I hold his head to my chest as tears of joy soak his hair. He is finally home.

I lay him next to Myrna and slowly rise to my feet. Out of the crowd emerges the Serpent. He walks straight toward me, dressed in red, his face as foreboding as I remember. His gait is powerful and intimidating, but I am not afraid. I think back to our encounter in the wilderness, Tira obliterating his body with a blast from a laser cannon. At that moment, my fear blinded me to the truth that I was walking in the will of God. There was nothing the enemy could have done to keep me from my purpose. Now,

I know the battle has already been won. I hold out my hands in surrender and smile. He pushes me forcefully in the chest and I fall backwards to the ground. He kicks me twice in the side and grabs me by the back of my shirt, lifting me to my feet.

"Do you think that is funny?" he growls angrily, inches from my face. He punches me hard in the gut and elbows me in the neck. I fall gasping to my knees.

"That's enough for now!" Colonel Justice orders hastily, running toward the Serpent with his hands outstretched. I would be no good to him in a coma or dead.

The Serpent spits on the ground in front of him and rolls up his sleeve. "You have no authority here!" he bellows, and kicks my stomach again. The pain is intense and I can barely catch my breath before another kick sends me sprawling on my side. He grabs me by the collar and pulls me up. I attempt to stand straight, but the throbbing is too severe and I double over once more.

"He will stand trial for treason," the Serpent growls and knees me in the mouth. Before I can fall, he grabs me by the shoulders and lifts me straight into the air, dropping me flat on my stomach. I lie there motionless, staring at Phil and Myrna, until I feel the cool metal of a restraining device press against the back of my neck followed by the incapacitating shock. "Take him away!"

Though I cannot move, I can still feel the pain. Two Dragons grab me by the legs and drag my limp body away from the square. The mob cheers as we pass through.

"Kill him and throw him with the others!"

"Look what your God did to us!"

"Justice! Justice!"

I feel a kick to my side, then another to my face as I lose consciousness.

Chapter 21

"Legend has it, this prison has housed some of the most notable figures in human history," a voice speaks. My eyes struggle open. I see the metal bars of a cell door. My hands are raised above my head, shackled to the wall behind me. I try to make out who is speaking, but it is too dark, though the voice sounds familiar. "In fact, tradition claims this structure was built on the ruins of the prison from which Peter escaped; which, I suppose, is one of the reasons they would bring you here: to reinforce how impotent your religion is."

"Who are you?"

"Why would you come here? After you saw what they did to your friends?"

"He led me here."

"Ridiculous," he taunts. "That is why man abandoned this religious nonsense. We became tired of forsaking our reason when circumstances did not go our way. Why sit around for the gods to make things right, when we could do it ourselves? We made our own heaven, twenty glistening jewels of hope, where our bodies no longer would be ravaged by the decaying of this wasteland."

"It pales in comparison to what my friends are experiencing now."

I hear rustling in the dark and then a loud banging, as if something metal were thrown down a long hallway.

"Who are you?" I ask again. Silence.

I glance around the cell. It is a primitive structure, the walls are chiseled rock and the floor is pitted concrete. I am definitely somewhere outside of the City. My shoulders are aching, and judging by the pain in my side, I must have a few broken ribs. I sit there quietly for a few minutes as the dull aching in my stomach grows increasing stronger and I notice how parched my mouth is. I have been here at least one day, maybe even longer.

"She was only a girl..."

"Dr. King?" I ask as the pain in the voice sparks my memory.

"How could you let this happen?"

"It was not my doing. She made a choice."

"A choice? She was just a girl!"

"No, she was more than just a girl," I reply firmly. "She was a symbol of all that was good in this world. When people saw her, they saw hope." I see two hands grasp the metal bars, and the figure of Dr. King emerges from the shadows.

"If that is true, then why is she now the scourge of the earth! I am sick of this religious garbage. I hope you enjoy *your* public execution! I will be there holding the axe!" He disappears into the shadows, and I hear his footsteps echoing away.

"Don't you see?" I say loud enough that he stops walking. He is quiet for a moment before I hear his steps grow louder. "Don't you see?" I cannot see him but I know he is standing just outside the cell. "Do you not see His love for her?"

He does not answer. His presence speaks for him. He did not wait here all this time to berate me and leave. He is searching for something, a resolution: something he knows he cannot find anywhere else.

"Don't you see what He did to win her heart? Can you imagine a love that deep? She did not know Him, yet He pursued her relentlessly. *He rewrote the laws of time to save her!*"

"I don't understand," he replies sternly. "Nor do I have any desire to continue this conversation."

"I have been there, blind to the truth." I smile and break open a cut on my lip. Blood begins trickling into my mouth. "You will not be able to understand until you let go of your selfish pride and allow Him to guide you."

He scoffs. "You seem to forget I am a soulless robot."

"We all are, Dr. King. Your nurse, Miss Laura, taught me that. No matter the choices we make; He loves us more. That is the wonder of His grace."

He growls something I cannot understand before walking away once more. This time I do not call out. His fate is sealed; his heart is hardened. He, like everyone else, knew there was more to this life – something more than he could touch and see. That is why the hatred was so ferocious. The truth tugged on desires in his being he could never quench by his own hand. He is lost in the endless desert between the darkness and the light.

I yank on the restraints, but they do not budge. The pain in my side is intense and is exacerbated by the position of my arms. I relax – the weight of my body now unbearably straining the joints in my shoulders. I sigh and rest my head against the cold prison wall.

I close my eyes and see the blue horizon of the Pacific. In front of me are the small woodland animals, dancing through the sunlit meadow. I see two deer, drinking from a trickling stream – their tails flicking peacefully, even though they realize I am there. Mom is sitting beneath a large oak, flipping through her Bible. I feel a gentle breeze on my face and a sharp longing in my heart, as she smiles and holds it up for me to read.

"I was reading Luke in my devotion time today – the passage where Peter confesses he believes Jesus is the Messiah of God

– and I realized how much Peter reminds me of you, Sardy. He was a bold, passionate leader; yet, he was gripped with an unspoken fear. The fear of what a decision like that would cost: to daily seek God's purpose, forsaking what he thought he loved most."

She hands me the Bible and I hold it softly in my hands. I look down at the words and then back into her eyes. "I think I finally understand."

She smiles. "Yes – you do. I am so proud of the man you have become." She takes the Bible and places it back at the foot of the oak. She reaches behind the tree and grabs her bow.

"You will need this. Now go – it is time."

I feel my arms fall to my sides, and I open my eyes to see the restraints lying on the ground. I painfully bring my arms into my chest, holding them tightly for a moment, before kneeling and rising to my feet. My body is deathly weak, but I barely acknowledge it, as I make my way to the cell door. I reach my hand to the lock, but the entire door falls crashing to the floor.

"Sardis!" I hear Dr. King scream from the other side of the dark hallway. I stumble out of the cell as he appears before me. "How did you –"

"He is coming!"

"What?" He raises a stun weapon, his hand shaking. "Don't move, or I will shoot!"

"This is the end of all things," I state as the floor begins to shake.

"What is happening?" he cries, his voice trembling.

"I have seen the future, Dr. King, and I can testify to the fall of man."

"I don't understand!"

"He has allowed the fullness of time to play out and is now coming to rescue His Bride!"

A large piece of ceiling falls, crushing his body beneath it. A shudder sweeps through the hallway as I stand still, waiting for the dust to settle. There are no guards, no one else in the ancient prison. They have all been summoned to the battle that is about to begin. I grab my bag lying next to his smoking corpse and run through the crumbling hallway and out into the bright sunlight.

I can see the Crystal City shimmering to the east, but I am led north up a steep hill. When I reach the crest, I see the two Great Armies spread throughout the valley below. To the east, toward the Great City, is Colonel Justice leading hundreds of thousands he has saved. To the west is the glittering Army of the United Elect. Their number is far greater, expanding so deep, I cannot see the end. They are covered in shining armor and led by a soldier dressed in blood red. I can see two bodies lying on the ground between the two forces. A large flag on a tall pole has been shoved through the chest of each. I am too far away to see their faces, but I know who they are. I watch as the Serpent and Colonel Justice walk toward the corpses and each grab one of the flags, taking them back to their respective front lines. For a long moment the valley is still, until the army to the east charges forth, followed shortly by their battle cry, the sound having lagged behind at this distance.

I slide the bag off my shoulder and reach inside for the gold pin. I stare at it for a moment before placing it on my chest. I close my eyes and take a deep breath, the raging sounds of hatred and bloodshed ringing in my ears, yet, through the noise I begin to hear the sound of a faint voice singing...

"Let the morning bring word of Your unfailing love,
For I have put my trust in Your hand."

I see Phil, dressed in white, singing and holding out his hand. He pulls me close and whispers softly into my ear, "Look down, Buddy."

My eyes well with tears as I see a vast ocean, powerful and deep – there is no shore in sight, only the crashing of the waves. I am standing. My soul is on fire. "*I have put my trust in Your hand,*" I sing as I fix my gaze upon the horizon. I take one step – and then another – each footfall landing firmly upon the water.

I open my eyes and look across the valley. It is then I see them: countless beings – shimmering, ethereal, clad with fire, and littering the expanse between my position and the enemy. It is the Angel Army, waiting for me to fulfill my purpose. I grasp the cross on my chest and sprint toward the threshing floor.

As I run, more angels appear, each covered with brilliant gold and orange armor that shines like the face of the sun. In their hands are large swords and golden shields, each seemingly made of fire. When I pass, they raise their swords into the air and fall in behind me.

I run until I reach a plateau, overlooking the chaos below. The army fans out around me, eager for my cue to attack. One hands me a bow and I reach over my shoulder and find a full quiver. I grab an arrow, its tip glowing blue with fire. Another raises its sword, "*It is time,*" it says, motioning toward the brightening eastern sky. "*The kingdom of the world has become the kingdom of our Lord and of His Christ, and He will reign forever and ever!*"

The Spirit within me leaps as I raise my bow. "For those under the altar!" I shout, firing the flaming arrow into the heart of the battle. Cries of horror rise from the writhing valley as my army descends.

I scan the scene for the Lawless One. "Justice!" I scream as I see him standing, bloodied, amidst the carnage. He lifts a laser cannon, his eyes wild with fear.

"Sardis!" he cries, as I race toward him. "Join us and we will defeat this menace together!"

I raise my bow at his chest. "The people trusted you!" I shout as I let an arrow fly, piercing his shoulder and causing his weapon to fall from his hand. "How many did you willingly lead astray?" Another arrow hits his chest and sends him spinning to the ground.

"You coward!" I scream as I stand over his thrashing body. I nock another arrow and aim it at his chest as he begins sobbing – his fate before him.

"Everything I did was for the good of humanity!" he cries, lifting his hands in defense. "All I wanted was for man to regain his rightful place in this world."

"I will let God be the judge of that!" I fire the arrow into the ground next to him and throw my bow at his feet. Two angels pick him up and carry him away. I lift my eyes to find the Serpent, but instead see *my friends* standing there.

"Come up here!" a voice thunders from above, causing the ground to shake. A brilliant white cloud descends from the sky and I watch Phil and Myrna ascend directly into the air. A hush goes over the valley as the gathered watch the two slowly rise, before disappearing completely as a brilliant white light, emanating from where they last were, explodes in all directions, blinding me for a brief moment and sending a wave of horrifying screams through the masses. The ground begins shaking harder, increasing the decibel level of the screams.

A blow to my back sends me sprawling to the ground. I turn to see the Dragon in red standing over my body, a sword raised above his head. I quickly roll to the side as his sword plows into the earth. He lifts it again as I struggle to my feet.

"Die!" he thunders as he swings again, missing wildly. I search the quaking ground for a weapon and find the tip of a sword protruding from beneath a smoking I-Mort corpse. I dive to the ground, frantically trying to pry the weapon from beneath the body, as he approaches.

"It is finished!" he bellows as he jumps toward me, lifting the sword over his head. Time seems to stand still as I futilely attempt to free my weapon. I watch his elbows bend and the sword begin to descend as a deafening trumpet blast, emanating from beyond the Crystal City, knocks him backward off his feet. I pry the sword free and thrust it through his body, pinning him to the earth.

I turn toward the trumpet sound as a streak appears across the eastern sky. Clouds begin to form as the streak grows brighter, until the clouds themselves billow with fire. Silence falls over the valley as the doomed turn toward the light and watch as the clouds descend upon Crystal City, completely demolishing it as they pass through. A figure begins to emerge within the cloud: a Rider dressed in a flowing white robe, riding upon a white horse. On His head are many crowns and a sash across the front of the horse reads, "Faithful and True." More riders in white appear behind the First, their number immeasurable. It is the Army of Heaven.

I walk to the Serpent and lower my face to his. "Yes. It is finished."

Within moments, the white riders have passed through, leaving none in the valley standing. The Lord motions toward the fiery angels who had been following me and giant sickles appear in their hands. He waves his arm and they take off in all directions in search of a Harvest. The Lord tugs on the reins of His horse and charges the hill where I had been standing. As He does so, the earth opens and swallows the hill as He moves past. He raises His arm once more and the rest of His army disperses, the ground disintegrating underneath their feet as they go.

A shadow begins to form across the land. I look up and see a darkness creeping across the face of the sun. Flashes of light become visible the darker the sky becomes. Soon it is as black as night and I realize the flashes are the stars being torn from their place in the universe – entire galaxies explode before my eyes. The last image I see is the entire earth quaking uncontrollably as the moon, red as blood, is swept away as if it were being rolled up in a giant scroll.

When I open my eyes, I am standing in the midst of a brilliant forest. I am reminded of my hunts, how at home I felt beneath the branches. Content, I would sit there, taking in the beauty around me. This forest, though, is unlike anything I have ever seen. The colors are so pure and so rich. It is as if I have been unable to see true color until this moment.

I reach out my hand and touch a green leaf and watch as a drop of dew rolls down the vibrant purple veins. I have witnessed this phenomenon a thousand times, but as the water drop slowly makes its way to the tip of the leaf, an excited burst of energy flows through me, and I quickly lower my hand to catch it before it hits the ground. The drop gently falls into my hand. As it slides across the creases of my palm, I can feel every hydrogen and oxygen molecule as they coolly spin and dive through the unique lines. It is unlike anything I have ever felt before.

I have no sensation of thirst, but the sight of the pure water electrifies my taste buds and I raise the drop to my lips. The only way I can describe the taste is ice mixed with fire. The sensation both burns and cools the entire surface of my tongue. There is a texture to the taste as well. It is both soft and smooth, coating my whole mouth, sending sensations through my body that literally make my knees so weak I have to sit down. The taste is unlike anything I have ever known.

As I sit, I am overcome by the intricate aroma that is surrounding me. My mind travels to the government building in Shiloh where they would pump beautiful fragrance to try and entice us to buy their feeble representation of what I am experiencing now. My body is calm. I am at complete peace. I close my eyes and breathe in the aroma, letting it wash over my senses. It smells so familiar, like the smell of Mom's hair or the perfume Lacy was wearing when I bumped into her on the street back home; but at the same time, it is unlike anything I have ever smelled before. It is as if the smell also has a unique color or a rich frequency. I concentrate, trying to hear the color of the aroma and am awed by the complexity of the sound. It is a complete scale in one intoxicating note. It is unlike anything I have ever heard before.

I open my eyes and see a brilliant creature floating away from my gaze, down a narrow footpath through the lush vegetation. I realize it is a butterfly and decide to follow it. I walk mile after mile in God's garden. Each step I take is a completely new sensory experience, so much so, my brain cannot keep up with the new information exploding inside. Eternity would not be long enough for one to fully grasp the beauty before me.

After what seems like a brief moment, I reach a mighty river. The clear and calm water is flowing away from the base of a majestic mountain. I look up and see a blinding white light emanating from the peak. It is so bright and pure that I cannot look directly at it. I close my eyes and when I open them, I am standing at the edge of a steep cliff, the dazzling garden miles below. Before me is a path made of *gold*, leading to the entrance of a Great Room at the top of the majestic mountain peak. The light is pouring out of the open doorway, and I am drawn to its presence. I hear a faint melody coming from inside, and as I pass through the *sapphire* gates, I realize it is a beautiful chorus singing, *"Holy, Holy, Holy."*

I shield my eyes with my hands and peer through my fingers, but I am unable to see past the blinding light. I decide to continue toward the Angelic chorus, when I see a silhouette approaching.

"Hello?" I address the figure as it continues to move closer.

"Hello, Sardis," my father gently says. I run to him and throw my arms around his neck. He is dressed in a radiant white robe and his face is glowing.

"Welcome home, my brother. Come; the others are here."

"Have you been waiting long?"

"There is no waiting."

He grabs my hand, and I feel the strength and tenderness I always admired most about him in his grip. As we walk, I close my eyes and see a five-year-old boy pulling his patient father toward the swing for one more ride. I hear him congratulating me after a good report from school. I smell his cologne and taste his famous apple pancakes. I wish this walk could last forever, and it does.

Soon another figure approaches and I let my father's hand go and run to it. Before I can make out who it is, I smell her hair and taste her venison stew. I dive headlong into her arms and bury my head into her chest. There are no tears. There is only love: pure unfiltered love.

"I love you, Mom."

She kisses my forehead. "Peanut, I love you, too."

Instinctively my thumb moves toward the wedding ring on my finger. I had worn it to remember the love my parents shared for one another, but as I look at it now, all I see is a piece of metal. It is the only shadow in this bright room. I open my hand and it falls, clanging, to the ground.

"Found you!" Phil shouts as he pops out from behind my mother. "That is the second time! You had better work on your hiding skills, Buddy!" He flashes his face. I grab him and pull him close in a heavy embrace.

"I'm sorry I didn't listen to you—"

"There are no sorrows here. There is only joy." He holds out the ring I had dropped a moment ago and places it in the palm of my hand, closing my fingers securely around it.

"There is someone else who would like to see you." He motions with his head toward the light. My heart leaps as I see Lacy, dressed in white, with a green leafy wreath on her head, slowly materialize through the light. She is staring at me, her eyes sparkling like that day in the basement and that night by the fire. In her hand is a bouquet of white roses, and her father is standing next to her with his hand on her shoulder. He gives her a quick hug and puts his hand on her back, and she walks slowly toward me. I look down at the ring in my hand. It no longer resembles the shadow I saw before, but it now is glowing, composed not of metal but of pulsating light. She reaches toward me and I grab her hand gently, sliding the ring on her finger. She smiles and stands by my side as another figure approaches. The light seems to move as the figure gets closer. This light is new – eternal and life-giving. Soon, He is standing before us.

"Well done," He states, holding out his hand. I reach for Him. My soul is complete as He pulls my body tenderly against His. I feel His hand on the back of my neck as His forehead rests softly against mine. Tears of ecstasy should be pouring down my face, but instead there is light emanating from my eyes. It is a new experience, something that can only occur in His presence. He kisses my cheek and releases His embrace.

"Come. We are about to partake in the Wedding Celebration. My Bride awaits."

We walk toward the light, my wife on one side and my Lord on the other. As we approach the Throne Room, the Heavenly Chorus erupts in shouts of adulation, *"Worthy is the Lamb who was slain, to receive glory, honor, and praise!"*

I look down and my clothes have been replaced by a flowing white robe. I no longer know what sin is – all I feel is light. I see One sitting upon a throne which is floating on a sea of glass, clear as *crystal*. I do not look directly upon Him, but His essence shines like *jasper* and there is a sparkling emerald rainbow surrounding the throne.

"This is my faithful servant, Sardis," the Lord says to the Father and the gathered angels, as we enter His presence. "When he was dead, he chose to heed My voice and follow; thus, his name will be, *Chayah,* and he will reign with Me forever."

"*Amen*," the Angelic creatures around the throne proclaim.

"This is my faithful servant, Laodicea," the Lord states as He takes Lacy by the hand. "She chose to become rich by seeking gold refined in the fire. Her heart was set ablaze and her presence was cool and refreshing. Thus, her name will be, *Ashar,* and she will walk with Me forever."

"*Amen.*"

"This is my faithful servant, Philadelphia." He takes Phil by the arm and pulls him close, kissing his forehead and speaking softly into his ear, "I love you, as you have loved Me." The Lord smiles and turns back to the gathered, as Phil's face beams.

"He will be made a pillar in the Temple of my God. His new name I cannot speak, because it is *My Name,* and also my God will write His name upon him. Since you have been faithful in a few things, now I will give you authority over many."

"*Amen,*" the creatures shout once more.

"Please, my servants, take your seat among the Worthy. We are about to begin."

Then I see her, standing at the edge of the crystal sea. She is dressed in white, her train flowing beyond the limits of my sight. She turns and I see her face, her *red hair and green eyes.* The Lord takes her by the hand and they walk before the Father, standing atop the still water.

"Have you chosen Your Bride?" the Father asks, His voice gently thundering.

"I chose Her from before the world began. I watched Her dance with great kings and beg with lowly peasants. I caught every tear and rejoiced with every triumph. I bent time and space, life and death, to win Her heart. No matter how far She ran or how deep She fell, I was always there holding and preparing Her for this moment."

"*Who can deny the perfect will of our Lord!*" I hear in chorus from the Angelic creatures surrounding the Throne.

"She will never shed another tear, nor ever again be afraid. Her days will be filled with our love and there will be no more night. We will walk hand in hand for eternity and then forever more. She is mine – the love of My life."

"Very well," the Father booms as cheers spring forth from every recess of Creation.

"*To Him who sits on the throne and to the Lamb be praise and honor and glory and power, forever and ever!*"

I grasp Lacy's hand as the most glorious words ever spoken rain down upon all of God's people.

"I now pronounce you Husband and Wife. You may kiss Your Bride."

CPSIA information can be obtained at www.ICGtesting.com
Printed in the USA
BVOW07*0623040814

361412BV00001B/1/P